# In the Shadow of Evil

THEYTUS BOOKS

Copyright © 2011 Beatrice Culleton Mosionier

Library and Archives Canada Cataloguing in Publication


Mosionier, Beatrice, 1949-

In the shadow of evil / Beatrice Culleton

Mosionier. -- Rev. ed.


ISBN 978-1-926886-01-5


I. Title.


PS8576.O783I53 2010      C813'.54      C2010-907081-X


Cover Design by Ann Doyon


Printed in Canada

www.theytus.com

In Canada: Theytus Books, Green Mountain Rd., Lot 45, RR#2, Site 50, Comp. 8
Penticton, British Columbia. V2A 6J7, Tel. 250-493-7181
In the USA: Theytus Books, P.O. Box 2890, Oroville, Washington, 98844

We acknowledge the financial support of the Government of Canada through the Canada
Book Fund (CBF) for our publishing activities. We acknowledge the support of the Canada
Council for the Arts which last year invested $20.1 million in writing and publishing
throughout Canada. Nous remercions de son soutien le Conseil des Arts du Canada, qui
a investi 20,1 millions de dollars l'an dernier dans les lettres et l'édition à travers le
Canada. We acknowledge the support of the Province of British Columbia through the
British Columbia Arts Council.

# In the Shadow of Evil

# The Wolves of Shadow Lake

The moon cast its silvery light across the quiet of the forest. High up in a black spruce a lynx lazily blinked, ever watchful for movement of prey. Its eyes widened; its head lifted; its nose quivered. In the distance, some of the surrealistic shadows created by the moonlight moved in and out among the trees. Gentle air currents brought the low sounds of anxious whines and the soft falls of padded feet racing over fallen leaves to the twitching ears of the lynx. Its short tail switched back and forth nervously as the wolves came into view.

Neka, the black female and mother of two pups, was in the lead, followed closely by Okimaw, her mate, and the leader of the nine-member wolf clan. Behind, and off to the sides, were seven more wolves of various ages. Of the three adult males, only Otakosin came from a previous litter and had the same markings as his father, Okimaw. The other two males, Oskinikiw and Kanatan, were older but not quite as large or as formidable as Okimaw. Nimis was an adult of charcoal colouring, not the deep black of her mother Neka, and she bore a white spot on her chest. Kisikaw and Wapan, the six-month-old female pups that had survived from a litter of five, were excitedly keeping up. Kehte-aya, the oldest of the wolves and once the matriarch, brought up the rear.

They were playing a game of tag. Oskinikiw shot by Okimaw to sideswipe Neka and bowl her over. She took it good-naturedly with a brief wag of her tail. Then she and the pack chased Oskinikiw. Okimaw brought the game to Shadow Lake. They lapped up water and, while five of the adults rested. Kanatan, the clown, and Kehte-aya, the old one, were drawn into more games with the exuberant youngsters.

Neka stood up and stretched, wagged her tail and nuzzled Okimaw affectionately. He, too, stood up to stretch and then he looked around. Curious, Oskinikiw raised his head. Neka pointed her nose towards the sky and gave a few low tentative howls. Okimaw immediately raised his head and blended his lower-pitched voice with hers. This duet brought the rest of the wolves racing back in delight. With tails wagging, they greeted each other as if they had been apart for weeks. The pups threw their higher-pitched, almost squeaky voices into the symphony. By then the rest of the adults joined in, all seeming to give the moon a disjointed serenade.

As abruptly as it started, it ended. In the intervening silence the wolves listened intently. They heard answering calls that carried over the mist of the night air from perhaps twenty kilometres to the west. Wapan whined impatiently and approached her father to nip at his muzzle. Kisikaw followed suit by nipping at Kehte-aya's mouth. Tails wagging, they were all soon nipping and licking at Okimaw, and the rest of the pack joined in, all looking like pups begging for food to be regurgitated. In fact, the young ones did want to be fed. It was time for the hunt.

Okimaw pointed his nose in different directions, sorting out the many scents drifting by on the placid air currents. Then he set out with a deliberate wolf trot, followed by Neka. All playfulness was now gone. The wolves were on full alert. They had an oblong summer route that they had marked out as their territory. But now that they were able to leave the den and the rendezvous area, they could expand into their winter territory, which covered roughly two hundred square kilometres. In some areas their runway overlapped the territories of neighbouring wolf packs. Elk, deer, moose, and caribou were their main large prey. From denning season to autumn, the wolf pack would spend much of its time in the valley containing Shadow Lake.

In the past, they had been a pack deep in the wilderness with little contact with humans, and they had remained healthy as traditional teachings had passed from generation to generation. Among the most important teachings was the warning to avoid humans, "Awasis, watch them if you like, but do not be seen."

Now it was the season for the hunters from the south, the ones with the telescopic, high-powered, automatic rifles. In the foothills of the Rockies, reports of rifle shots cracked like thunderclaps, reverberating back and forth across mountainsides. In the lower forested regions, the sounds were more like muffled snaps. The smell of gunpowder in the air meant the days were dangerous times, and most of the wildlife took deeper cover.

That night, Okimaw led the pack away from the south shores of Shadow Lake towards the north. He soon scented an elk nearby and stopped to sniff the air. He circled, trying to get a visual fix on the prey. When he saw the young animal casually browsing on the sweet sapwood of a black spruce and then turning its head to scan its surroundings, the wolf froze. The others froze likewise. Lowering himself close to the ground, the wolf stalked forward to close the distance to the prey. Whenever the elk raised its head, Okimaw would freeze. Neka was just to his rear. When they saw the elk twitch its ears and look in their direction more alertly, the whole pack sprang forward.

The elk merely turned its body so it was facing them, stopping the wolves in their tracks. Oskinikiw circled to the elk's right side. Without moving his head, the elk eyed Oskinikiw, Okimaw, and Kanata as they moved up one by one. So far he still had some lead time. Escape to the left seemed like the best choice. With a sideways leap he was off and running.

The chase began. The elk was young and strong. The distance between him and his predators began to increase. When the elk sensed that the pursuers were giving up the chase, he turned and watched the wolves trot off, then browsed on the vegetation around him. It was useful for both prey and predator to conserve energy. The elk would live to see his first rutting season, if a hunter's bullet didn't get him first.

The wolves rested after the fruitless chase, then, one by one, the adults left in different directions. The youngsters with Neka and Kehte-aya made up a smaller unit. It was another way of hunting. The wolves could cover more ground by spreading out. At this time of the year, when the smell of gunpowder was released into the air, chances of finding wounded prey were possible. More than once, the wolves had seen and heard the two-legged predators stumbling through the woods.

The next day, when the wolves regrouped, it was Nimis who returned carrying the scent that she had been successful. She had found and fed on the fresh carcass of a mule deer. Whenever they met, the wolves greeted each other by nuzzling and sniffing. The wolves backtracked over her trail, Okimaw in the lead, and soon they joined the ravens already feeding on the carcass.

Ravens, crows, and jays, all members of the crow family, kept company with the wolves, sometimes leading the wolves to carcasses and sometimes following the pack on their hunts. The crows were quite daring around the wolves, settling down in their midst, regardless of whether the wolves were feeding or resting. Only the young inexperienced wolves would try to pounce on the birds, but they soon learned it was an exercise in futility.

One afternoon, after gorging on a moose carcass, the wolves with their bloated stomachs were napping. With his muzzle resting on his front paws, Kanatan was sleepily watching one of the crows hop among the other wolves. The crow approached Otakosin's head, deliberately pecking at the ground in front. Sensing some fun, Kanatan raised his head to watch more closely. Now the crow was pecking closer and closer to Otakosin. With one swift movement it pecked the sleeping wolf right on the nose. Otakosin jumped straight up in the air, yelping, but the crow easily managed to avoid Otakosin's pounce. Otakosin spotted the amused Kanatan and, since he couldn't vent his indignation on the agile crow, he went after Kanatan.

Kanatan took his licking and showed his subordination to Otakosin by rolling onto his back with his tail tucked between his legs, pleading for mercy. When Otakosin had satisfied himself, he returned to his resting spot, circled to settle down, and gave Kanatan an icy stare. Kanatan immediately turned his eyes away from Otakosin's. Some wolves have no sense of humour.

Until the mating season, when a change in leadership might occur,

Okimaw was the alpha male. He was also a breeding male. Later, he might still retain the leadership, but the breeding male might be one of the lower-ranking males. He was from Kehte-aya's second litter and was now in his eighth year. Okimaw decided when, where, and how a hunt would proceed. He always ate from the kills. All the members of the pack were submissive to him. Neka was the alpha female and was submissive only to Okimaw, but, as his mate, she could be more persuasive than submissive, and sometimes Okimaw allowed her to lead the pack. They were affectionate with each other all year round. If a female wolf were the largest, strongest wolf of a pack, it was possible for her to be the alpha wolf. But Neka was a docile, gentle wolf for most of the year.

Oskinikiw was the beta male. If Okimaw were killed or seriously incapacitated, Oskinikiw would assume the leadership and could take Neka as his mate, or he might choose Nimis or even a wandering female. He had been adopted by Neka and Okimaw when his mother was killed by a grizzly. Four years earlier, Oskinikiw's mother had detected the presence of a marauding grizzly bear. She had already moved two pups to a new den a kilometre away and was on her third trip. There was one pup still in the den when the grizzly located the entrance. Panicked at being alone, the pup had disobeyed his mother and wandered out of the den to look for his littermates. His whimpering immediately attracted the bear. The mother wolf tried in vain to save her pup, but the grizzly turned on her and, with one swipe of his large paw, caught her across her head and broke her neck. When the rest of the wolves returned at the end of a long hunt and discovered the remains, they moved out of the area.

Neka and Okimaw had been on a romp while Kehte-aya remained with Neka's litter. The romp became a hunt and the hunt took them into the overlap of their runway, where markings had already become aged and where the abandoned den was located. Neka heard the cries of the pups and began sniffing the area until she found the den. Deep inside, she found the two three-week-old pups still alive, but barely. She nursed them both and then, picking one up by its belly, she brought it out and Okimaw followed her back to her own den. For some reason she did not go back for the other pup. Perhaps it was too sick or weak, or perhaps she didn't have enough milk, or perhaps she simply forgot about it.

Otakosin was a year younger than Oskinikiw and had begun to challenge Oskinikiw for beta position. This past summer, Otakosin had left the pack for a few weeks and, on his return, he reassumed his standing in the pack hierarchy. Any of the subordinates could leave to start their own families or join another pack. Occasionally, a wolf from another pack stayed for a few days before rejoining its own pack. It was a way of overcoming inbreeding and, possibly, it was also a way of exchanging information from distant places. However, a pack of wolves could just as easily turn an intruder away or even kill it.

One cool sunny afternoon in the late fall, as the wolves were sleeping after eating their fill of a bull moose, the sound of a rifle shot snapped. They were immediately up, scattering in different directions into the surrounding stands of black spruce and jack pine. One wolf did not get up. Oskinikiw had flipped to his side with his legs splayed in a sudden tense spasm. He shuddered a few times, then his body went limp and he died. That evening, back near the south end of Shadow Lake, Okimaw raised his voice to call his wolves to him. They all eventually returned, except for Oskinikiw. When they howled the next time, it was a mournful song. Afterwards, Okimaw led the wolves farther to the northwest. It was time to travel deeper into their winter territory.

In December the wolf pack was again marking its winter range and they were hunting more often during the day. In their hunts, they attempted to get as close to the quarry as possible, hoping for a quick rush and a kill, their strong jaws ripping and slashing. Today they would split up and some of them would feed on hare. Many times they made their rushes and chased elk, deer, and moose, and many times they settled for beaver, hare, and marmot. For some of them, long periods without food were not unusual. Their stomachs were made for the feast-and-famine way of the wild.

Between September and January the days and nights in the lives of wolves were spent hunting, resting, playing, and marking out their expanded territory. By January the pups, Kisikaw and Wapan, born in the previous March or April, could take part in kills of larger game. Only a discerning eye could pick them out as youngsters. They would be fully mature at about twenty-two months, after which they might wander off to form new packs or join others, or they would establish a place for themselves in this pack.

The mating season began in January, and the normally tolerant dispositions of Neka and Okimaw changed dramatically. Okimaw became testy, mostly towards his son, Otakosin, taking every opportunity to show his brute strength. And Neka enforced her dominance over Nimis, over every real or imagined transgression. This show of dominance passed down the line, and the wolves avoided eye contact and kept their tails well tucked between their legs. Only the alpha pair went around with their tails raised high.

Neka and Okimaw finally left the pack after three weeks to carry out the remainder of their courtship in private. After they had successfully completed their mating ritual, life among the wolves returned to normal.

In March the pack returned to Shadow Lake, where they had their denning area. Shadow Lake was seven kilometres long and, in some places, three kilometres wide. If seen from the air, it was shaped like a tight S, and it supported a family of common loons. The lake at the southeast end became marshland, an attraction to moose and fowl. On the opposite side where land indented the lake, the wolves had their den.

Neka prepared the den, making some slight renovations. It was located about one hundred yards from the water, and high banks provided views of the surrounding clearings and of the entrance. Stands of trembling aspen, black spruce, jack pine and hemlock protected three sides, and thickets of willow shrubs along the lake hid the den's entrance. The interior was a narrow twenty-foot tunnel, winding through the root system of the trees above, and it widened slightly at the end, where Neka would give birth to the pups.

At the beginning of spring, about two months after conception, Neka crawled in to give birth to a new generation. Six pups were born. Of these, two might survive to adulthood. The wilderness can be a harsh environment. For now, the whole pack celebrated the birth of the pups. With tails wagging, they danced around outside, whining and licking each other. Then, remembering that Neka might be hungry, they performed their pre-hunting ritual, nipping and licking at Okimaw's jaws, and he led them off to the hunt. He and other members brought food back, either swallowing it so they could regurgitate it on their return or, if portable, bringing back chunks of meat.

By the third week, all the puppies' eyes had opened and most of them were no longer deaf. Some of them were already crawling towards the entrance. Neka decided it was time to introduce them to the rest of the family. On that day, all the wolves gathered at the entrance, watching with anticipation. Each pup was greeted with much fuss. Neka, proud mother, watched her grunting, squealing pups.

Wapan, now thirteen months, was especially intrigued with the pups. Kehte-aya, Nimis, and Kanatan often took turns staying at the den while the others were away hunting. When Wapan was allowed to stay with the pups, she was quite pleased. She would settle down and allow the pups to climb all over her. If she went on the hunt, she made sure she brought back food but she preferred to be the one to stay with the little ones, although, more and more, Kehte-aya also remained at the den.

Kehta-aya was still agile, but she had become slower and stiffer with age. One day, she joined the hunt while Wapan remained behind. The pack came upon a mule deer, chased it, cornered it, and closed in on it. Kehte-aya was at the front while Okimaw and the others were tearing at its flanks. One of its sharp front hoofs caught Kehte-aya in the shoulder. It wasn't unusual for wolves to be struck. They healed well, and quickly, from such injuries. When the deer was down and the feeding frenzy began, Kehte-aya limped up to the carcass, but Okimaw chased her away and would not allow her to feed. Kehte-aya limped off to a thicket of willows to watch the feeding wolves and lick at the wound from which she would not heal.

The pack could afford to raise a healthy new litter to continue a generation of wolves. But when food was hard to come by, when each adult member had to carry its own weight to stay strong and sustain the pack, the pack could not carry the injured and the weak. Kehte-aya would not recover, and instinct dictated that she be excluded from the pack. Even if she had not been wounded, her age and condition would have guaranteed her exile sometime in the coming year.

That night, the howls of the wolves seemed to have an intensely lonely sound, almost as if they were in mourning once again. Kehte-aya, now feeding on what was left, raised her head to listen, knew her fate, and accepted it. She sighed and lowered her head to resume her meagre feeding. In time her pack would drive her further into the bush. Her time of usefulness to the pack had come to an end. From then on, when Neka was away, it would be Wapan who watched over the pups.

# 1

PREMONITION

The Chinook winds had blown by, teasing us with their higher temperatures, but soon full warmer days really would be here. The morning had been warm only briefly, and then the temperature had dropped drastically. Now the wind that had brought the cold was howling intermittently. Buffered from those winds inside our small log cabin, Peter had set up the chess game. Todd, our three-year-old, was asleep in his bed, and Lady, our collie, was lying at my feet. All the elements to ensure contentment were there, but I was miserable.

A few months back I had accepted an invitation to do readings in Norway House in northern Manitoba. The sessions would start on Wednesday afternoon and end on Friday morning, and I had decided to attend an Aboriginal writers' conference in Winnipeg on the Saturday, so I wouldn't be back until Sunday. The date of departure was closing in. No matter how reassuring Peter tried to be, I had a strong feeling that one of the flights was going to crash. I tried to remember if I had felt so certain before, but while I hated flying, once it was done I never remembered the details of my anxieties, only that I had had them.

"Let the games begin," Peter said cheerfully, holding a pawn in each hand behind his back. I picked the white pawn and made my usual opening move. After the initial play, each successive move took longer and longer.

Peter loved playing chess. His first mystery book, *Check and Mate*, was about a deadly game based on chess moves between an old man,

Gregory M. Thomas—the protagonist in his subsequent books—and an elusive stalker obsessed with a young lady. Of all the books he had written since, that one remained my favourite.

Since moving up north to the Fort St. John area, in the foothills of the Rockies, we had a routine of ending our days with a chess game, or sometimes two, skipping the games only if Peter was into his writing. When my ever-so-perfect sister Leona and her twelve-year-old son Michael had come to visit last summer, Peter had taught Michael the game, and Michael had taken my place for a while.

As I responded to a move and lost my bishop, I studied Peter's face, wondering what he thought about when we weren't talking. Probably plots. Because he wrote novels, Peter had to leave home more often than I did to do his research, maintain his contacts, and earn extra income with speaking engagements. In contrast, I spent my time trying not to think of the secrets of my past.

Lady stood up, shook herself, and trotted to the door, looking back at us expectantly. As I rose to let her out, Peter shushed me: "Listen."

At first I could hear only the snaps of wet wood burning in the stove. Then I distinctly heard them above the howling wind. The wolves were somewhere in our vicinity.

Peter and I exchanged smiles and we rushed out to the screened porch. Lady's nose quivered as she sniffed the night air and let out a soft high-pitched whine. I crouched down to pet her while we listened intently, reveling in the primeval excitement that the wolves awakened. The howling never seemed to last long enough and tonight it had an especially mournful quality.

"There's no answer," Peter noted, after a few minutes of silence. Sometimes there were answering calls in the distance, but not tonight, or they were beyond our hearing. Once, when Peter was away and I had let Lady out around five in the morning, I heard them, young ones and older ones, and it seemed they were just around the bend. They reminded me of people at a cocktail party: some excited voices rising above others. Unable to resist, I had let out a howling sound and that had silenced them immediately. Back in my bed I'd pictured them rolling around on

11

the ground, laughing at my effort. Or maybe I had insulted them in wolf language.

"They sound so forlorn tonight," I said. We walked back in, Lady following us, and settling again at my feet. "Or maybe it's just me."

Peter moved his black rook into place. "Check."

"Are you sure you want to do that?" I asked coyly.

"What?" Peter studied the board again. "Oh, I see. Yeah, well, it's too late. I already moved. So we're feeling forlorn, are we?"

"Well, I am. I'll miss you and Todd. And I have a really bad feeling about this trip. You can take it back," I said, indicating his lost piece.

"I can't. Rules are you can't take a move back."

"Like this is a championship game?" My queen was at the kitty corner from his rook. Was it a setup? If I took his rook, would I lose my queen? I should have delayed my trip to Norway House until late May when I imagined the snow would be all gone, but no, I had let my publisher tell them I'd come in the middle of April. Without caring too much, I made my move. If I lost my queen, I deserved it.

Closing in for the kill, Peter made another move. In doing so, he had left me an opening. He had once said I had a wicked mind, in that I pretended to play defensively, eventually pulling him in.

Smiling wickedly, I made my final move and said, "Check and mate." I sat back with exaggerated satisfaction. Inside, I was like two people. One wore the mask of a normal person. The other was always thinking, dwelling on comments like the one Peter had made about my wicked mind. He'd been joking, but maybe he sensed that I had more than just a wicked mind. Maybe he instinctively sensed that I had a wicked soul.

Peter looked at the board, seeing only now what he had missed. "Okay, okay, what if I had taken that move back?"

"You mean rules are made to be broken?"

"Let's just try it. You still win."

"I know," I said in jest. We put the pieces back in their positions before my queen had taken his rook and he had returned the rook to its original place. We played from there for another fifteen minutes, when I once again put him into checkmate.

"Another one?" Peter asked, refusing to retire as the loser.

"Oh Peter, I hate killing your men," I said jokingly.

We grinned at each other. He leaned forward and said in a lower voice, "One more."

"Okay. You set them up. I'll go check on Todd." Before I left, I put the kettle on the wood stove.

Todd was sleeping peacefully, a corner of his blanket tucked into his mouth. He was my angel, who roused feelings of gratitude in me, though at times he also roused feelings of guilt. Lady had followed me and she now settled herself on the rug beside his bed, almost as if it was her job to keep watch over him. Later during the night she would curl up or stretch out on the rug on my side of the bed.

I returned to the table with two cups of hot chocolate and picked a black pawn from Peter's right hand. "Too bad," he said, smiling gleefully. He knew I wasn't as good when I played black and that he would probably win. "Remember, we can't take back any moves."

"Yeah, right," I agreed.

"What you need is a killer instinct," he said, trying to psych me out in advance.

"Okay." I picked off a pawn, unable to resist, even though I knew I was leaving myself vulnerable.

"Are you sure you want to do that?" he mimicked me from our previous game.

"Yup." Only two more nights at home. I squirmed at the thought. Peter noticed.

"What?"

"I seriously have a real bad feeling this time."

"You already said that, and you always have bad feelings about flying. Flying is safer than driving. That's because pilots are well trained and there's not as many planes in the air as there are cars on the ground."

"But that doesn't make me feel any better. The man who owned this place before us died in a plane crash."

"Yeah, but they say Wayne Schumack mixed drugs with alcohol," Peter recalled.

"Well, this time, I have an extra, extra bad feeling."

"Why don't you cancel?"

"Can't do that now. I committed myself. I should be committed for committing myself."

"You could have said no. You should have said no."

"I know. I vow this is the last trip, unless I can drive or take a train."

"That's what you said after the last trip. We always go through this."

"Before I only promised. This is a vow, and a vow is more serious than a promise. You can take that move back if you want."

"Okay."

The next morning, Colin Sayers and his friend Howard Norach dropped by for coffee. Colin said he was in the area on business. He was in oil explorations, and Howard was retired. Because they always seemed to be together, I assumed Howard had been in the oil business, too. Colin was my sister Leona's latest "love of her life." They had met last August when she was visiting us, and then she had moved in with him in Fort St. John instead of returning home to Winnipeg like she had planned. Because he was living with my sister, I resented him almost as much as I resented Leona, but I was more civil with him than I was with Leona. Now, to be polite, I asked him how Leona and her son Michael were doing. Colin glanced at Howard and didn't seem to want to talk about them. All he said was that they were okay.

Howard had come with Colin a couple of times in the past few months. I always sensed that he tried hard not to look at me, yet I could feel his eyes on me as I made coffee or tended to Todd. Maybe the old man had a thing for me—and if so, dream on! Over coffee, Peter mentioned that Todd and he would have to "bach it" for a few days because I was going on a trip. Right away, I thought Peter was hoping to get an invite to Leona's for supper. Colin was very curious about the details of my trip. He seemed to have something else on his mind, but he kept whatever it was to himself and he and Howard left after their second cups of coffee.

By the middle of that afternoon, anxiety had me pacing back and forth and it wasn't only about travelling. Pictures of Peter and Leona sitting across from each other, talking and laughing, filled my mind. Peter was so much more attractive than Colin. At the same time I could not envision Peter cheating on me. He had never done anything to deserve my suspicions. He wasn't Nick, I said to myself. To burn off my nervous energy, I decided to go outside and split some wood.

Peter, who was revising another chapter before sending his manuscript off to his publisher, brought Todd outside and we went for a walk down to the lake.

"Loon!" Todd suddenly exclaimed. We were at the edge of the lake and most of the ice was gone, but the loons had not yet returned.

"No," Peter said. "The loons aren't back from the south yet. It's a duck."

"Duck," Todd repeated. That set him off on a rhyming spree. "Duck. Muck. Suck. Luck."

Peter and I looked at each other, waiting for the "F" word to come. We smiled.

"The loon will be here soon," Peter said, in an attempt to ward him off.

Todd merely looked up at him and continued, "Duck. Muck. Buck. Guck."

"The ice is nice," I said helpfully.

Peter looked at me. "The ice is nice?"

I shrugged. "Look in his eyes. He's toying with us."

Peter studied our son. Todd seemed to know his game was up because he giggled gleefully. He knew that the "F" word, which he heard from movies we rented, was a no-no. Peter picked him up and swung him around in the air. Todd laughed all the more with delight. His eyes, shining with pure joy, looked down into his father's eyes, and the wonderful sound of his laughter echoed out across the lake. The pleasure in their faces was evident as they enjoyed life as it was meant to be. They both had the same smile that held a hint of good-natured mischief. I didn't know that in a short while, the memory of them at this moment would return sometimes to haunt me, and sometimes to sustain me.

Once we returned to the cabin, I began to pack a bag while Peter added more wood to the woodstove. When he was done, he brought Todd in for his afternoon nap. A little while later, he came into our bedroom carrying a binder containing his manuscript *A Dick Named Tom.*

"Take this with you," he said. "I'm almost done, but I'll wait till you get back before I email it."

"Did you ask Amber if she had Word? It'd be so much easier to send it from their place, than having to go to Fort St. John." Amber was our closest neighbours' teenaged granddaughter. She'd been living with Kit and Mona since before her mother died in Vancouver. Apparently, Amber had gotten into some kind of trouble, which I found hard to believe because she seemed like a great kid. She knew how to use the Internet and send e-mails, which was handy because the telephone wires ended at their place and the cost to put in poles and wiring to our cabin was exorbitant.

Peter said, "Good question. If she doesn't, I'll get it for her."

I always packed light for flights so I didn't have to wait for baggage to be unloaded. Unfortunately, my winter clothing was too bulky, so I had to bring down one of the larger suitcases from the attic. I looked everything over and made sure I had my plane ticket. I would leave for the long drive to Fort St. John extra early in the morning in case the roads were icy, fly from there to Edmonton, and wait for the flight to Winnipeg. I'd stay overnight in Winnipeg, but I had to get to the airport by six-thirty the next morning for the seven o'clock small-plane flight to Norway House. Besides flying, I hated staying alone in hotel rooms—I'd rather be nestled in Peter's arms—and then there were all the small worries, like not being able to get my morning cups of coffee with real milk. Satisfied that all was in order in my luggage, I went to Todd's bedroom.

Lady raised her head and wagged a greeting. Not wanting to disturb my sleeping son, I sat on the rug and let Lady rest her head on my lap. She liked me to stroke her head. Todd's mouth moved a few times as if he were sucking on his blanket. Unable to resist, I moved his thick dark-brown hair, thinking I'd have to give him a haircut when I got back. His clear skin still had a rosy pink glow from being outside.

Although I'd never told Peter, I was glad that Todd had fair skin. He wouldn't get the name-calling I'd had to take as a kid. Now when I saw other kids his age, I thought none of them were as perfect as he was— none were as good-natured, as eager to please or to smile that unique special smile that he'd inherited from Peter. And he could be so funny. I had only been guessing he had been toying with us out at the lake and was surprised I had been right. He was smarter than the average bear.

He must have sensed he was being watched because he woke up and immediately held his arms out to me to be hugged. I obliged, and then took him to wash up before supper. Already I knew I was going to miss him so much.

On Wednesday morning, F-day—F for flights, I became all silent.

Peter, knowing my silence was due to distress and not to anger, paid cheerful attention to Todd during breakfast. Todd was in a talkative mood but I was too distracted to pay attention. I'd woken up with a feeling of dread and now, over my third cup of coffee, I was actually feeling terror. Six different planes and I knew one of them wasn't going to make it to its destination. Premonitions were silly, I chided myself. My fear of flying was just getting worse. That's all it was.

I looked at my watch. I was five minutes behind schedule. "I guess I should leave now. Do you think the roads will be icy?"

"No, they should be dry. Are you sure you don't want me to drive you?"

"No, no. From the way flight schedules are these days, I might not get back until Monday." I answered.

"Don't worry so much. Before you know it, you'll be back accepting another invitation to fly to another school."

"Yeah, right!" I kissed him, and gave him and Todd extra-tight hugs.

Carrying Todd, Peter saw me out to the truck, where we said more goodbyes.

"Say goodbye to Lady, Mommy." Todd said, pointing down to her. Thinking I was taking her for a ride, she was all excited. I leaned down so she could lick my face and I could say goodbye. The goodbye word meant she had to stay behind and she quieted down.

"You always say goodbye like you'll never see us again," Peter remonstrated.

I shrugged and said lightly, "I don't want to leave you guys."

"Take your time going but hurry back." He gave me one last kiss, and he and Todd waved to me as I drove out of the yard. In the woods to the far north, I thought I saw a flash of light, like when the sun's rays bounce off chrome or glass, but I quickly forgot it when I glanced in the rear-view mirror and saw Lady following me. After a short distance, she gave up and sat to watch me drive away.

I followed our road, a cantankerous, sparsely gravelled road, six kilometres down to Kit's place. A winding road, it sometimes went east, sometimes south, and I'm sure at times it headed back west. Kit's real name was Martin Kitsewasis, and he and Mona were our closest neighbours and friends. Mona had come from Halfway River and had inherited a traditional trapline that included our two sections of land. When we first moved up here from Vancouver, Kit had come and asked Peter if they could continue trapping on our land. Catching cute little animals and skinning them was something I found distasteful, but since it was their way, and they had been here first, I was pleased when Peter gave them permission. Besides, they were pretty old, and I didn't think they did much trapping. I passed by their driveway on my right where, even in winter, evergreens, young and old, hid their house from view.

Here, at Kit's, the road widened. It was the turnaround for the school bus, and the village of Dodging maintained it year-round only to this point. About two kilometres past Kit's, a private road went north. At its entrance, a sign—NAK-WAN inc. / keep out / trespassers will be prosecuted—was posted at the entrance. Mrs. Martens, owner of the Dodging grocery store, had once grumbled that it was a biological laboratory that got all its supplies from Fort St. John. On one of his hikes, Peter had come across a high, seemingly endless chain-link fence topped with barbed wire. Whatever the place was, they had invested a lot of money to prevent trespassing. I had read an early draft of Peter's new manuscript and I knew he had gotten the idea for it from NAK-WAN inc.

I passed through the village of Dodging. Except for the gas station on my left and the sprinkling of newer buildings visible from the main road, the village had a Western Frontier feel to it. The facing of most of the buildings was constructed from jack pine poles and in many places the wooden sidewalks were protected with overhangs.

Like all the old frontier settlements, here in Indian country, white people controlled the amenities of the town. Dodging had a Presbyterian Church, a school, Mrs. Martens' general store and gas station, and the two-storey Castaway Motel and Restaurant, which featured the only pool table in the area and housed the local drinking hole, the Palomino Saloon. As I passed the post office on my right I exchanged glances with Mrs. Springer, the local reporter for Fort St. John's Peace Valley Voice. She was getting out of her car, no doubt to get her latest piece of gossip from the lady who ran the post office.

Whenever Peter and I stopped in Dodging for our mail, we seemed to run into Mrs. Springer, who always gushed over Peter. She adored him and Todd, and she probably wondered how come he had married me, a Métis woman. About a year ago, Peter must have talked her into doing a piece on me, and my picture had appeared in the paper. Because I had always thought she didn't like me, I was surprised the article was so promotional. I guess I could thank Peter for that. Ever since then, when strangers stared at me, I never knew why.

Leaving Dodging behind, I entered the portent of more destruction to come. When we had first moved up north, and I looked at our road map, I'd thought the whole area was untouched, but bulldozing equipment had already bullied its way into the wilderness, cutting open ugly wounds for the heavy trucks that followed. Chainsaws buzzed as tall trees toppled and crashed to the ground, their silent screams unheard. Unlike our road, where towering old-growth evergreens spread their boughs overhead, herbicides were sprayed along these new roads to subdue vegetation and, consequently, the animals that grazed on them. Something about these roads reminded me of the desolation of the prairies, where nothing impeded the winds. All of this frenzied activity took place to feed man's hunger for oil, lumber, and other commodities and, in my case, for the gas in my truck and the fuel for the planes I'd be taking—another darn good reason to quit travelling.

Three hours after leaving our cabin, I settled myself on the first plane.

19

Though I appeared to be reading, I was braced for takeoff. Trying to think of good things only, I pictured Todd, Peter, and Lady back at our cabin, imagined what they'd be doing right now. If I gave up writing children's books, I thought, I would never be tempted to travel like this again. When I felt the plane speed up for its ascent, I closed my eyes and held my breath until we were high in the sky. Then I spent the rest of the time listening for changes in the droning sound of the engines.

When my last flight finally reached Norway House without incident, I was able to relax enough to enjoy the classroom visits. As planned, Peter called me during the lunch hour at the school to assure himself I had made the trip safely. On Wednesday afternoon and all day Thursday, I spoke or read to students, and I had a tour of the local sights. In the evenings I had supper in the company of my host and other people, and spent the balance of my nights restlessly reading Peter's manuscript. I wished we had a landline at Shadow Lake. I knew I could phone Kit's place but Peter and I had agreed that only emergency phone calls would go through them. When my loneliness for Peter and Todd got to be too much, I tried to think of an urgent message but couldn't come up with one.

On Friday I flew to Winnipeg, and having already met many of the writers at other events, I enjoyed the conference. If I had liked my mother, I would have made time to see her but I had no desire to see the woman who'd given me away to foster care when I was five. On Sunday morning I was happy to be getting on the flight to Edmonton, only because it was homeward bound. When my last plane taxied in at Fort St. John, I got the urge to jump and yell for joy. Instead, I chided myself for all the dumb feelings I had expressed earlier. From now on, I vowed to myself again, no more airplane trips—that's it, no more!

A perfect day with a clear blue sky kept me company on my drive home, but freezing rain must have hit the area earlier because there were still shaded icy stretches. As I was driving by Kit and Mona's, a muddy but happy Lady came bounding out to greet me. I backed up the truck and pulled into their driveway. Mona must have heard me because she came out on her porch right away and after we exchanged greetings, she told me she'd had a phone call.

"Some man. He said Leona asked him to make the call. That was on Friday. We were just about to go to my sister's for the weekend. Yeah, he said that Leona wanted Peter to come to Fort St. John, Saturday morning. This man, he didn't give a name, like who he was or what it was about. He just hung up, eh."

"Oh, it was probably Colin. Her boyfriend," I said.

Mona pulled her cardigan tighter around herself and added, "Yeah, so Kit went right away to tell Peter about the phone call and then we left."

Flip-flop—my stomach turned over. Leona had made her move. Had Peter run to her side? Colin must have told her I'd be out of town. Hiding the feelings churning inside me, I asked Mona, "How is Mary?"

"Oh, she's much better. My other sister, Elsie, she's coming back for a couple of weeks, so Mary will have someone with her."

"Well, that's good. Thanks for taking that message to Peter," I said, lying through a smile.

Lady was going down the driveway already so I called her to the truck. She sat and barked at me. In no mood to play games, I got in the truck and drove slowly after her. When she got to the road, she looked over her shoulder at me as if she wanted me to follow her into the woods on the north side of the road. I wanted to get home quickly, to find out exactly what was going on. I opened the door on the passenger side and called to her to come. She was waiting at the edge of the woods, as if she expected me to follow her. She barked at me, so I barked right back, "Lady, get in the damned truck. Now!"

She didn't know what to do with such a direct order. For some crazy reason known only to her, she had a need to go traipsing off into the woods, and she wanted me to go along with her. She stood, lowered her head, looked over her shoulder towards the north, then very slowly came to the truck and jumped in, whining all the while.

I drove carefully on our icy road. I was mad as hell at Leona for her phone call, and at Colin, too. Didn't he have the brains to see what she was up to? And I was going to be a lot angrier at Peter if he had gone to Fort St. John. Lady, sporting a rank swampy smell that permeated the whole inside of the truck, continued whining. Distracted from my thoughts, I said, "Lady, where have you been that you stink so much?"

As soon as I drove around the last bend, I began to tremble with anger. Peter's truck was nowhere in sight. He must have been in such a rush to get to Leona that he hadn't even bothered to make sure Lady was inside. I forced myself to think of other reasons why he wasn't here.

Leaving Lady outside on her own just wasn't like him. Maybe he'd only gone there today, expecting to see me on the road, or maybe he'd gone somewhere else and would be back shortly. But inside on the table was a scribbled note on a card from his Rolodex: "Christine, I had to go to Fort St. John. Be back as soon as I can. Peter."

He had gone to her! I sat at the table staring at the card; there was something wrong with it. Then it came to me. I realized he'd used our full names. When he wrote, he worked late into the night and he might leave notes for me for the mornings but he always used just our initials. The only time he ever called me Christine was if he was really furious with me, and that had amounted to maybe four times over the past ten years. Usually, it was just Chris. He must have been so anxious to get to Leona—that was it, I thought. I was suddenly filled with rage, not at him, but at me. I had spent all these years trusting him. I should have known better: trust no one. I revised my thought to: trust no man around Leona.

The rage gave way to self-pity, and I began to cry. I couldn't lose Peter's love to another woman, I just couldn't. That special smile of his? It was only for me. In all our years together I had never seen him share it with anyone else. And why would he, because in that smile was his desire for me. So no, I didn't want to share it with anyone else, especially not with Leona!

I lit a fire in the wood stove, put the kettle on for coffee and returned to look at the "kiss-off" note. Later, with my coffee, I settled on the couch to wait. Plans of what to do came to mind. I'd pack for Todd and myself so that when Peter returned, I'd be all ready to leave. I'd move back to Winnipeg because living in Vancouver as a single parent would be too expensive and it was Peter's hometown. Smiling wryly to myself,

I thought I was like a yo-yo. Over a decade ago, Leona and Nick had driven me to Vancouver, and now Leona and Peter would drive me back to Winnipeg.

Leona! I hated her!

Before I left for good, I'd go to her place and give her a piece of my mind. Then again, I couldn't really spare a piece of my mind. Well, I was going to do something to get back at her. I turned on the TV for distraction from my ugly thoughts. The sudden bout of depression brought on a fatigue so intense I couldn't think clearly enough to figure out how I was going to get back at her. Gulping back the last of my coffee, I leaned sideways to rest on the arm of the couch—and that was all I remembered.

When I woke up, it was dark. I found that I had my jacket on, but I was very cold. No wonder—I was sitting behind the wheel of the truck. I got out and made my way to the porch. I was totally disoriented. When I finally made it to the side porch, I looked back and noted that I hadn't parked the truck in its usual spot.

Inside the cabin, it was pitch black. Lady poked her nose into my hand. I vaguely remembered that the TV had been on when I went to sleep. At the couch, I removed only my toque and, in spite of feeling that something was drastically wrong, I sat down, leaned over, and fell asleep again.

When I woke up, I was still on the couch, still in my clothes, and in my jacket, and it was seven in the morning. My body was aching from the way I had slept. My first thought was, if Peter had come home and seen me asleep on the couch, he would have woken me up and got me to bed. I went to check the bedrooms but they were empty. That meant Peter had spent the night in Fort St. John with Leona. The fact that Michael and Todd were with them wouldn't have mattered.

The toque had come off in my sleep and I had a strange sensation to do with my head. Touching my hand to my hair, I was shocked. What happened to my hair? I rushed to the bathroom, where I saw long strands of coal-black hair coiled on the floor before I looked up at the strange image reflected back in the mirror. Sometime in the night I had driven the truck; sometime in the night I had cut my waist-length hair. All that was left were short, jagged spikes. Yet I had no recollection of doing either of these things.

Sometime in the night my mind had snapped.

Another wave of depression hit me and zapped any energy I had left. All I could do was light a fire for coffee, put food and fresh water down for Lady, and prop both the kitchen and porch doors open so she could come and go as she pleased. The odour she carried reminded me that I would have to give her a bath. Then I sat on the couch drinking the coffee, pondering my bleak future. My last thoughts were that I was going to raise hell with Peter when he did come home. Then I'd leave for Winnipeg.

When I next awoke, the clock on the wall said it was close to 4:00 p.m. Time for another coffee, and prepare for my trip to Leona's and that didn't just involve the driving. I imagined Peter telling me, "I'm sorry Christine. I fell in love with Leona. It just happened." What my reaction was going to be in that event, I didn't yet know. While I waited for the kettle to boil, I returned to take another look in the mirror, trying to call up even a flash of memory of having cut my hair. Nothing came. For me, shearing off my hair was a form of self-mutilation, one that I'd done before. What was really weird was that I didn't have the emotions that I had had back then. Right now I was angry—big-time angry, a little bit jealous—okay, a whole lot jealous, and I was very hurt. But if I could recognize these feelings, then how could I possibly be crazy? I must have hacked off my hair in my sleep. Obviously, I'd been sleepwalking. That was something new and therefore, alarming.

The water in the kettle boiled over and I went to make my coffee and something to eat. The thoughts that filled my mind brought on another wave of grogginess, so I abandoned the idea of eating and returned to the couch to finish off my coffee. This time I knew I was drifting back to sleep, but couldn't stop myself.

When I woke again, I felt as groggy as I had when I went to sleep. Still, I managed to put more wood in the stove and to tend to Lady's needs. She seemed to want me to come outside with her, but, being too tired, I just propped the doors open again—I must have closed them during my sleep—and headed back for the couch.

The next time I woke up I looked at the clock and was amazed that the hands were in a perfect vertical position, with the short hand on the six. My next thoughts were that I'd force some food down, tidy myself up, and then make that drive to Fort St. John to reclaim my son from that bitch and bastard. But with my coffee in hand, I found myself gravitating towards the couch once more, to sit for just a minute.

Lady poked at me with her nose until I sat up. It was light out so even though I'd slept through Sunday evening and right through yesterday, I had managed to sleep right through the night. What was the matter with me? The sleeping had to be my reaction to the stress of losing Peter to Leona—that was it. I heard a car door slam shut. From Lady's lack of excitement, I knew it wasn't Peter and Todd. I figured it would be Kit so I put a fire on in the stove for coffee. I heard heavy footsteps on the porch steps, the porch door squeaking open, and loud knocking at the door. When I opened the door, Kit was standing there and behind him was a uniformed RCMP officer.

My hands went to my hair to pat what was left of it into place. Kit's eyes widened in surprise when he saw me, and I knew I looked a mess.

"Chris," he said, "I've got some bad news."

# 2

MISSING

We all sat at the kitchen table and the officer introduced himself as Sergeant Trolley. He told me that Peter's truck had been found in the Peace River.

My mind grasped at what he wasn't saying, that both Peter and Todd had died in an accident. My body began making erratic movements. My hands twitched, my arms moved upwards, then down, and an involuntary smile flashed across my face. Shaking my head no, I denied the possibility that Peter and Todd could be dead.

"What about Todd?" I asked, dreading the answer. My words came out sounding slurred and my mouth was dry. Even though it was warm inside the cabin, I was shivering.

"I'm sorry?" Sergeant Trolley asked, not understanding my question.

"Todd. Her son. He's three," Kit explained.

"We didn't find either one. My men are working at getting the truck out but there was no one in it. I'm very sorry, Mrs. Webster," he said, sympathetically. "Was your husband in good health? Was he on any medications?"

Listlessly, I replied, "Peter's health was good, he wasn't on any medications. All we ever took, if we had to, were aspirins."

"What about his doctor? Did he have a regular doctor?"

"In Fort St. John."

"Do you have his name and address?"

Zombie-like and not even bothering to wonder why he'd want

to know about Peter's doctor, I crossed the room to the Rolodex on Peter's desk and copied down the information on a scratch pad. When I returned to the table, I noticed that the officer's eyes now seemed more alert than sympathetic.

"Are you alright, Mrs. Webster?" he asked, "Have you been drinking?"

"No, I'm not alright. And no, I don't drink." With Todd and Peter gone, I'd never be all right, again. Not ever. Tears rimmed my eyes, but I didn't want to break down in front of a stranger. I didn't have the energy to resent his second question.

"I just meant you seem sluggish," he explained.

"Oh that. I've been away on a trip. Ever since I got back on Sunday, I've been feeling so tired. I don't understand it. I've never been like this before." His stare was so intense that I went on, "I had to go to Norway House. That's in northern Manitoba."

A hissing noise came from the woodstove as boiling water sloshed out of the kettle. "I was just going to make coffee. You want some?"

Both Kit and Trolley nodded, so I got up, went to the counter, spooned instant coffee into three cups, and brought them back to the table. Because of a joke Peter had cracked once, at my expense, I usually prepared my coffee at the counter but right now I didn't care. My eyelids were so heavy. I went back for the sugar bowl and milk. Lady quietly followed me and lay down as I counted out spoons. Turning to go back to the table, I tripped over her and fell. The sugar went flying everywhere as I concentrated on holding the milk container upright. Under my breath, I swore at Lady. She tried to make up by licking my face, as I just sat on the floor, forcing myself not to cry. Kit came over to soothe me and help me back to the table, then got more sugar from the bag in the cupboard and refilled the bowl.

Eyeing me, Sergeant Trolley said, "I'm so sorry, Mrs. Webster. I know how you must be feeling, but I have to ask these questions. I couldn't help seeing this here," he said picking up Peter's note. "This note is from your husband?"

As I rubbed my eyes, I looked at the note, wishing I had put it somewhere else. I wondered again why he had used my full name. Had he been angry with me and, if so, why? To answer the officer's question, I nodded.

He asked, "Why'd he go to Fort St. John? Do you know?"

I looked at Kit for him to explain. "The phone call?"

Kit understood and said, "Friday afternoon, we got a call from a man. He was calling for Leona—that's Chris's sister—said she wanted Peter to go there on Saturday morning. Didn't say why."

"What time did you get the call?"

"I don't know," Kit said. "Sometime after four. Amber—that's my granddaughter—was home from school and we were just going to leave for the weekend to go to my sister-in-law's place. Yeah, I came here right after Mona told me."

"How did he react when you told him?"

"He just said thanks and invited me to stay for a coffee, but I had to get back, so I left."

"He seemed normal to you?"

This question coupled with the one about Peter's doctor sunk in.

"You think it wasn't an accident? That Peter deliberately . . ." I couldn't finish the sentence. The idea was just too preposterous.

Sergeant Trolley watched me shake my head and asked another question. "Were you getting along?"

"Yes, we got along fine." From the corner of my eye I saw Kit nodding his head, and I was grateful. "Why do you ask something like that?"

"We have to consider all the possibilities, and those who are closest know the most. They can help us more than anyone else. If they're not hiding something, that is." The way he looked at me was both an accusation and invitation to come clean.

"Well, Peter was happy. He's a writer and he had just finished another manuscript. He was doing what he wanted to do and he had everything he wanted." Perhaps not, I thought to myself. Perhaps he had wanted Leona instead of me. This was speculation on my part, and I told myself that it would not be at all helpful to a police investigation. I sure wasn't going to share this with anyone else. So I continued, "He's the one who wanted to come live up here in the first place."

"From where?" he asked.

"Vancouver," I said, yawning.

Strangely, the exhaustion I'd felt for the past few days was beginning to lift. "When did this . . . the accident happen, do you know?"

"At this point, we don't know, exactly. From what you've told us, it must have been Saturday, maybe Sunday."

"I have to go to where Peter's truck is," I said. "Are you going back there? I could follow you."

"In your condition, you shouldn't do any driving."

"I'll drive you, Chris," Kit said. His kindness touched me.

Before we left, Sergeant Trolley asked me for Leona's address, so I returned to Peter's Rolodex, copied her address for him, and put her card in my pocket. Sergeant Trolley must have thought it strange that I didn't know my own sister's address, but I had refused to memorize it. In turn, he gave me his card, in case I thought of anything else or had further questions. Or perhaps he was thinking I might want to come clean with what I knew. In Peter's novels, Gregory M. Thomas, a former police detective and present owner of a large detective agency, could always sense when someone was lying to him. Maybe Sergeant Trolley was like him and had sensed I was holding back information.

Excusing myself, I went to the bathroom, wiped my face with cold water, and ripped a comb through what was left of my hair. Then we were all on our way to the Peace River, with me in Kit's truck. I was quiet as if I were holding my breath, perhaps expecting some kind of actual evidence at the scene that Peter and Todd were dead. Eventually, I told him I'd been sleeping almost constantly since I got back on Sunday. Then I told him I'd had a really bad premonition about my trip. And here it didn't have anything to do with me after all. It had been about Peter and Todd. After that we drove on in silence.

When we turned left onto the highway towards Fort St. John, Kit surprised me by saying, "We thought we heard you drive by our place on Sunday night."

"Couldn't have been me 'cause, like I said, I've been sleeping." One thing I knew for sure was that I could not have driven anywhere and still remained on the road. On the other hand, I wasn't totally convinced of that myself. What was going on with me?

"Well, I'm just saying we thought we heard you. We didn't want to tell the police, though. They might jump to all sorts of conclusions."

"Sounds like he already has," I said. "The questions he asked—it's like he doesn't believe Peter really had an accident."

Kit didn't answer at first, but as we drew closer to the accident site and saw lots of vehicles parked on both sides of the highway, he said, "I'm sure Peter and Todd are okay." In that moment he seemed more like a father than a neighbour.

Sergeant Trolley's police car rolled to a stop behind the last car parked on the south side and Kit pulled up behind it. We got out and followed him along the shoulder of the highway. The officer explained that Peter's truck must have been coming from the west and gone out of control. Although the trees were sparse along this side of the highway, they would have prevented a vehicle from going all the way down to the river. Where we stopped, the incline down to the river was bare of trees, and looking straight down the steep path, I saw Peter's truck on the narrow shoreline, water dripping from it.

Kit surveyed the scene. "How did you find out about the accident?" he asked Trolley. "Nothing's really visible from the highway."

"We got a call early this morning," Trolley responded. "The fellow wouldn't give his name. Just told us he'd had a flat and saw what he thought was a truck in the river last night."

There were signs of activity and sounds of men yelling out directions. One of the officers saw us and called out that they had found something. He began climbing up towards us carrying a small plastic bag. Sergeant Trolley moved forward to take the bag from him

He held up the bag, asking, "Do you recognize this?"

I had been staring at the activity down below. When I turned to see what was in the bag, I almost choked on the words, "It looks like Todd's running shoe." It had maroon spots on it, which could only have been blood, and I steeled myself against the tears that threatened to flow. Until that moment I had been able to stop myself from thinking that Peter and

Todd were dead, but now, wasn't this proof?

"Was the truck submerged?" Kit asked the officer.

"Yeah, the front part was almost straight down. The back was sticking out a bit. And the door on the driver side was open."

"Is it okay if I leave?" I mumbled.

Sergeant Trolley nodded but said, "We'll be by later."

Kit led me back to his pickup, and I saw Mrs. Springer pull into our spot as we drove away. I couldn't give in to my grief, just yet. "Could you take me to Fort St. John?" I asked Kit. "I should tell Leona what happened."

What I really wanted to do was find out even though his truck was coming from the west, whether Peter had gone there before the accident and, if so, whether he had spent the night with them. The police didn't know when the accident had happened and, if they hadn't received the anonymous call, Peter's truck might not have been discovered for quite some time. The other thing I needed to know was why Leona had wanted Peter to come to her place when Colin must have told her I would be away. In a weird way, I felt that if I had lost Peter to Leona before the accident, it would somehow make his death a little less painful. As for Todd, nothing would ever take away the pain of losing him.

In Fort St. John at Leona's, no one answered the door. An elderly neighbour was outside doing some spring yard work, so I asked him if he knew where Leona and Colin were. The man took off his hat, scratched his chin, and said, "Well, I imagine Colin's at work. Who are you?"

"Christine Webster. I'm Leona's sister, and there's been an accident. I need to find her. Do you know where she is?"

"Don't know. Saw her leave, must have been a couple of months back."

"You mean she moved away?"

"Yeah, her and Michael, they got in a taxi one morning and they had their bags with them. Haven't seen them since. That's all I know."

Stunned by this news, I got back into Kit's truck. "That man who made the call for Leona? What exactly did he say?" I asked. "Did he leave an address or anything?"

"No. Mona would have taken it down. Just asked for us to pass on

31

a message that Peter should go to Fort St. John on Saturday morning. Why? She's not home?"

"Apparently she and Michael moved out a couple of months ago."

On Colin's visit to us the day before I left for my trip he hadn't mentioned that he and Leona had split up. Maybe he'd only come over to see if Leona was staying with us. Maybe Peter and Leona had been talking to each other all along. But when and where? No, I couldn't see that happening.

My confusion, I thought, would have to wait because just then I had a lump in my throat. My grieving could no longer wait. I had to get back to Shadow Lake where I could be alone. Todd and Peter gone! It couldn't be, and yet it was. The sight of Todd's running shoe had confirmed it. All the way back I wanted to let go, but I didn't. Except for patting my hand before he started driving, Kit didn't make any vain attempts to comfort me.

We were already in my driveway before I thought of Peter's parents, Barbara and Barry. They had to be notified, but I couldn't bring myself to return to Kit's place. As soon as I was inside, I went into Todd's bedroom and threw myself across his bed. I writhed in pain, wanting to get out of my skin, wishing for relief through tears, but the tears wouldn't come. Lady followed me inside and showed her concern by nuzzling at me and whining anxiously. If they were dead, what was I going to do without them? That they would never again be in my life was just not possible.

That night I gathered Todd's blanket and pillow along with Peter's favourite sweater, and, bunching them up as a kind of pillow, I lay down on the couch, waiting for sleep to take me, comforted a little by their vague scents. The next day, after washing up, I tidied the cabin, sweeping up the hair on the bathroom floor. Afterwards, I headed for Kit's, dreading the phone call I had to make to Peter's parents.

Peter's mother answered the phone and, as strong and capable as she was, I couldn't make myself tell another mother her son was dead. I asked to speak to Barry. He took the news quietly and then asked, "Are you okay? Why don't you come down here?"

"No, I want to be here in case they have more news," I said, trying to keep a steady voice. "Tell Barbara that I'm very sorry. I just couldn't bring myself to tell her directly."

"I understand," he said. After asking me a few more questions, he concluded, "You take care and call us when you do hear something new." I gave him Sergeant Trolley's phone number at the RCMP detachment in Fort St. John.

Declining an offer of lunch from Mona and Kit, I went back to the spot on the highway where Peter's truck had gone off. Another RCMP vehicle was already parked there. Not wanting to talk to anyone, I passed by until I found a place where I could turn back. I decided to return here later that night.

Back at the cabin, I sat on Todd's bed. At times, I remembered something funny he'd done and it made me smile. The clock in the living room was ticking away, and the more time passed, the more guilt I felt. The more guilt I felt, the more I hated myself. How ironic that it had taken such a loss to think about all the reasons for the guilt, now when nothing could be done.

When it got dark I got up enough energy to head back to the accident site. In spite of my flashlight, I groped my way down the embankment, slip-sliding part of the way, not much caring whether I hurt myself. Sitting there on a cold rock, I wished I knew what had happened, wished it could be undone.

If only I had burned Leona's very first letter. But I had been curious. And I had allowed Peter to read it and talk me into inviting her back into my life, my sanctuary. Now I was sitting alone on a rock, hopelessly wishing for the impossible, that our lives were what they had been before Leona came to Shadow Lake. My thoughts focused on her. I had challenged the fates, knowing I would always lose.

Even though I knew that, I had always trusted Peter. Until her letter came.

———

One day Peter had gone to Dodging and upon his return had given me an envelope from my publisher. I opened it to find another envelope, and when I saw the name in the return address, my stomach turned over. My first thought was to burn it in the stove with the rest of the junk mail, but I put it aside to read later in private.

Peter, curious as always, looked up from his mail to ask, "A fan letter?"

"No, I don't think so," I answered.

I went to Todd's bedroom to sit for a while and watch him sleep, but, mostly, I went there to avoid further questions from Peter. I tried, unsuccessfully, not to think about what might be in the letter.

Later that day I went down to the lake and read it. It was addressed from Leona Pelletier—not Leona Scarlos but Leona Pelletier. So they hadn't married after all. I turned the envelope over, looked at the postmark, and saw it had been mailed from Winnipeg. Why did she have to go and write to me? Why couldn't she just leave me alone? Why was I letting a simple letter control my emotions? The solution to the problem of this letter would be simply not to answer, or to flip it into the lake and just let it go. But if I didn't read it, I would always wonder. Maybe it was about our mother being dead. So what? I wouldn't go to her funeral anyways. I smelled the envelope expecting to get a whiff of perfume. Nothing. Finally, I tore the end open and pulled out a pink sheet of paper. That figured—nothing common for the "queen."

*Dear Chrissy,*

*How are you? Bet your surprised to hear from me, eh? A voice from the past. I only recently got the bright idea of writing to you through your publisher. I need your help but if you can't, that's ok. I'm sure I can do something else, but I would love to see you again.*

*I have to have an operation soon, nothing serious, just a gallbladder operation. So I won't be able to work for a while. I'm a waitress and they won't be able to keep my job open for me. Before I go on, I have to tell you I have a son. Michael's 12 years old and he's the most important person in my life. I guess that means we haven't seen each other for around 14 years. I've got a friend he can stay with while I'm in the hospital. But the doc says I need 2,*

*3 weeks after to recuperate. There's not enough room at my friend's for both of us.*

*I'm holding off on this operation till July. That way, Mikey will be on summer holidays. So if you have the room and it's not a problem, I'd like to visit with you. But it wouldn't be a big deal if its not a good idea.*

*Not a day's gone by that I haven't thought of you. About a month ago I was talking about you to one of the women at work and she asked if I was related to you because she had a children's book written by Christine Pelletier Webster. She brought it in the next day and I saw your picture. I can't tell you how proud I was, am of you.*

*Chrissy, I have so much to tell you. I really hope we can visit with each other. To be honest, its hard writing this letter after all this time and here I am, asking for your help. Oh yeah, remember that doctor you lived with? I ran into Gerry Caruthers, that social worker. He told me that doctor and his daughters drowned in a boating accident in the Caribbeans. Time flies!*

*You can write to me at the return address until the end of June. Thanks no matter what you decide. Bye for now.*

*All my love to you and yours.*
*Leona*

By my calculation Nick was Michael's father, and a wave of jealousy washed over me. She had kept her child. I heard Peter and Todd behind me about the same time that Lady came and put her wet nose into my hand, the one holding the letter.

"Bad news?" Peter asked, sensing my distress.

"No," I answered and tried to hide the letter. I didn't want to have to explain Leona to him. All he knew about my past was that I'd grown up in foster homes in Winnipeg and that I had a half-sister I didn't know well. The only thing of interest was the news about Dr. Coran. I was glad he was dead. Too bad his daughters had died, too.

He tilted his head, focused on the letter in my hand and asked, "Want to share?"

To say no was not an option, so I handed him the letter and stooped down to adjust the hood on Todd's jacket. His instant smile restored good feelings in me.

"Fourteen years since you last saw each other?"

"Something like that," I answered. "But we weren't close or anything. She was only a half-sister."

From his perspective, this letter should have been an exciting moment for me.

"Yeah, but now you'd have a chance to get to know each other. Family is family. And she has a son. Wow!"

"Wow, wow," Todd piped up. We both looked at him and laughed. Simply watching Todd and Lady too, could put a smile on my face no matter what else was happening.

"You have to write back and tell her they should come as soon as they can. These people who drowned, you lived with them?"

I nodded but I felt myself being backed into a corner from which only the belated truth could rescue me, but for some reason I couldn't bring myself to tell Peter I had been wronged by my own sister and I definitely didn't want to talk about Dr. Coran. For some reason! Who was I kidding? Telling him anything meant telling him more belated truths, which would lead to even more belated truths.

"Yeah, write back and offer to send them plane tickets," Peter said, looking over the letter again. "It's too bad she didn't include a phone number. We could have phoned from Kit's place tonight."

Maybe Leona had put a secret seductive scent on her letter, detectable only by men. He didn't know a thing about her, yet he wanted her here. My mind was too slow to come up with a reason why I should not invite her.

"Come on, you can write back to her right away. You must have been shocked, huh?"

Grinning, Peter handed the letter back to me, took hold of Todd's hand and led the way back. As I followed, I considered the possibility of telling him what Leona had done to me. Instead of the truth, it was a lie that came to me. I could tell him that Leona was an alcoholic and that I didn't think it would be a good idea to have her around Todd. But then he might say that was all the more reason to have her come. And if she didn't have a drinking problem, I'd look like the liar I was. Scratch that one. I could say she was a heavy smoker, but Kit smoked and it didn't bother us. Instead, I said that having Leona here would arouse all the ill feelings I had towards my mother and it would remind me of the bad times in foster homes. That was the best I could do.

Peter's response was that talking to my sister might bring a different perspective to my childhood and my mother. That's when I gave up and wrote the damn letter.

Two weeks later I got her reply.

> *Dear Chrissy,*
>
> *Thanks for your letter. I didn't know if you would answer me or not. I pictured you living in Vancouver, since that's where your publisher is. So much time has passed since we last saw each other. We have so much to talk about.*
>
> *Right now, I want to congratulate you on your children's books. They are so lovely. I didn't know you had that in you, a talent for writing. It took me forever to compose my last letter so that it would open doors. Chrissy, I want to see you so much. Besides thinking about you, I used to worry about you.*
>
> *The second thing I wanted to tell you was a confession. I don't really need an operation. I thought if I asked for your help, you might answer. I remember how soft-hearted you were and I'm sorry I used that. If I just sent an I-want-to-make-up-with-you letter, you would probably have tossed it out, right? And of course, I wouldn't blame you. Now that you know I lied, you may not want me around so please send me a note at least telling me to stay out of your life and I will understand.*
>
> *Otherwise, Mikey and me will have our bags packed on June 29 for a short visit. Speaking of Mikey, you will simply love him.*

*If you are going to kick me out of your life, just tell me more about yourself. It said in the book that you were married to Peter Webster, a mystery novelist. That is so neat. Do you have children? Dogs? Cats? Horses? Knowing you, you probably have them all, right?*

*I am so looking forward to hearing from you again, soon.*

*Love, hugs and kisses,*
*Leona*

Darn, if I'd known she was lying about her operation, I could have told my lies and maybe stopped Peter from bugging me about contacting her. He had no idea that what was being opened here was a can of worms. He had picked up the mail and made a big production of handing this letter to me, so now he would want to read it. Although he was tapping away at his keyboard when I handed the letter to him, he immediately read it as if he wasn't doing anything important. Must have been that secret scent.

"Ah, so you had a falling-out with her?" he said, looking up at me.

"It seemed important at the time but now it's nothing," I countered.

"You are going to tell her they're still welcome, right?"

Sighing, I turned away and flopped down on the couch. "I've been happy without her in my life, without all the memories she will invoke. I've never missed her. It's not like we grew up together."

"But it's not just about you and her. She has a son. You have a son. They're cousins, and they should at least get to meet each other—get to know that they have family."

An appeal to my soft-hearted side usually ended with Peter getting his way. I tried to convince myself that having Leona come back into my life wasn't going to be such a big deal. Peter's commitment to me was real. And if Leona did manage to catch his interest, well, he would never leave Todd. I wasn't going to be afraid of my sister, so I retrieved the letter from Peter's desk and wrote a nice civilized letter saying we were looking forward to seeing her and Michael in June. At the time, I thought I could ride out a two-week visit.

At the end of June, Peter, Todd, and I went to the bus depot in Fort St. John to pick up Leona and Michael. She had refused my offer of plane tickets, saying she preferred to take the train and then a bus. As we waited inside our truck, my insides churned, and the churning sped up as the bus pulled in and passengers began to disembark. I hoped that maybe she had aged ungracefully and let herself go. Then I saw her in the doorway of the bus. Two men got off before her, and one turned to take her hand and help her down. The other handed her carry-on luggage back to her. Damn, I thought, she was even more beautiful than ever and still with that feline grace in every movement. Behind her, a miniature Nick got off and, for the moment, she ignored him to laughingly make her goodbyes to the two men.

Reluctantly, I got out of the truck and went over to the bus where she was waiting for her other luggage. When Leona saw me, she glowed. Peter, carrying Todd, joined us. I made the necessary introductions and I was relieved when she refused my offer of the front seat beside Peter. Instead, she squeezed into the jump seat of the extended cab. On the drive back, she and Peter exchanged good-natured banter. I focused my attention on Todd and Michael and tried not to imagine innuendoes between Peter and Leona. That night over supper down by the beach, Peter asked Leona how long she could stay and she jokingly replied. "The whole summer. It is so beautiful up here."

"Done," Peter said. "Right, Chris?"

I smiled and said, "Why not? You don't have anything pressing in Winnipeg, do you?"

"Well, no; well, okay. But if we get on your nerves, you have to promise me you'll send us packing. Okay?" Leona said, smiling at both of us.

The mental picture of me kicking Peter in the butt was my only comfort, as I smiled, smiled, smiled at everyone sitting around the picnic table.

In the following weeks, Peter, Michael, and Todd went canoeing and trekking. In the woods to the north, they played hide-and-seek with Lady—Michael was really impressed with Lady doing that, and he told us about this cave he found on our side of the gully to the north. One hot afternoon, he took Leona and me to see it and when we got back, I was secretly delighted to see what a mess she'd become, with her makeup and hair askew.

Peter taught Michael how to drive the truck, providing me with a good excuse to snap at him when we got a private moment. "He's only twelve. You don't teach a kid that young how to drive."

He replied that rural kids learned that kind of thing at his age in case of emergencies. My source of irritation was the way he had been joking with Leona earlier that morning and I didn't want to let go. "So grinding your gears away, that's okay?"

Peter looked at me and asked, "What's really bugging you?" I backed off but carried the grudge for the rest of that day.

Peter took them over to Kit's place to visit and Amber made Michael go horseback riding with her. At night after Todd went to bed, Michael took my place at the dining-room table and played chess with Peter while Leona and I sat in the living room, talking about nothing. Mona had given me some leather hides she had tanned and I had planned to make things with them, but had never gotten around to it. When Leona saw them, she insisted on making each of us moccasins. She went around drawing outlines of our feet and I hated the way she so easily joked around with Peter. Later, while she sewed, I twiddled my thumbs and wished I could get her out of my life. For good.

One Friday night we decided to go to Dodging for supper. Weekends were my nights off from the kitchen, and Peter, Todd, and I often ate out or he did the cooking. We were all sitting in the restaurant when I felt someone watching us. It wasn't that unusual because people did recognize Peter on occasion. When I got the feeling again, I looked around again and sure enough I caught an old man staring right at me. He was sitting with a man around Leona's age. Now why would he be staring at me and not at Leona?

I forgot about him when our food came but while we were choosing desserts, the two men suddenly appeared at our table. The younger one said to Peter, "Excuse us, we don't want to disturb you, but aren't you that mystery writer? Oxford or something?"

That made Peter laugh, as he said, "Webster, Peter Webster."

The man also laughed and said, "Yeah, there was a write-up about you in the Peace Valley Voice a while back. I'm Colin Sayers and this is Howard Norach."

The three men exchanged brief handshakes and Colin continued, "My sister really likes your books. Would I be disturbing you greatly if I asked for an autograph?"

"Well, it's the fans who keep us going," Peter said, taking the paper placemat from Colin. "What's her name?"

While Peter wrote, I looked up at both men. Colin was eyeing Leona appreciatively, and they exchanged smiles, but the older man was staring at me. I was sure we had never met before but maybe he'd recognized me from my picture in last month's newspaper article on me.

"Thank you very much. Sorry again to disturb you," Colin said, still smiling.

Peter nodded to him and they left.

"It's the fans that keep us going?" I asked Peter, smiling.

Peter laughed and said, "It was all I could think of."

The following week, Leona and I went to town while Peter took the boys fishing. We decided to have lunch at the same restaurant before doing some grocery shopping. Colin was there again and, when he came over to our table, Leona invited him to join us. I had forgotten my grocery list, so I began to recreate it while I finished eating, leaving Leona and Colin to carry on with their conversation. When I heard him ask if he could see her again, I was glad. So far, Peter seemed immune to Leona's many charms although they joked around more often than I liked. I couldn't read his mind, so I wasn't absolutely sure, but I thought that if she got herself a man while she was up here, that would be a good thing all around.

A few days later I was in the backyard hanging a second load of clothes on the line when Colin came calling on Leona.

"Colin invited Mikey and me to dinner in Fort St. John tonight. Do you mind?" she asked.

"No. Not at all," I replied and carried on with my chores. I was folding clothes in my room when Leona came in and said, "You know, Colin kind of wanted tonight to be like a date. I wondered if you think Mikey would mind not coming along with me."

"You'd have to ask him that," I said.

"I know that, but I had to run it by you first. I don't expect you to baby-sit for me while I run off on a date," Leona said through a smile.

"We don't mind having Michael here. I just meant as long as he doesn't mind staying behind."

Peter and Colin were now having coffee, and Leona went outside to look for Michael, so I joined the men at the table for a coffee break. Colin watched as I dumped two heaping teaspoons of sugar into my coffee.

"She likes a bit of coffee with her milk and sugar," Peter joked.

Hiding my annoyance with Peter for that comment, I finished my coffee without taking part in their conversation. Colin mentioned he was in oil explorations and asked Peter if he was interested in leasing some of his land. Without hesitation, Peter said we were not at all interested in that. Colin tried to get him to change his mind by talking about the benefits, but Peter held his ground. Leona returned and just before she and Colin left, he joked to Peter he wouldn't give up on trying to lease our land. After they left, Peter looked upset. Right away, I thought he didn't like Leona going out with another man. I was tempted to ask him if he was upset by that but at the same time I didn't want to get into an argument in front of the kids. More than that, I didn't want him to know I was jealous of Leona.

Trying to suppress this feeling, I busied myself with preparing supper.

Because he was still upset as we were getting ready for bed, I finally asked, "What is bugging you?"

"Well, I don't want to upset you."

"About?"

"If I told you, you might get upset."

"Jeeze, Peter. I'm already upset that you're upset and I don't know why. So tell me."

"It's Colin—his interest in drilling on our land for oil. I'm pretty sure that oil companies can drill anywhere they want."

I was so relieved it wasn't about Leona, and I figured all my other suppositions regarding her and Peter were wrong. I asked, "Wouldn't they think twice about antagonizing you? You're somewhat famous."

"That would be no match to the millions they think they could make. Are you upset now?"

I smiled at him. "Things will work out. For us."

He had no idea I wasn't talking about oil companies.

Later, I heard Leona as she settled herself on the couch, and for the moment I was almost happy to have her and Michael here with us.

While Michael was friendly, we didn't talk much to each other. The first time he addressed me as "Auntie Chris," I felt a momentary surge of affection for him, maybe because that made me feel like I was a part of his family. Still, I felt awkward with him, perhaps because he reminded me so much of the man I had once loved and now detested. Actually, I didn't really detest him because I just didn't care at all about Nick. Michael had been taking karate, and one night when Kit, Mona and Amber came over, Leona talked Michael into performing the katas for us. Before he started he told us about each kata he would do. He also explained that he had started with a white belt, then a yellow belt, and, when he got back home, was going to get his green belt. Michael's demonstration gave Peter the idea to create a younger character who was an expert in martial arts to join his Gregory M. Thomas.

One rainy day in the middle of August, Peter took the boys to Fort St. John to a movie and to do some shopping. Leona and I had the whole afternoon to ourselves.

"I'm in love, Chrissy," she volunteered.

"The way you were with Michael's father?" The words came out so suddenly that they shocked even me.

Leona looked at me as if she had been slapped. Then she answered slowly, "Yes."

"I didn't want to talk about it back then. But I can talk about it now. Nick stopped being important to me the moment I saw him in your bed," I said, not quite truthfully. Nick was still important in one way: never forgive, never forget, because if I did, I could get seriously hurt again.

"Chrissy, do we have to talk about that? It's ancient history."

"It's not. You have Michael. And he's the spitting image of Nick. You asked me if you could come here, supposedly to talk things out. So what you did to me is not ancient history."

Jealousy of my sister had resurfaced. Actually it had never gone away, but this time it was far worse than before. One reason was that she had Nick's son and, besides being each other's best friend, Leona and Michael had a mutually respectful relationship that allowed them to be relaxed with each other, even playful. Leona was the lioness with a cub, doling out the perfect combination of affection and discipline. Peter was like that with Todd. What I did mostly was watch like an outsider. As a mother, I felt I was lacking, that everything I did was thought out or copied. Peter had to have noticed and perhaps by now he had also noticed Leona's natural ability to mother in sharp contrast to my lack of it.

And Peter was the second reason. Since her arrival here, the wound she had inflicted had resurrected, and it brought out the worst in me. If she set her sights on Peter, I knew I would be helpless to do anything about it. For now I wanted so much to trust Peter because I hated living with this fear of my sister. Maybe if I aroused her conscience, she would leave Peter alone.

"I'm sorry, Leona. You're right. You said you were in love. With Colin?"

"I know, I know, I just met him, but we talk; and we talk about everything. So it's like I've known him for years." Her beautiful eyes glowed as she talked.

I was so relieved that she wasn't interested in Peter and vice versa that I was genuinely happy she had found love with Colin.

Before the end of August, Leona told me that she and Michael were going to be moving in with Colin in Fort St. John. I had been looking forward to her return to Winnipeg, a nice safe distance from us. Even though she and Peter might not be interested in each other now, anything could happen in the future. With her, anything was possible. One side of me wanted to trust her and one side was always on the alert. My mood often hinged on which side had taken over. So once she was gone, it was my intention not to stay in contact with her. Fort St. John—well, at least she was focused on another man.

When Peter heard about her plans, he said there was something about Colin he didn't trust. A trickle of jealousy rose up in me. Well not a trickle exactly, more like a flood, but I was able to dismiss it later when he told me he liked Michael and Leona but was glad he could now get back to his work.

Over the following months, Colin brought Leona and Michael to Shadow Lake for visits. Colin seemed completely enamoured with Leona and he said silly things to Peter, such as, "Leona did this, isn't she cute?" As if Peter would say yes, in front of me. He noticed the cold way I treated her. I would never be able to trust her completely. Without knowing our history, he must have thought I was out of line, and that was another reason why I detested her. Whenever we went to Fort St. John, Peter would ask, to my annoyance, whether I wanted to drop in and visit with Leona and Michael. I always said no.

At the end of December we went to Vancouver for three weeks and stayed with Peter's parents. For the first time I was happy to be there, and they both seemed so pleased to have us with them. It made me wonder if I had misread Barbara in the past. I went with Peter as he renewed contacts and did research, and we took Todd out with us as much as possible. A week after we celebrated Todd's third birthday, we returned to Shadow Lake.

---

In the past four months, Leona and Colin had not come to visit us. I assumed it was because Leona was fed up with me. Sometimes I felt sorry that I had behaved badly, but then I'd remind myself that she was a woman with no scruples and should be avoided. I remembered how many times Peter had gone to Fort St. John without me. Because I had thought she was happily living with Colin, I hadn't paid attention. And if she had nothing to hide, why didn't she contact me when she left him? Colin must have suspected something between Leona and Peter, and that's why he had come for a visit. Now, realizing that she had left

Colin months ago, my suspicion that she and Peter had been involved deepened.

Oh, Peter, did you fall for her, too?

In spite of my warm clothing I was shivering; not because of Leona but because of Todd's blood-soaked running shoe.

Heedless of my pain, the waters of the Peace River drifted by in silence, with only the occasional sound of water slapping at rocks. Being there brought no soulful connection to Peter and Todd, and, in spite of Todd's running shoe, I could not, did not, believe they were somewhere in this river. If they weren't, I wondered where Peter was right now. Perhaps he was with her, making love to her, while I sat on this cold rock. If that were the case, I deserved it. I deserved it because of the bad thing I'd done in my own past, and I deserved it for having allowed Leona back into my life.

My trembling and the darkness impeded the climb back up the steep embankment. The thought that I might slip and fall, hit my head, and die from a head injury, or hypothermia, was a tempting one. Then all the pain and the guilt would end. But I was Christine the Coward and I made sure I got back to the truck safely.

Back in my truck I turned the heater and the fan on high so I could warm up quickly. Unable to accept that Todd and Peter were dead, I had to surmise that Peter and Leona were together. They had to be. As much as the picture of them together hurt, they just had to be. The alternative meant that Todd had died and there would be no relief from that pain. Not ever.

# 3

---

## CAPTURED

Howard Norach sat in his study remembering the wonderful last few days. He had downloaded all the video images from the laptop he had installed in Christine's attic to his computer. Now he could watch the parts he really relished over and over. Like Christine inside her cabin, dazed and confused. When he'd been there on Saturday to take Peter and Todd, he had thought it a stroke of genius to add the sleeping powder he'd used on Peter into the sugar bowl.

Too bad there weren't more hiding places to set up cameras, like in the bathroom. He had missed her reaction when she saw her new hair cut. He had taken so much delight in cutting off her hair. And then Archie had suggested making her think she'd driven her truck somewhere. That was genius, too, even if it had come from Archie. As it was he had a good view of the dining room and living room. He and his men had been able to come and go as they pleased since the time they took Peter.

Thinking about this, he laughed with wicked glee. So far his cat-and-mouse game was working beautifully.

He watched the segment of Christine tripping over the dog. He should have had it killed when he took Peter and the kid. But that would have aroused Christine's suspicions. On the other hand, her falling and spilling the drugged sugar had worked to his benefit. If her visitors had used the sugar, they might have gotten drowsy too and become suspicious that something else was going on. He should have foreseen that the police or her neighbours would visit her because of the accident,

47

which his men had staged with Peter's truck. The downside was that he would no longer have easy access to her cabin while she was in a drug-induced sleep. Oh well, he couldn't have her sleeping throughout the game—that would be too boring.

Colin had provided a lot of useful information about the Websters that he had gained from living with Leona. Sometimes it seemed like a useless detail, like phone messages going through their neighbours, but that later became useful. He had had Archie call and leave the message that made everyone think Peter had driven to Fort St. John but had an accident on his way there. Now everyone would think he was in the river.

Now he would wait for Christine's next move—her reaction to the supposed deaths of her husband and child. The very last thing the police would suspect was that Peter and Todd were his guests; instead they'd be focused on finding their bodies. Meanwhile he'd have all the time he wanted to carry out his plan. He now had a toy with which to occupy himself. He would derive a great deal of amusement from matching wits with the mystery writer. Peter was jailed in one of the compound's outbuildings, separated from his child. He had given Todd to his daughter Queenie as a kind of gift.

Peter sat on the cot wondering what the hell was going on. Where was Todd? He remembered Howard visiting him just after lunch. They'd been talking about his books when there was a knock at the door. He answered, and three men forced their way in and grabbed him. Lady had started barking. She jumped at one man but another picked up the cast-iron frying pan and smashed it down on her. Struggling, he looked to Howard for help and was shocked to see him holding Todd. He was smiling and silently threatening to break Todd's neck.

They forced him to write a note to Chris saying that he had to go to Fort St. John. The only clue that he could give her that something was wrong was to use both their full names. They never used Christine and Peter, in their notes to each other, just their initials. He hoped she would notice; but what she could do about it, he didn't know. At least it was something. After that, Howard handed Todd to one of the men who took him outside. Peter made a move, but Howard told him to sit back down. He ordered Peter to finish his coffee, and stitched Lady's bleeding wound closed. Peter thought it strange that he did that.

When Howard was done, he rinsed the cups, wiped one and put it away. The other he left on the counter. That's when Peter began to get drowsy. They walked him out to the van where Todd reached out to him and settled himself on his lap. That was the last he saw of Todd and the last that he remembered.

Now he was here, imprisoned in a small windowless room, much like a jail cell with only a cot, a toilet and sink. The meals so far were served on paper plates with plastic spoons that were passed through the lower of two small openings in the steel door. The fluorescent lighting was recessed and only a vent protruded from the ceiling. He had no idea how long he'd been here and no idea where he was. He had looked for a weak point in his cell but there was none. He knew yelling for help would be useless. He'd already tried it.

Nothing like this had ever happened in his books, and he wondered what his protagonist, Greg Thomas would do. He knew he needed to put a plan together, but that seemed ludicrous right now. His books—were they the reason that he found himself a prisoner? Had he drawn a psychopath into their lives with his books? Was Chris okay or did they get her, too?

The upper panel on the door slid open, revealing Howard's face. Peter got up and went to the door and asked, "Howard, what's going on? What are you up to? Where's my son?"

Howard smiled and replied, "One question at a time, Peter. How do you like your amenities?"

"Where is Todd?"

"He's fine. Don't be worrying about him. Worry about yourself."

"Why are you doing this?"

"Oh, stay cool. I'm just having a little fun. And just so you know, your truck ended up in the Peace River and you and your son got swept away in the current. Everybody is mourning for the death of Peter Webster and his son. No one will be looking for you. My condolences." He smiled

BEATRICE CULLETON MOSIONIER

and began to slide the panel shut.

"Wait! Let's talk."

Howard slid the panel open again. "Consider yourself lucky," he said. "You're not dead—yet. Hope you're enjoying our hospitality. You even get room service. Nothing but the best for our guests," and with that, he laughed and slid the panel shut.

Peter grabbed the knob and jiggled it, trying to force the door to open even though he knew it wouldn't. What had gotten into Howard? He'd gone so far as to stage an accident to make it look like he and Todd were dead. Why? Was it something to do with Chris? Maybe he wanted Chris. Maybe that was what this was all about. He had always seemed too interested in her even though he tried to hide it.

From the meals he had been given so far, he figured he had been in here for three days. Chris would have gotten back on Sunday. If they hadn't taken her, she must be convinced they were dead. If so, her grief would be overwhelming. Otherwise, her instincts about people might make her aware of Howard's deviousness. She watched people and while she might not notice or care that they were wearing the latest fashion, she had good instincts of what they were about. He knew she wouldn't turn to her sister. For some reason, she didn't trust Leona, although he couldn't understand why.

He'd had a long talk with Kit before starting his last book, because he had decided to introduce a new detective, Tom Crow. Crow was the unknown son of Greg Thomas and an Indian woman from a reserve in the area. From Kit, he had learned that many Indian people retained a traditional knowledge that didn't necessarily have to be taught. It came from having the genes of Indian ancestors. It was powerful and spiritual, and even if many Indian people had been removed from it, many could and did return to their roots. At the time, he had thought Kit might be referring to Chris since his book's character would know his Aboriginal roots, while Chris had no traditional knowledge and did not make her cultural heritage a part of her life. Yet sometimes she surprised him— she seemed to have an instinctive connection, and he wondered where that came from. That was why he encouraged her to attend Aboriginal gatherings like the recent writers' conference in Winnipeg. She needed to make contact.

Right now she was his only hope and he prayed she didn't leave Shadow Lake, move back to Vancouver or even to Winnipeg. He sent out the first of his mind messages to her: We're alive! Don't give up on us. Look for us, Chris.

Reality was, she would not be looking for Todd and him. Not if she thought they were dead. Still, he had to find out what was happening to her and Todd.

It was obvious to him that this Howard wasn't just a retired senior; but who was he really, that he had a set-up for prisoners? Was this the NAK-WAN laboratory? He'd come across the fence, topped with barbed wire, surrounding the lab last year, and while he didn't think it was a place of evil, his imagination had kicked in. What if? At the time he had tried to research the place for his novel but had come up empty. Everyone in Dodging speculated that it was either some sort of government lab or an American oil business.

The only certain thing about NAK-WAN was that nobody knew anything about it. No one from Dodging had taken part in building it. In his book, Peter had decided to fictionalize a place like it as the headquarters for an anti-government, supremacist organization with ties to the Ku Klux Klan. At his first meeting with Constable Bob Cormier in Fort St. John, the RCMP officer had said his boss believed NAK-WAN was a private laboratory and that it was above board.

Except for a handful of people close to him, no one knew what was in his manuscript and he was probably way off in his deliberations on why he and Todd had been kidnapped. That left him to think of all his previous novels in case they were the reason for his present predicament, and if Howard was after Chris, to concentrate on every visit he had made to their place.

# 4

A GOOD CHOICE

As I was driving back to the cabin, Lady startled me by dashing out from the north side of the road. I stopped the truck, opened the door, and she jumped in, licking my face in excitement. I was puzzled. I knew I had left her inside, so she wouldn't follow me. She didn't know how to open doors, especially locked doors, so how did she get out? Could she have slipped out before me so that I had locked the door on an empty house? As I drove into our yard, I saw the cabin was in darkness, yet I remembered leaving the kitchen light on.

I was thankful that Lady was with me. Alone, I'm not sure I would have gotten out of the truck. Now I was scared, yet less so than an hour ago, when I thought an accident to end my life was just what I needed. The cabin was locked. Inside the porch, I had the usual trouble unlocking the door, but once inside, I flicked on the light switch as I entered the kitchen. I thought I could smell beer, and I looked around for its origin. Nothing was out of place, so I reckoned it was a combination of my imagination and forgetfulness.

Inside my bedroom, I looked at our empty bed. I didn't want to sleep in it, knowing Peter would never share it with me again. If I reached for him during the night, the loss would overwhelm me.

As I prepared to sleep on the couch, I thought of the contradictions in my feelings: die or live.

When I opened my eyes the next morning, the weight of depression bore down on me, pinning me to the couch. I lay there, staring at the knots and the swirls of the tongue-and-groove pine ceiling. Lady finally coaxed me into getting up and, while I moved about in slow motion, doing only what I had to, I mourned. Today, I thought, I would give Lady her bath after taking one myself. When Lady heard the bath water running, she immediately went under our desks at the far end of the living room. Like Todd, she hated baths, and they both hated getting combed, too.

"Don't worry, this one's for me," I said to her.

The mirror was all steamed up. I wiped a hole clear, thinking I should cut my hair evenly. I must have picked up lengths of my hair and just cut it right off because it was long here, shorter there—a total mess. I started cutting when I heard the sound of a vehicle. I hurried to dress as I remembered that Sergeant Trolley had said they'd be back. I braced myself, in case they were here to tell me they had found Todd and Peter.

Thankfully, the sound belonged to Kit's pickup, not Trolley's police van. Kit and Mona had brought a pot of venison stew with them and some pie. Mona had guessed that I hadn't eaten and she took charge of my kitchen. Despite my protests that I wasn't hungry, I found myself eating.

Later that afternoon, Sergeant Trolley came knocking at my door. Accompanying him was an Aboriginal officer, Constable Bob Cormier. My shivering, in spite of a warm cabin, began as soon as I saw them.

Sergeant Trolley began asking me something. I interrupted to ask, "Did you find them?"

"No, we didn't," Sergeant Trolley said, "but we'll continue searching. Mind if we sit down?"

I nodded, still shivering. I sat down with them, and then got up to get my jacket, feeling their eyes on me. Maybe they thought I was going to walk out and just leave them sitting there. "I'm just so cold," I explained as I returned to sit at the table.

Sergeant Trolley continued talking, "There is something about the accident. You're sure you told me the truth about your husband?"

"There's nothing more I can tell you," I interrupted.

"You're sure? Because now's not the time to hold anything back."

The sudden turn of the conversation took me by surprise. "I told you what I know."

"We have to ask," Constable Cormier said, and he seemed sympathetic. "I'm sorry. Someone phoned in about seeing your husband's truck in the river, and we'd like you to come in and listen to the tape to see if you recognize the voice."

Because of the contrast in the tones of their voices, I was thinking they were playing good cop, bad cop, when it dawned on me why they wanted me to listen to the tape. "You think it might be Peter's voice!" I said.

Sergeant Trolley said, "Too many things about the accident really don't look right. Besides that particular location, for instance, there were no skid marks, and . . ."

Constable Cormier said in a gentle voice, "We should have found their bodies by now. Unless they got hooked on to something . . ." His voice trailed off as he caught Sergeant Trolley scowling at him.

It dawned on me what they were implying. "You think Peter staged the accident? Peter would never have done something like that. He was—is—the most decent straightforward person I ever knew."

"Mrs. Webster, it's hard to ask about sensitive matters at a time like this, but is it possible he was involved with someone else?" Sergeant Trolley asked.

"Another woman?" Even as I asked, I was shaking my head no. "If he had met someone else, he would have told me, and if he had wanted to leave me, he would have told me."

"And what about your son? Would your husband have walked away from him?"

Since that thought had already crossed my mind, that question stumped me momentarily. I finally answered, "We both loved Todd very much and we would have arranged something that was beneficial to him. Another thing, that running shoe had bloodstains on it, didn't it? Peter would never hurt Todd. Never."

For me to doubt Peter was one thing, but for these strangers to come here and bandy about suspicions was unacceptable. I was almost snarling as I continued, "Besides, the whole idea of staging an accident means he'd have to cut himself off from everything—from his parents, from his friends. You just talk to them—they'll tell you what he's like. And like I said, he just finished another book. Writing is his life. He wouldn't abandon that. He wouldn't abandon anything here. I don't know how to convince you what kind of person Peter was. Is."

Before they left, Sergeant Trolley assured me they would continue with the search. What he didn't say was the alternative—that they might find proof that Peter had staged the accident.

At the end of that day, I felt overwhelmingly lonely. At times, I accepted the idea of Peter running away with Leona and I wondered how I could let him know that I wanted to see Todd—just see him. I may not have been a woman with natural mothering abilities like Leona, but I would never take part in cutting a mother out of her son's life. Doing that would be psychopathic and when that thought came to me, I knew neither Peter nor Leona had such traits. In their own ways, they were loving, generous people. The alternative was to believe that Peter and Todd were dead. Either way I would always love Peter.

I turned off the table lamp and sat on the couch in the darkness, Peter and Todd's clothing on one side and Lady on the other. Right now she was my only friend, the only one who could try to comfort me. What was I going to do without them, without Todd? One thing I knew was that I would not leave Shadow Lake until they were found. Yes, no matter what Peter might have done to me, I knew I would always love him. When I met him, I was adrift going nowhere and he had been my lifesaver.

————

In the two years after fleeing Winnipeg for good, I hung around with a girl named Emily and her hippie friends. The hippies had a language all their own which I was slow to learn and quick to forget. No matter where I went, I was always the outsider, never really part of the group. Even though I had many one-night stands, even though I got drunk and smoked whatever they smoked, the watcher in me kept me apart. The watcher in me tried to figure out what their problems were—it was easier to ignore my own—why they led such hopeless lives.

I was too much the coward to get in trouble the way they did. For instance, I smoked pot if they offered it, but I never bought it myself. And I refused the heavy-duty drugs. Most of them were happy to lie around, living off welfare or panhandling, the girls turning tricks for money to buy drugs, the guys going out to score—whatever that meant. Police raids and arrests were not uncommon. I think it was part of a game of suspense we all played. Twice I had near misses, leaving with a guy and learning later that the cops had raided the house we'd just left.

I got a job at a FabriChoice store, mostly because I knew materials, thanks to Leona. It was the last place I would have thought of, but when I saw the sign in the window, I'd gone in on a whim. I told myself that working in a FabriChoice store would remind me that I should trust no one ever again; thanks or no thanks to Leona.

Emily's group was forever changing—some left, others came—and I think what we all enjoyed was our easy acceptance of others. Andrea was new to the group and she and I became good friends, spending Saturday afternoons together, starting with brunch, and sometimes going to movies on weeknights. She was crazy about movies and occasionally she'd drag me to the theatre too. Sometimes she would drop in on our weekend parties, entertaining us with her lively mimicking or having us in stitches with comedy routines she'd picked up. Then she would go out on the streets, for she turned tricks for a living. That was distressing and I worried about her, but I wasn't going to lecture her. She wanted to be an actress, and her weekdays were devoted to theatre school.

One Saturday, on a cold February day, she dragged me to an audition for a play at a small local theatre called Goblins. That was how I met Peter, who was the playwright. Although he stood out from everyone else, it wasn't love at first sight. I still had Nick on my mind. Not that I still wanted him, but he had made me think all men were untrustworthy. I did however, quit with the one-night stands and everything else I thought Peter would disapprove of. He just seemed so straight, one of the reasons he had stood out. For the longest time I was able to resist that smile of his, or so I thought, but I soon realized I was seriously attracted to him. I told myself he must be married or have a girlfriend, but he was never in the presence of another woman. I began to meet Andrea after her rehearsals and sometimes we all went out for coffee. Peter would stare at me and when I returned his stare, he would smile with a combination of mischief and desire.

Andrea soon noticed and told me, "You've chosen well, Grasshopper. Go for him."

That made me laugh because I thought my reluctant attraction to him had gone unnoticed.

Peter and I began going out and then he proposed to me. My first thought was that I hadn't told him any of the secrets from my past.

Seeing my hesitation, he said, "I'll love you forever."

"No matter what?" I responded.

"No matter what."

"What if I killed someone?" I countered.

"You're too kind and good-hearted to do anything like that."

There it was—a chance to tell him what I was really like. Once again, I let it go by and I said I would love to be married to him because that was a truth.

Rarely, but still on occasion, I'd compare him to Nick. Where Nick had swept me off my feet, Peter was secure and steady. Peter was tall, and though he had a powerful build he moved with a masculine grace. And I noticed he gave that special smile of his only to me. Any defense I still had against his possible untrustworthiness vanished.

The play he had written, and which Andrea starred in, was called *Check and Mate*, and he had based it on his unfinished novel. Long after the play, he finally finished the book. When he sent it out and got all those rejection letters, I thought it was me who was jinxing him. I was like a magnet that attracted only bad luck. Most times we lived on my wage, eating macaroni and cheese six times a week. We had lots of fights, mostly about money or lack of it, because I felt he was trying to control everything.

There were times I packed my two suitcases and that stubborn streak I'd always had forced me to go for the door. He would ask me to stay. I told myself I stayed because I had nothing better to do but, in reality, I was relieved and more than happy to stay.

One time I was so upset that I told Andrea about a fight and she said, "Oh he probably picks fights to make up."

"Why would he do that?"

"Well, don't you guys make up, you know, in the bedroom?"

"We don't need fights for that."

"I know, but there's that added passion isn't there? Yeah, I think I could do a comedy routine with that."

Indignant, I asked, "Are you making fun of me?"

"Not yet, kiddo, but I will." She nudged me a couple of times until I smiled.

When success as an author came to him, it came in a gush. I was able to quit working, and we no longer ate macaroni and cheese. In the months that followed, we enjoyed lazy days, making our meals together or going out, taking long walks, shopping for clothes, going out at night to the theatre followed by dinners with Andrea and old friends from his theatre days. Our private times were filled with a passion that far exceeded those making-up times. That was when the fights that made me head for the door ended. We still had spats but never anything major. In all that time and in the years that followed, I never found the right moment to make the confessions from my past.

Too soon for me, Peter had to get back to his work. After those months of togetherness, I felt excluded from this part of his life. In his study, he happily worked on novel after novel. He began to travel a lot, taking me along wherever he went. That part I liked. Eventually, he talked me into trying my hand at writing books. When I came up with my first children's book, he helped me get it published. My success was nothing compared to his, but I did get asked to give talks at schools. Sometimes I'd end up talking about his writing rather than mine.

Sometimes I felt I loved him too much and I needed to pull back. At parties, my insecurities would come out and I would be positively jealous when all these talented, attractive females gathered around him, practically pushing me aside. Thankfully, he never flirted. He'd answer questions and talk to people, then look across the room at me and smile that smile. That's when I would relax and enjoy the rest of the evening. He made me feel we were one.

His first book was optioned for a movie, and when he got paid for the rights, he broke the news to me that he wanted to leave the city and move to an isolated place in the foothills of the Rockies. He and Al Roberts, his life-long buddy, had found the place when they'd gone for their yearly hunting trip along the Alaska Highway. A hunter from another party almost shot Al, so they had taken time to find a more secluded area where they could hunt in peace. I didn't like the idea of moving, and I liked it even less when Peter confessed he had already put an offer on a cabin with two sections of land.

As usual, I had no real say. When he made up his mind about something, nothing would change it, and we ended up here at Shadow Lake. Like a child in a time of upheaval, I was sullen and silent, hating everything in sight. The first time we saw Kit, he was just an old Indian man on horseback with a packed mule trailing behind. Peter stopped his truck to say hello. The man had looked over at us with piercing, cold eyes and merely nodded. Without any apparent movement, he urged his mount onwards.

"There's a taste of your new neighbourhood," I snorted. Even though he didn't have to, Peter continued his sales pitch about the new place. "It's a great place for kids. We won't have to worry about perverts grabbing them or their getting hit by cars or any of the other things that happen in the city."

"I told you already, I don't want children," I said, irritated by the mention of kids.

Peter ignored my protests and continued. "We'll get a boat, a snowmobile, two snowmobiles. We'll get skis." He looked eastward across to the grassy meadow between the lake and the treeline and added, "And dogs and horses. I'll build a barn and corrals."

"You said there'd be no distractions up here. You'll have to cut wood for the winter, lots of wood, and tend to horses after you've built a barn and corrals for them. You'll have to go and buy food for them, lots of food. You don't even know how to build things, or take care of horses, or even dogs for that matter."

"I had a dog when I was a kid. And I'll learn or get help from the locals. Chris, look around. This place is ideal for us. It's everything I've ever wanted."

Well, he was the boss of us and in a way, I liked it that he was so independent, and grudgingly I came to accept our new home.

In our very first autumn up here, Al wrote to say he couldn't come for their yearly ritual of deer hunting because he'd broken his leg. Perhaps to make up for my childish behaviour, I offered to go with Peter on his hunting trip.

Peter scoffed, saying, "You? You couldn't shoot a deer if it was looking up your nose."

"Sure I could," I said confidently. "I took a course once."

"You took a course on how to shoot deer?" His cynicism dripped all over my confidence.

"Not on shooting deer," I responded. "At one of my foster homes, the Knights of Columbus sponsored a whole bunch of kids in town to take rifle-shooting. I used to have a certificate."

"I can't see them doing that," he replied.

"Well, maybe it was a Hunters and Anglers group. Mr. Gerard was a member of them, too. Or the Rifle Association."

"Ah-hah, another piece of your mysterious past comes to light. Anyhow, you probably only used a twenty-two, and with deer you need a three-oh-eight or a 30-30."

"What's the difference? I was a good shot." Realizing I didn't know anything about rifles, my confidence was evaporating.

Peter set some cans up for target practice, and I started with the twenty-two, pleased when I hit all my targets. Then he had me try his 30-30. When the recoil hit me hard in the shoulder, he burst out laughing. I yelled at him for not warning me about it, but the more he tried to say he was sorry, the more he laughed. He made a shoulder pad, and I practiced until I no longer flinched from the recoil.

The very first day we went out, I saw a deer and I was the one who shot and killed it, out of pure reflex. Peter was pleased, but I felt such regret, such sorrow, for killing a living thing—for what—to show off? The buck I had killed was young and healthy. Earlier that day it had run and fed, and life for it was good. Then I had come along, and a beautiful living animal became a carcass. The worst part was that I preferred store-bought meat to venison. Talk about being assimilated. Okay, let's not.

Yet, at the same time, I'd had a millisecond of vicious delight when I squeezed the trigger. As with all the other secrets of my past, I kept that to myself. After that, I never went hunting again, and I hated that Peter went, and that Al and Iris came up here in the fall for hunting season.

While we never did build a barn and corrals, we built a garage to house two snowmobiles and an ATV. To bring in all the lumber and supplies, we got two trucks and a trailer, which was useful for gathering firewood. We had a plan to build another garage for the trucks but so far we hadn't gotten around to it. We did get a puppy, a Collie puppy, and I called her Lady because when we picked her, she already had these lady-like qualities compared to the rest of her littermates. And besides that, I was never good at thinking up names.

When I first learned I was pregnant with Todd, I couldn't believe it. There had been no indication, not until I vaguely remembered that I might have missed my period once or twice. While the pregnancy excited Peter, it churned up turmoil in me. This was the time to confess to him, but when he came with me on my first visit to a doctor and I was asked, "Is this your first?" I said yes, and added to the lie by saying I was hoping for a girl.

For the rest of that pregnancy I was miserable, trying to drum up the courage to tell Peter at least one of my secrets. Peter had taken me, and Lady, to Vancouver in December so that we wouldn't be at the mercy of bad weather or impossible road conditions, and we stayed at his parents' place.

Years before when we had gotten married, Peter's parents had attended. His mother, Barbara had seemed disappointed that her only son was marrying a Métis woman. I still held that against her, and whenever we stayed at their place, I still got the impression she didn't like

61

me. Any advice she gave me sounded like reproach.

On January fifth, our son was born and we named him Todd. With this baby came my first-ever protective mother's instincts. I was afraid my baby would sense the tension I had at my in-laws, so I told Peter to get us a place of our own. He must have been aware of my feelings, because he agreed without objecting. We stayed in Vancouver until February, and my time with Todd was totally relaxed, totally enjoyable, totally unlike the first time.

———————————

I had given away one child. God had given me another one, and because I didn't deserve anything good, he had taken that child away, along with a husband who might have once loved me.

While I considered Peter an excellent father, I had doubts about my own mothering instincts. In the beginning I'd held Todd to feed him, bathe him, and change him, but Peter held him just to enjoy the contact, and he talked to Todd the way I talked to Lady. I had a more natural rapport with a dog than with my son. While I often petted and stroked the dog, touching humans was something foreign to me. I realized that when I grew up, only Leona had touched me, and then Nick, and, at times, even his touch annoyed me. Peter was different. I loved his touch. Gradually I had learned to demonstrate affection towards Todd from watching Peter and by responding to Todd's own needs.

Sometimes I wondered why I lacked parenting skills. I put it down to the fact that I'd been in foster homes, but even before that I never recalled my own mother having any kind of bond with me. Maybe that's what it was. I had bonded to Peter but not to Todd. I had often questioned whether I truly loved Todd, unconditionally. And then just this past winter the answer had come in a dream.

In the dream, Todd and I were down by the lake, and the ice was just beginning to break up. We were building a fort with wet snow. My attention was focused on building the fort and perfecting a comfortable seat for Todd. A small plank of wood on the seat would prevent his bottom from getting wet. As I looked around for one, I saw Todd way out on the lake, balancing on a rocking slab of ice. One minute he had been right beside me, and the next he was out there, helpless. I screamed at him to stay still and began running towards him. I was still too far away when the slab of ice tilted, one edge rising above the main body of ice. Todd slid right down into the icy waters. The slab of ice levelled itself, closing the gap over my son.

I had woken then, crying and paralyzed from the horror of seeing my son swallowed by Shadow Lake. Unable to move, I wanted to go back into the dream so I could save him and, at the same time, I wanted to go to his room to reassure myself that he was all right. Watching him sleep that night, I knew in my heart that I did love him, very much, just like a real mother.

That dream hadn't been an answer, after all. It had been a premonition. Shadow Lake had not swallowed Todd, but the Peace River had. Why had I ever thought I could have a good life? I wiped my tears away. I felt so utterly sorry for myself. I couldn't possibly go on living this way, with only memories for company. I wanted Peter and Todd back. No matter what Peter might have done, I wanted both of them back.

# 5

BETRAYALS

As I tended to my morning rituals, I forced myself to think through a scenario that had Peter leaving with Leona. They would have had to plan it months ago, maybe when Peter first knew I would be away on a trip. That was back in February, the month that Leona had left Colin. Come to think of it, I was going to turn the invitation down until Peter had gone to the library in Fort St. John, to do some research. When he came back, he had not only told me about the Winnipeg Aboriginal Writers' conference, he talked me into going to both. But why had he bothered making a phone call to Mona? He could have just left the day that I left. And that 911 phone call, the one I was supposed to go listen to, what was that all about? If it had been Peter who made that call, why did he want the truck to be found?

For the moment I disregarded those two anomalies. The best time for an accident would be at night, when the risk of being seen was minimal. And icy road conditions, while handy, would not have been necessary to their plan. That spot on Highway 29 was well chosen because a vehicle going down that embankment would only stop when it hit the river. After planting Todd's running shoe inside, Peter could have driven the truck to the edge and jumped out, so the gear would still be in drive. But how would he know the back end would stick out so that some mysterious stranger could phone it in? Unless he phoned it in. But again, why would he want the truck to be found?

The blood on Todd's running shoe could have been from a nosebleed.

He could have propped his door open, so investigators would assume the currents carried their bodies away. All the while, Leona would be waiting nearby with another vehicle so they could drive away together.

But why, if Peter wanted so badly to get away from me and be with my sister and keep Todd, did he have to have such an elaborate plan? As a mystery writer, he knew a lot about the procedures of police investigations. If he and Leona had done this to me, it meant that Peter was evil. And Leona, well, it was already a given that she was evil.

With this scenario in mind, I was both anxious to go listen to that tape and afraid. The only comfort was that if Peter had run away with Leona, then Todd was still alive. The police had planted the seed in my head, and I had been fertilizing the idea with the knowledge I had of my sister.

Besides the phone call to Mona, another thing that didn't fit was Peter being capable of such actions. Surely there would have been indications that his commitment to me had waned. In the few months before my trip to Manitoba, Peter had been the same as always; he was usually thoughtful unless he was focused on his writing. Okay, so sometimes he was snappy with me and I with him, but mostly, he did those thoughtful little things that showed he cared. And, he couldn't smile that special smile if he wasn't in love with me, could he?

Later in Fort St. John, at the RCMP office, I sat in the interrogation room, waiting apprehensively for Sergeant Trolley. When he let me listen to the tape, I was so relieved when I heard a stranger's voice and not Peter's. Because the operator was trying unsuccessfully to get the stranger's name, her interruptions and static overlapped some of the man's words.

"Uh, hi. I was driving . . . I was driving home . . . had a flat tire, and when I was changing it, I thought I saw something shining, down in the Peace River in the moonlight . . . binoculars . . . it looked like the back of a truck. You should check it out."

After the tape played out I was visibly relieved.

"So you did think it might be your husband?" Trolley asked.

"It's not."

"But from the relief you showed, you thought it might be. So you're not telling me everything you know. Mrs. Webster, is there another woman involved?"

If I told him what I suspected and not what I knew for sure, which was nothing, they would focus on that and not continue to try to find Peter and Todd. We had read enough about all those cases where innocent men were convicted because of police blinders. I did not want to run the risk of that happening here.

Knowing I was no match for a police interrogation, I looked up at Sergeant Trolley and said definitively, "I've never heard that voice before. As far as I know, Peter was not involved with another woman." I stood up and walked out.

As I drove home, I was more confused than ever. To me, the man on the tape sounded like he was lying. Maybe he was the one who had caused the accident. I pulled over and considered returning to the station. Had the police considered that, and if so, why continue with questions that cast doubt on Peter's character? It wasn't as if they had met Leona. My words, "As far as I know," was the truth because I wasn't one hundred percent positive that they were together. Peter would never have brought a third party into the plan, if it were a plan. For Todd's sake, I fervently wished it were a plan. Peter was a mystery writer, capable of plotting devious schemes. But was he really capable of carrying them out?

Less than an hour after I got home, Colin himself came calling. Howard was with him, and when he followed Colin in, Lady reacted to him strangely. She growled and withdrew under my desk. Howard laughed and said he'd always had that effect on dogs, and cats, too. Both were openly sympathetic and so easy to talk to that I told them almost everything that had happened so far, leaving out my suspicions about Leona and Peter.

I asked Colin if he had left a phone message for Peter on Friday night to come to Fort St. John. He said no and told me that Leona had left him in February—his fault—and that he was surprised I hadn't heard from her at all. He confessed that his last visit to us had been to see if she was here. I noticed his glances at Howard; he was nervous. I wondered if he was embarrassed to be talking about Leona in front of his friend. Colin and I promised to let each other know if we heard from her. I wished Howard wasn't there because I really wanted to ask Colin if Peter had ever come to see them. Alone with Colin, I might have been able to be more open with him, even if such a question made me transparently jealous.

After they left, I was left with the big question: who had left that message for Peter? Maybe Leona had gotten some man to make the call for her because Mona would have recognized her voice. But that simply did not make sense. And if she and Colin hadn't seen each other since February, how would she have known I was away? My heart sank even further, because she could only have found that out from one person— Peter. It must have been part of their plan. And the phone call to Mona could have been part of staging an accident.

The caller had asked for Peter and that meant they knew I was out of town. There it was—the proof that Peter had betrayed me. Leona was a taker. She had taken Peter and Todd from me. I didn't want Peter back now. But I wanted Todd so much. I felt so sorry for myself because I had an overwhelming feeling that I would never see him again. All thanks to Leona. Once, a very long time ago, she had been my best friend.

———————

When I turned eighteen and was released from Children's Aid, she took me in. Living with her was liberating. I dropped out of Grade twelve, having lost the motivation to finish, and I happily settled for a job as a waitress. Leona modeled part time, worked as a hostess in an expensive steakhouse, and devoted her free time to sewing clothes for us. In return, I cooked and cleaned. Weekends were party times for her, and I sometimes joined her.

We had vague plans to buy a house but first thing I wanted was a car. If I had a car, I'd feel even more liberated. After getting my driver's license, I got babysitting jobs for evenings and weekends through the YWCA and finally saved enough to buy a used car.

I loved reading and hated when Leona called me a bookworm. If I was into a really good book, I skipped going out with Leona and her friends, and I'd end up in a restaurant I really liked, treat myself to fries and a hamburger and read my book. That was bliss. And that was how I met the love of my life. One night someone sat on the stool next to mine.

"Could you pass me the salt?" a male voice asked.

I took no notice until I was tapped on the arm. Realizing that the question had been asked of me, I quickly reached out to pass the salt.

"Here you are," he said, handing me back the saltshaker. I put it back in its place and resumed reading.

"Could you pass me the ketchup, please?"

Slightly annoyed, I finally looked to my right and hot damn, this really cute guy was sitting right next to me, grinning.

"A napkin. You must need a napkin," I said to cover my sudden interest.

My tone must have sounded sarcastic because he said, contritely, "I'm sorry, but I was only trying to get your attention."

"Oh," was my great comeback, so I added, "Well, it's this book. I'm almost finished. See? I got caught up in it."

"Yeah, I saw you reading last Saturday. It's hard to compete with a book." He spoke in a serious tone of voice, but he had an amused look in his eyes.

He had noticed me last Saturday? Wow. A wonderful feeling washed over me.

"You were here last Saturday?" I asked.

"Yup. Most Saturday nights now. I'm Nick," he said, and then waited briefly before asking, "What's your name?"

"Chris. Christine for short." The ending of my book was forgotten.

"Okay, Christine for short. Want to have a coffee with me? My treat."

Without waiting for my answer, he ordered two coffees and took them to a booth. I followed him. When we sat down, I brilliantly said, "It's really Christine for long and Chris for short."

"Oh, and you were just testing me?"

"That's right."

"Okay. So why does a pretty girl like you end up reading in a restaurant on a Saturday night?"

"Well the same question goes for you. Except you're not a girl and you weren't reading."

"Oh? But I'm pretty? Anyhow, I asked first."

"I just love reading." I took a sip of coffee because the way he was staring at me made me nervous. I added, "And eating. Out. Now you."

"Since I don't have anyone to cook for me, I always eat out. Usually different places but last Saturday I saw you . . . reading. And I wanted to see if you'd be here again."

We talked over more coffees. By the time we walked out, I thought Nick was the coolest guy I had ever met. Actually, he was the only guy I had ever met. Well, that I had an interest in. Later I thought he must have thought I looked exotic because of my long, straight, shiny black hair. It helped that Leona had taught me how to apply makeup.

The next week I walked on air. People at work commented that it was great to see a smile on my face. Friday night I went back to the same restaurant, hoping he would be there, but he wasn't. He had probably gotten off work and gone out on a date. Come to think of it, he may not have been married, but a guy like that would definitely have a girlfriend. By the end of that evening I'd convinced myself he did have a girlfriend and, if I ever saw him again, I would be cool and distant. On Saturday night, though, I made sure to take a booth. He walked in and came straight to my table. Butterflies started fluttering inside me as soon as I saw him.

"Hi, Christine for short," he said, as he took off his jacket and sat down.

"Hello, Nicholas for long . . . I presume," I joked back. Okay, I wouldn't be cool and distant. I would joke around and be like a little sister.

We spent a couple of hours eating and being nonsensical and then he asked, "Want to come to my place? Watch some TV?"

That put a stop to my merriment. I had never been alone with a man in his place. I never even had a boyfriend before. Nick reached over and tilted my head so my eyes met his. "Hey, I'm not going to try anything funny, if that's what you're worried about."

"It's not the funny stuff I'm worried about. It's the serious stuff."

That made him laugh. "Okay, then I'll only do the funny stuff."

I smiled, and he made up my mind for me by putting on his jacket, saying, "Come on, Christine for short."

As we went out to the car, he took my keys and led me to the passenger side. Apprehensively, I got in, wondering if I should be allowing a semi-complete stranger to drive my car. It turned out he only lived a few blocks away. I learned his last name was Scarlos, he was twenty-six years old—same age as Leona—and he worked at the CN. When I asked why he didn't go to bars after work, he said he didn't like that scene.

For weeks we met that way, and I never told Leona about him. One night Nick and I were sitting on his couch when he suddenly turned and kissed me long and hard.

Startled, I drew back and said, "That borders on serious stuff."

"I know. I'm seriously attracted to you."

During the week, I tried to keep my feelings in check by telling myself he had one or more girlfriends for the rest of the week. Quite possibly, I was his Saturday night girl. About a month after we first met, we ended up in his bed. When he put his arms around me and we just talked, a wonderful lazy, carefree feeling engulfed me. That aura of being warm, cozy, and protected remained with me for the rest of the week, no matter what else happened. But then, too soon, he wanted to go all the way. I just couldn't.

One Sunday afternoon Leona was working on a blouse for me, and, as I was trying it on inside out so she could pin it, she asked, "So who is he?" She said this with pins between her lips.

I answered with a question, knowing very well what she was asking about. "Who is who?"

"Come on, Chrissy! You get this dreamy look on your face. You smile a lot to yourself. You hum. You're glowing. So who is he?"

"Just a guy."

"Yeah, right, just a guy."

"His name's Nick. Nicholas Scarlos."

"And when are you going to bring this Nicholas Scarlos home to meet me?"

The dreamy smile on my face vanished. I hadn't really thought of it before, but if Nick met Leona, he'd fall in love with her immediately. They were both irresistible, so how could they not be attracted to each other? I was glad that Leona was working behind me because I didn't want her to see the insecurity written all over my face.

"He doesn't like the bar scene," was all I could think of saying.

"So? I didn't say at a bar. Bring him here for supper. There. You can take it off now." Leona moved some things off the table so she could sew the blouse together.

Tossing the blouse over to her and pulling my old sweatshirt back on, I said, "I don't know why you keep making me these fancy clothes. You know I just like my old jeans and sweatshirts." I said this mostly to change the subject. Leona always dressed up and we would always be opposites. To my relief, we didn't talk about Nick again that night, and I was left wondering how I was going to keep them apart for the rest of our lives.

When Nick asked me to stay over one night, I told him I would the next time because I had to let my sister know. That was a little white lie, and I told it to delay the inevitable. I didn't really have to tell Leona anything because she herself stayed overnight at different boyfriends' places or brought them home to our one-bedroom apartment. The first few times I'd been shocked by her promiscuity, but now I just silently disapproved. Back when she had one of her modelling jobs, she'd come home with a fur coat as a bonus. Something in her demeanour made me suspect that she had slept with the gift-bearer to get it. To my way of thinking, she was too casual about sex. I guess she never had the hang-ups that haunted me.

By now I knew I was Nick's only girlfriend, and he'd given me a key to his place so I could come and go as I pleased. I got into the habit of staying at Nick's on weekends and at Leona's on weekdays.

One night, right out of the blue, he asked me to marry him.

Thinking he was joking, I asked, "Why?"

"Why? Because we love each other. Don't we? And I want to spend the rest of my life with you."

I don't know why I hesitated. It was most likely because it had never occurred to me he'd ask. I looked him in the eyes and asked, "You're absolutely sure?"

"I wouldn't ask if I wasn't absolutely sure."

I smiled, and said, "Yes!" Inside I was elated.

At the end of June, Leona arranged a special party for my nineteenth birthday. She had friends who had a cabin at Winnipeg Beach and, because it was a long weekend, a group of us went up and spent the whole weekend there. Having resigned myself to the fact that Nick was going to have to meet Leona some day, I decided they should meet beforehand at our place. Nick came for supper on a Thursday night. I watched closely for signs of fireworks between them and was relieved when they both seemed disinterested.

Winnipeg Beach was great—at first. Nick took that whole weekend off work to be with me. Still, I was watchful because Leona was the centre of attention, and Nick couldn't help being drawn in by her incredible charisma. Knowing by now I didn't have a father of any kind, Nick jokingly asked Leona for my hand in marriage. The way he asked, and the way everyone else laughed, made me feel the same way I had during the few family visits where Mom and Leona had talked and laughed and excluded me. I was also sure that some of Leona's girlfriends were wondering why Nick was with me and not with Leona.

Later that month on a Tuesday morning, I woke to the sound of heavy rain pelting at the window. I was at Leona's place. Nick had wanted me to move in with him and although we were engaged, I still stayed at Leona's during the week and Nick's on the weekend. The thunder was still crashing overhead in the early part of the afternoon. At work, we could see constant flashes of lightning. After an especially loud crash, the fluorescent lights stopped humming and everything went off. After the few customers in the restaurant left, we hung around to see if the blackout was temporary. Then our boss told us we could go. Of course that was the day that Leona borrowed my car since she had the day off. When I got home, I was soaked. I walked up to our side entrance, thinking of the long warm bath I was going to have as soon as I got inside.

What I noticed first when I entered our apartment was a pair of men's sneakers because I almost stepped on them. The first thing I heard was the radio coming from Leona's bedroom, meaning she had company. She could have at least closed her door. The bath was out because I couldn't pass by her open door. Not wanting to go back out in the rain, I went quietly into the living room to read and wait, regretting that I had come home early each time I heard her bed squeak. I wondered what kind of guy she'd picked up this time. I thought about tiptoeing back into the hallway and reading and waiting there or making some kind of noise. I knew they'd be surprised to find me there when they came out, and it would be me who'd feel the most awkward.

I decided to go back out, return, and yell, "Hi Leona, you home?" Yeah, that would be the proper thing. I put my book down, took my keys, and got up to sneak outside.

That's when, above the sound of the radio and the droning rain, I heard a familiar voice ask, "Wanna smoke?" Something inside me turned upside down. In the next instant, Nick's voice came again, "You got the lighter on your side?"

Whoosh! A rage washed over me and, irrationally, I marched right to her doorway. Nick was in the act of lighting up a smoke and, although a sheet covered them, they were obviously naked underneath. My mouth opened and closed as much as theirs did. I backed out, shutting the door behind me. They both called to me simultaneously. I grabbed my damp sweater and went out the door. Outside, since Leona had my car keys, I walked and walked and walked. I'd left my purse behind. I had no money, and no place to go, and I was shivering. As I walked, I squeezed my house keys in my hand as though they were Leona's neck, until I finally thought, "Why the hell am I out here in the rain? Damn them. They can leave."

Back at the door to Leona's apartment, I paused before I stormed in. Leona was now dressed in jeans and a T-shirt. I didn't look her in the eye. I felt so much contempt for her.

As soon as she saw me, she said, "Oh, Chrissy, I'm so sorry."

"Shove it, Leona," I growled as I went into the bathroom, slamming the door in her face. Because I was shivering now, I ran hot water for my bath. For what must have been hours, I soaked in that bathtub, thinking. First thing I'd do is move out. Emily, at work, had been asking around if anyone wanted to drive to Vancouver in the near future. She had started a few months back and we had never talked much, but now her question interested me. Move out and put distance between us—a really good idea. When I finally got out of the tub, I realized I'd forgotten to get fresh clothing. I dressed in my damp clothing and immediately started shivering again.

Leona, sitting at the table across the room, jumped up as soon as I opened the door. "Chrissy, we've got to talk. You have to understand we didn't mean to. It just happened."

"Just shut up, Leona," I said, and flopped on the couch. I pulled my book from underneath me and pretended to read.

The next day at work, I went over to Emily and asked if she was still looking for a ride to Vancouver. Her face lit up and she nodded. By the end of that day we both gave notice that we'd be leaving. I had the car, and she had the gas money and knew people in Calgary, where we could stay over. When I told her I didn't really have a place to stay right now, she invited me to stay at her place. That night I found she was staying with some friends, and no one had washed the dishes that day or done any other cleaning. A pile of dirty laundry sat in one corner of the living room, which contained only mattresses on the floor. They gave me a mattress for the night.

The next morning the smell of home-rolled cigarettes hung so heavy in the air that I felt nauseous. Unable to handle Emily's place, I decided to return to Leona's at night. For two weeks, I refused to talk to her. Nick came over one night and Leona let him in. I picked up my purse and walked by them, leaving in my car.

On my last night at Leona's I almost wanted to talk with her. Not to make up with her, but to give her a taste of her own medicine. I'd pretend to forgive her and the next day, I'd be gone. I'd begun to see these two people whom I had idolized in a totally different light. Unfortunately, love doesn't get rinsed away like soap. I still loved Leona. I wasn't so sure about Nick but I sure hated what they had done to me. Forgive and forget? I think not. And by going to Vancouver, I wouldn't be tempted.

The next morning Emily had no idea there was a broken heart in the car with us. I hid it well by laughing and joking and singing along with her. She told me she had come to Winnipeg with her boyfriend and a couple of friends, and he had taken up with his former girlfriend, leaving her stranded. She could easily have called her mother to get home, but it was a matter of pride. I asked why she hadn't just taken a bus back.

"Because of this," she said, rolling a homemade joint. "Can't toke up in public. Want a drag?"

I declined and immediately glanced in the rear-view mirror and all around, looking for cops. For some time lately, I hadn't liked the taste of booze, and even the smell of cigarettes in the morning gave me a headache. We took turns driving and late that night we reached Calgary. After a few days with her friends, we drove all the way to Vancouver, a long, tiring drive, during which I was oblivious to the majesty of the mountains. In Vancouver, rain greeted us late that night. Emily found us another flophouse, where she was warmly greeted by anyone who wasn't spaced out. Someone made us a meal of scrambled eggs and toast.

The next morning, with plans for job hunting, I went out to look for a store so I could get a paper. The first thing I noticed was that my car wasn't where I had parked it, so I went back in and woke Emily to tell her. One of the other kids said the cops probably had it towed away. Another said it was probably stolen. In either case, I most likely wouldn't see it again. I knew I couldn't call the cops about it, because of the smell in the flophouse and the residue of Emily's pot smoking in the car.

Oh well, I thought, at least I won't be tempted to drive back to Winnipeg, and I wouldn't have to worry about repair bills either. The car had been on its last tire anyway. If it had been stolen, the thief was probably swearing at me by now. Emily got up late that afternoon. My losing the car did not seem to concern her at all, and my idea of going out to look for a job right away only amused her.

"You don't just go knocking on doors," she said.

"Why not? I did in Winnipeg and it worked."

"Do you know how big Vancouver is compared to Winnipeg?"

"Then what should I do?"

"We'll go to my mother's place. She has a phone and she's usually home. I'll tell her to take messages for us."

"And she'll do that?"

"Yeah," she said, not explaining further.

Emily's mother had a large place. She was a widow and rented out the two top floors to roomers. Within two weeks I got a job as a store clerk in a department store. By now the smell of morning coffee made me nauseous, and its taste was horrible. I started drinking orange juice or milk, figuring that Vancouver coffee or the water was different from Winnipeg's.

Emily and I went to her mother's a few times a week to eat. I suspected they must have been rich at one time. Mrs. Brett always had wine with her meals. Besides not liking its taste, I didn't want to be like my mother, so I always refused. All I knew about my mother was that she liked to drink.

One night Emily said to me, "Mom asked me if you were pregnant. Are you?"

Shocked, I looked at her and said, "I don't think so. But gee, I don't really know."

"Well, do you get your periods?"

I realized I didn't remember having periods recently. "They've always been irregular," I said. "I read once that stress could make a woman irregular and I figured that's why."

"Well, Mom said—God, I hate it when I say 'Mom said this, Mom said that.'"

"Don't you like your Mom?"

She gestured with her hand that it was so-so. "You should go see a doctor."

"I can't afford one."

"Sure you can. You're covered by Manitoba insurance for three months."

"No, I mean I just started working. I can't take time off."

Emily shrugged, and I was left to think about the repercussions if I was pregnant. Nick's last present to me. Just great! After he proposed, he stopped using condoms.

When I finally got around to seeing a doctor, he confirmed that I was pregnant. He made me feel embarrassed that I hadn't come sooner, telling me I was already into my fourth month. I hadn't put on any weight and I was still wearing my usual clothing, so how was I supposed to know?

I worked right up until my supervisor told me I had to leave, because of my pregnancy. Partly because Vancouver was too expensive for someone out of work and mostly because I felt more at home in Winnipeg, I decided to return there to give birth. Maybe I was part salmon.

January in Winnipeg was miserably cold. I took a room that I had to share with another boarder in a rooming house near the Women's Pavilion. One day, my water broke and I walked over to the hospital, went into labour and less than three hours later I gave birth to a beautiful little girl.

And then I gave that beautiful little girl up for adoption.

When I was released from the hospital, I returned to the rooming house and when my roommate went off to school, I let myself break down. I cried and cried. I'd read about postnatal depression. The act of giving my baby up for adoption was an act of betrayal to her. Yet what could I have offered her? I was a loser, a total loser going nowhere. And I would have dragged her down with me, betrayed her over and over again, kind of like my mother. No, I could not have kept her and I blamed myself for not having a choice.

An idea came to me sometime the next day, and it grew over the next few days. I made an appointment to see a doctor and I told him I had trouble sleeping and that it was seriously affecting my job. He gave me a prescription for Valium and a stern warning that I was to follow the directions. One night at the large kitchen table, I kind of said goodbye to the other boarders. They had all been so nice to me, and sometimes a few of them had come to my room and tried to cheer me up.

When I was alone the next day, I cut my waist-length hair. It was my hair that had attracted Nick's attention and, if I hadn't met Nick, I wouldn't be where I was now. When I was all done, I sat on my bed and opened my bottle of pills. One by one I swallowed them and when they were gone, I lay down on the bed

I woke up in a hospital bed. My throat was dry and really sore, and I ached all over. There was movement all around me, and I heard an impatient voice saying my name. "Christine Pelletier!" I didn't care about anything. I must have been charged and arrested because after I was out of the hospital I was in a courtroom. One of the repercussions of not having done the job right was that I had to see a psychiatrist twice a week. Since I wouldn't have another go at doing myself in if I was sitting in jail, I agreed to the terms.

At my first few appointments, I refused to talk except to tell the psychiatrist that I was in his office only because I had to show up or go to jail. Gradually, the man tricked me into saying more than I intended. He already knew my recent background and, when he asked how I felt about giving up my baby, I answered with my own question, "How would you feel?"

"You suffered a great loss and you're mourning for her."

"Whatever," I said, and added, "but I shouldn't be mourning because this kind of stuff runs in my family. It should be natural for me."

"Natural to give up a child?"

"Yup, like mother, like daughter. Do you know I don't even know who my father is?"

"Does that bother you a great deal?"

"No, of course not." Then I smiled and sat back.

"What is it that you find humorous?" he asked.

I looked at him and dropped the smile. "If I became a hooker, I couldn't do older Indian guys because one of them might be my father. Or, for that matter, a brother. With my mother, anything's possible." I added that one to show what a contemptuous woman my mother had been—is—and I smiled again.

He didn't return the smile. "Were you afraid that would happen to your daughter?"

78

"My daughter isn't going to become a hooker. She's going to have good parents. And she's going to come out clean and healthy."

"And you didn't?"

"I'm shit."

"You don't really believe that, do you?"

"What does it matter? I'm here because the court says I have to be here." Shut the fuck up, I wanted to tell him.

"I understand that. But as long as you're here, why not talk to me?"

Sitting back, I said nothing. I looked around. Spotting an ashtray on his desk, I asked, "Got a cigarette?"

"I don't smoke."

"Neither do I. Just wanted to see if you had any bad habits, but you wouldn't, would you? So what would you know about shit? Nothing." I spit the words out with all the contempt I could muster.

"So why don't you tell me about that?"

"Because I'm not a teacher. And you, you can't even say the word 'shit,' can you?" The sudden taste of soap filled my mouth. Nonetheless, I enjoyed a rush of power I thought I had over this man.

The sparring continued for another three weeks before I gave it up and spilled my guts about the feelings I'd had for Nick, my mother, Leona, and the daughter I'd given away. But that lasted for only an hour, and then it was time to pull myself together and walk out of his office to make an appointment for the next time. One time he gave me a book by Dale Carnegie to read. I asked him if he gave books to all his customers, and he said no, only to clients who might benefit from them. That made me feel a little better about myself. But then, whenever I talked about trying to get my daughter back, he gave me these words to live by, "Let her be, Christine. Let her be." That told me he didn't think I was good mothering material.

I never did tell him my most private secret, the affair I'd had when I was thirteen—with a foster father who was "doing" his own daughters.

During the daytime, I often went to the library downtown. One day, I was heading home on Graham, when I saw them walking hand in hand. At first I couldn't believe it was them, but sure enough Leona and Nick were coming towards me. I pulled my collar up and lowered my face, glad that it was a cold day. I wondered if Leona would recognize my winter jacket.

I didn't have to worry. They had eyes only for each other as they passed right by me. I was briefly tempted to follow them, eavesdrop on their conversation, tap them on their shoulders, and say hello. Ruin their intimate moment. Enjoy their shock. But I merely watched them walk by, and continued on my way, suddenly chilled not from the outside but from deep inside. I went over to the building I saw them come out of and guessed right off they had been there to get a marriage license.

That night I coaxed the other boarders to lend me some money, telling them I probably wouldn't pay it back. With what they gave me, I had enough to buy a one-way ticket back to Vancouver. The next day as the bus rolled out of town, I vowed I would never, ever return to Winnipeg. By the time the bus reached Portage la Prairie, I'd decided my vow wasn't good enough and I revised it. What I had really meant to say was that I would never ever see my sister again. I had no sister. I had no mother. I had no daughter. My life in Winnipeg had ended.

# 6

## A MANIAC'S GAME

Peter awoke in a state of deep despair. Howard had come to see him the day before and in that crazy, amused way of his had told him, that he had accidentally given an overdose to Todd.

"Unfortunately, your son has passed away."

Peter had known that Howard would want a reaction, so he had pounded at the door with fury and hurled insults at the man on the other side. Laughing merrily, Howard had slammed the panel shut. Peter continued to vent his rage until it was replaced with a sorrow so deep that he cried.

When he could cry no more, he had sat on the cot, his back against the wall. To anyone watching it would have appeared he'd gone into a stupor. Peter knew that a man like Howard would be watching him at all times. He was sure that a small camera lurked in the vent on the ceiling. He thought if he appeared to be defeated, Howard might underestimate him and the next time he came into the cell, he might relax his guard. He wouldn't come in alone, of course. He'd have others for backup and no doubt, they'd be armed, but he might have a chance of escaping. Would they do anything else to him? If Howard had wanted him dead, he'd be dead already. He was positive that Todd was fine but imagining that he had died had helped him put on his display. It seemed as if Howard were playing some kind of maniac game and by now he was thinking that it had to do with Chris.

Chris might be smart but she was also vulnerable and fragile. That wasn't quite right: part of her was fragile, the part she kept hidden from him. He'd already figured out that something horrible had happened to her in her past, maybe in one of the foster homes, but she had never shared that part with him. He'd always felt that when she was ready, she would either share or she would rid herself of whatever it was that haunted her. He passed the time thinking of her and of Todd. While he thought of their good times, he kept his face impassive.

Seated at his wall of monitors, Howard watched Peter. If by some fluke, Peter and Christine ever got back together, she would have herself a man who was so broken he would never recover. However, that wasn't going to happen. Christine didn't know it yet, but she was his and his alone.

Earlier that day, he'd gone with Colin to visit her. He had sat there watching her pour her broken little heart out to them. It had taken everything in him not to burst out laughing at the irony of his being her source of grief.

And that dog of hers—he really had to do something about it—growling at him like that. He had never even touched it. Archie or one of his men had held it captive while they went about their business in her cabin. His plan was to make Christine think she was crazy. If later, she began to figure things out, no one would believe her. Most importantly, she wouldn't believe herself. If she'd had any brains, she might have wondered why her dog was suddenly growling at him when it had never done that before. But she was too focused on herself. That's the way they were, full of self-pity, always yapping that they were victims of this and victims of that.

And Colin—what an ass he was. The plan last August was for him to pretend to be interested in Christine's sister, but the ass had gone and fallen in love with her. Three months were gone and he'd only learned recently that Leona had left him and gone back to Winnipeg. That Colin had held back that information had been infuriating. Before Leona, Colin had been his most trusted disciple, but now both of them would pay, she for seducing him away from the fold and he for allowing himself to be seduced. At the moment, she was out of his reach and for his whole plan to work out the way he wanted, he needed her back. What he really wanted to do was get rid of Colin, but since he could still be useful he would let him live. Almost as much as he wanted to laugh at Christine, he had wanted to punch out Colin for continuing to glance at him, earlier today, when he was talking about Leona. Thank the Lord that Christine didn't have the brains to catch that interplay. From now on he'd "visit" Christine alone, unless he absolutely needed Colin to be there.

As it was, the game was beginning to be b-o-r-i-n-g, and he needed to prod that woman into making some kind of play. Right now, her husband was more interesting to watch. Correction: had been more interesting; he was breaking down already. Maybe tomorrow he'd take the boy out to show Peter. Put some life back into the writer.

Suddenly, the way to prod Christine came to him. He'd get Archie to take Adolph for a night visit.

# 7

## In The Shadow of Evil

Sometime during the night, Lady woke me to let her outside. I didn't want to wake up because I knew I'd have a hard time going back to sleep. Heavy rain poured from black skies, and now that she had me up I almost had to force her out into the rain. I returned to the couch, just to sit for a few minutes while I waited for her.

The sounds of a dogfight woke me, and then I heard the high-pitched squeal of a wounded animal. Realizing with horror that Lady was still out there, I jumped up and raced out, thinking the wolves had gotten her. The rain had stopped, and the only night sounds were water droplets falling from leaves and from the edge of the roof.

"Lady!" I yelled out into the night. A barely audible moan came from the direction of the truck. Grabbing a flashlight, I made my way toward the truck, calling for her. She walked slowly and stiffly into the beam of light, her fur matted and covered with mud and blood.

"Oh baby, I fell back asleep. I'm sorry. I'm sorry."

Lady gave a feeble wag of her tail. I led her back inside so I could get a better look at her. She lay down heavily on the floor and began licking at herself. When I saw that blood was oozing out of a long gash on her side, I thought of Mona. She knew about medicines and could help Lady. I dressed quickly, wrapped a towel around Lady's middle and carried her out to the truck. When I got to Mona's, I honked the horn until their lights came on.

We got Lady inside to their kitchen, and while Mona looked Lady over, Kit asked if I'd seen any stray dogs.

"You mean it wasn't a wolf?" I asked.

"Doesn't seem like it. It's hard to tell. A wolf would have killed her right off."

Mona put the kettle on and made some kind of salve mixture with dried leaves and herbs. She cut away Lady's fur around the main gash. I watched as she checked Lady for other wounds, and we were both surprised to find what looked like stitches from a recent but older wound just behind her left ear.

"She must have been hurt while I was gone. Peter must have taken her to the vet," I said, wondering if she'd been in a previous dogfight.

"Look at this here," Mona said, pointing to a spot just under her throat where the fur seemed to have been rubbed away. "It's like a rope burn. Maybe she got caught up in wire somewhere."

Lady squirmed, impatient at having to lie still. I soothed her as Mona dipped a needle and thread in the cooling herb mixture and began to close the wound with stitches. Lady gave a deep, low, moan, but didn't try to bite or anything. Afterwards, Mona coated the area and the other lesser wounds with the salve. She put some gauze over the gash, wrapped Lady's body tightly with a clean towel and pinned it closed.

"She was lucky. You must have scared off whatever attacked her," Kit said. "You notice any animal acting strange?"

"No, I haven't even seen any animals lately," I answered and then realized what he was talking about. "If you mean rabies, Lady had her shot for that. But then, that was last spring. She's due for another one, I think. But maybe Peter had that done if he took her to the vet while I was gone."

"She should be okay," Kit said.

"She should stay here," Mona said, petting Lady. I can check on her and change the dressing. Amber can help me out."

The next day I returned to Mona's to see Lady before I went to Dodging to pick up some groceries and the mail. Lady seemed much better, but I had a plan in mind, so I thought of asking Mona keep her. Since their granddaughter, Amber, was isolated at their place, I figured she could use a friend, and Lady was the best friend a girl could have.

Amber came in from outside. "Hi Christine. Jeeze I'm sorry about what happened."

"Thank you," I replied, not knowing if she was talking about Peter and Todd, or Lady.

"Hey! Tomorrow, do you want to go horseback riding with me?"

Unable to think of an excuse, I said, "Sure, okay."

In Dodging, I was stunned by people's attitude toward me. If anything I thought a few might be sympathetic, but everyone I ran into eyed me with hostility. The owner of the grocery store, who had always been friendly said, "You have a lot of nerve showing up in town."

"What?"

"The article in the paper—we all know you're involved in some way. Don't come back in here."

I spotted the Peace Valley Voice with Peter and Todd's picture on the front page. I added it to my purchases.

"How can you live with yourself?" she asked, while I paid.

I responded only in my mind, I can't.

On the drive home, I resumed thinking of ending it all. By the time I got to Mona's, I decided to ask if I could leave Lady with them from now on. Mona said Amber would be very happy to have her. On the drive home, my eyes got blurry from tears. At home, I looked at the front page picture of Peter holding Todd and noted that Mrs. Springer had written the article. One phrase caught my eye, "A source tells me that the remaining family member, Christine Pelletier, is a person of interest." That meant the police felt I was a suspect. No wonder everyone in town hated me. I didn't bother reading the rest. Because of the picture of Peter and Todd, I didn't put it in the stove to burn.

Being depressed zaps one's energy. I didn't have the energy to be hungry so all I did was make a coffee. I thought that maybe reading the rest of Peter's manuscript would distract me from the mood I was in. I went to my suitcase, which I hadn't bothered to unpack from my trip, and got out my copy. It occurred to me that he might have made changes while I was gone, so I went to his desk to get his copy. I couldn't find it

86

anywhere. Of course—I immediately thought—he had taken it with him when he ran off with Leona. Why else would it be gone?

Picking up my copy, I distanced myself from the rifle and thoughts of suicide by going down to the lake with Peter's manuscript. No sooner was I in the hammock than I got the feeling of being watched. Turning, I looked all around, saw nothing, and looked around again. That's when I caught the flicker of movement by the edge of the tree line to the east of the cabin. A tawny grey wolf emerged from the underbrush and stood watching me, its ears bent forward, its tail raised high. I felt honoured to see it. We stared at each other, and I wanted so much to know what it was thinking. The wolf tilted its head, gave the slightest wag of its tail and turned to disappear back into the underbrush.

It took me a while to get my mind off the wolf and refocused on the manuscript but I was soon caught up in the story and so focused, I didn't hear Howard's van pull into our driveway.

"Must be really good, whatever you're reading there." At the sound of his voice, I nearly fell out of the hammock, and clumsily got out of it.

"Oh, you really startled me. This is Peter's manuscript and, yeah, I really got into it."

We began walking back to the cabin.

"Would you like a coffee?"

"That would be great. That manuscript—his latest?"

"Yeah. I just started reading it." I said, so he wouldn't ask me what it was about.

Inside, he told me that he had just wanted to look in on me. "I hope you don't mind," he added. As if I were going to tell him that I did.

"Anything new from the police?" he asked.

"No. They should have found them by now. It's been a week."

"Well, if there's anything I can do for you, Christine, let me know. I'll drop in on you as often as I can, that is, if you really don't mind."

"You don't have to do that. I'm okay. And Kit and Mona live nearby."

"Well, I like you very much, Christine. I really would like to just come by and visit."

Liked me very much? I got a queasy feeling in my stomach. Was he hitting on me? The idea was revolting and I tried to figure out how I could say 'no, I don't want you coming back here,' in a nice way. All I could think to say was that I wasn't really good company these days. Later, I walked him out to his van, feeling quite awkward with him.

Walking him out was a mistake because he turned to me and gave me a hug that lasted too long, and said, "If you need anything, anything at all, just let me know. I want to be here for you."

After he left, I went back outside to the hammock. I was disturbed by Howard's behaviour, and I knew I would have to find a way to let him know I really didn't want him to call on me anymore. In the meantime, I picked up Peter's manuscript and started reading where I'd left off.

The protagonist was Gregory M. Thomas's son, Tom Crow Thomas. Thirty years earlier, Gregory had met an Indian woman and fallen in love. She was the reason he had never married. Gregory was investigating a white supremacist group implicated in the disappearance of Aboriginal women. When he learns he has a thirty-year old son, Tom, he talks him into joining his agency as a detective, which is why the working title for this novel was *A Dick Named Tom*. After Gregory is shot, he asks his son Tom to take over the investigation. Tom Crow Thomas is a look-alike to Billy Jack from the movies and come to think of it so was Constable Bob Cormier. I wondered if Peter had met Bob Cormier before, in Fort St. John.

The story was really interesting. There was no Leona-type woman in it. It was mostly about a group of racist men who were anti-government and anti-visible-minorities, and the mysterious things they were doing to get rid of undesirables. At one point I stopped reading and just lay back, thinking how lucky I was to have met Peter. His good guys were strong moral characters. I'd read once that actors had more fun playing bad guys because they could do different things with those characters. Maybe Peter had crossed to the other side because Leona was more fun.

As I lay there, a wind came up. It was strong enough to rock the hammock, and I dozed off and began dreaming that something scary was licking at my fingers. Something told me it wasn't a dream, and I woke up with a jolt. I jerked my arm back into the hammock and looked down just in time to see a little puppy streak for cover under my truck where he joined another puppy already there. They looked like German shepherd pups but very scrawny ones. I thought they might be wolf pups, but I knew, from one of our books about wolves, that they avoided people. The wolf I'd seen earlier was probably their mother.

My freezer was packed with meat that I would never eat, so I got out of the hammock and headed for our cabin. I got a hare out of the freezer. I hated rabbit stew, but Peter had loved it, and so he had shot them, skinned them, and put them on our menu. I wondered if I should cook the hare first but then I remembered that wild animals often ate from frozen carcasses in the winter.

I carried the carcass back out into the sunshine and put it down by one end of the truck; the pups moved to the other end. Then I went to sit on the steps, wondering if the pups would dare come this close to me, now that I was awake and watching. When the larger grey pup got the scent of meat, he edged forward cautiously. The black pup eyed both its sibling and me. The grey pup tugged the hare back under the truck, and I could hear the two of them make little growling noises as they chewed the carcass.

They had the hare in pieces when their mother, the one I'd seen before, came looking for them. She could not have been a very good hunter because she had allowed hunger to make them desperate enough to come near me. She got on her belly to retrieve what she could of the hare. Perhaps her desperation prevented her from being afraid of me. I remained very still and quiet because I didn't want to scare her. When she finished, she drew one pup to her and began washing it. It squealed and tried to get away and could have, too, but didn't. The other pup took the opportunity to pounce on its exposed belly. When she was done with the pups, she licked at her paws, then got up, glanced in my direction, and led them back into the bush.

One wolf sighting was amazing but seeing the pups with their mother this close up was beyond belief. Or maybe it was common, and people who'd had these experiences wisely never talked about them.

Against my better judgment, I went back inside to the freezer and got three packs of meat out. I walked into the bush, beyond where I'd first seen the mother wolf and set down the meat.

The wind that had picked up earlier was turning the day cooler, so I decided to continue reading inside. Before long, I heard Lady barking a greeting. I went outside, and she jumped up on me, her tail whipping back and forth. It was as if we hadn't seen each other for weeks. She wasn't even like this when I returned from my trip, I recalled. Amber and Kit followed on horseback. I hadn't expected them until the next day, so I was surprised to see them. Kit and I went into the house for some tea while Amber remained with the horses down at the lake, where she let them drink. Lady chose to stay with her.

"Her and that dog of yours are inseparable already," Kit observed.

Smiling, I said, "I kind of told Mona it might be a good idea for Lady to stay at your place."

"It would be a good thing for Amber. Yes. Thank you."

After his tea, Kit took the canoe out to do some fishing while Amber and I went for a horseback ride. It felt great, as long as I focused on the scenery, as long as I concentrated on moving as one with the horse, as long as I did not think about Todd and Peter.

"I've got to thank you about Lady. I just love that dog." Amber said as we rode side by side.

"Well, since she already goes to visit you, I thought it would be better for her to stay at your place." I said.

"Really? You don't mind?" Amber asked, excitement in her voice.

"No. She was attacked by something out here, maybe a wolf, although Kit doesn't think so," I replied, " but I just saw one earlier today. I think she'd have more protection at your place. Kit told me once that mule of his, I-ee-mon, keeps all the predators away, even grizzlies."

"Yeah, he's crazy, that mule. But when Kit puts his bridle on him, he turns completely docile. Anyhow you don't have to worry about Lady. We're like glue, eh. And we're getting her used to the horses."

Later, as they were getting ready to leave, Amber asked Kit, "Did you give her that telephone message?"

Kit slapped at his shirt pocket to dig out a piece of paper. "I'm sorry, I forgot, and I know how important this is to you. This was why we came here in the first place. Mona got this call earlier today. This woman said she was a friend of Leona's. She wants you to call her. That's her number, there. You could go over right now."

As soon as he mentioned Leona's name, I began to tremble. My pretense of the good mood I had been able to display with them vanished. Telling Kit I would go right away, I got my keys and left.

Emma, the woman who answered my call, said she was a good friend of Leona's. "Leona asked me to call you because, um, she wants you to look after Michael for a while."

"Why? Is she sick?"

"Um, no." I heard the woman sigh before going on, "She's in the Remand Centre."

"What? Why?"

"She's been charged with assault. And she doesn't want to risk Children's Aid taking him. He's staying with us right now but I can't keep him here."

I closed my eyes and thought how ironic life was. Leona was asking me to take care of Nick's son, of all people, while Nick's daughter was out there somewhere, alone. She was asking me to take care of her son while my own might be dead. No. No, I didn't think so.

"So could you?"

Unable to make myself say that I didn't want Nick and Leona's son anywhere near me, I simply said, "I'm sorry but I'll have to get back to you. Bye."

I returned to the cabin, having made an awkward apology to Mona for leaving so abruptly. Kit and Amber passed me on the road, and not wanting to talk, I simply waved as I went by.

As soon as I was inside, I went into Todd's room and, hugging his Teddy bear to me, I cried. When I was all cried out, I went into my bedroom, still hugging the bear. As I was sitting on the edge of my bed, my eyes rested on the rifles nestled in their places on the wall. I set the stuffed toy aside and brought down the .22, cradling it in my arms.

I thought of how life was one big joke; Leona, in jail for assault, asking me to take her son. That meant Peter and Todd weren't with her, never had been. That meant they were dead. Here, I'd had all those horrible thoughts about him. Because I was really the evil one, I had thought he was evil, too. The past really does have a way of catching up, I thought as I sat with my back against the headboard, the rifle beside me. I tried to make my mind blank, but memories of a time I wished I'd never had came back to me. I heard that just before you die your life flashes before you. Maybe memories just forced their way back into the present.

---

When I was five, my mother gave me to Children's Aid. She kept Leona with her and I never knew why she didn't want me. I must have behaved badly because I went into a series of foster homes and had a series of social workers.

When I was thirteen I landed at Dr. Coran's house. Miss Branzil was my social worker at the time. Dr. Coran was there to greet us and show us around the house. It was a spotlessly clean spacious split-level, and my bedroom, with a bathroom right next to it, was on the lower level. Miss Branzil was walking ahead of us, but I heard her tell Dr. Coran that I could be very willful. Behind her back, he looked at me with a smile and said they were very good with willful children and then he winked. I thought I was going to like this foster father. He was tall and even though he wore thick black-rimmed glasses, had a hooked nose and a large mole on his cheek just below his right eye, he didn't seem at all ugly. I even thought he was kind of good-looking for an old man. Maybe it was because he was nice to me.

After the first few days, I noticed his two daughters Queenie and Darcy and his wife were very submissive to him and that his word was law. I looked down on them for that. While he ordered them around and was arrogant with them, he seemed delighted by me. I thought it was because I was the only one who talked back. Where he might have ordered the others to go to their room, including his wife, he would laugh with me. Sometimes he'd make a lemonade or iced tea, just for me. He was always kind and interested and for the first time in my life, it seemed someone cared about me. He was the first foster father who treated me like a daughter.

Not long after I moved there, he called me into his study one morning and showed me how to file a pile of papers for him. He had made me some lemonade. I was careful to wipe the bottom of the glass before setting it down anywhere. Sometimes he could change from being really nice to being really nasty. That part I didn't like about him. By lunchtime, the pile was almost gone. He came up behind me and started nuzzling my neck. At first it just tickled and I knew it was wrong and I should stop him. But maybe knowing it was wrong is what made me curious. He turned me to face him and kissed me hard on my mouth. He led me over to the couch and began running his hands all over me whispering between kisses what I should do to him. And I did it. That first time on the couch, we didn't go all the way, but I wanted to.

He came to my bedroom one night and woke me up. At first I was alarmed when he lay beside me and started kissing me but it wasn't long before I was in the mood to do more. It was as if I were possessed. When he asked if I wanted him to take off his pajamas, I said yes. He removed them and climbed under my sheets beside me. He helped me take my pajamas off, too, and it was like I was another person. I didn't know what got into me but I wanted him, I needed him, and I somehow stopped myself from thinking about his wife right upstairs. That is, until I woke up the next morning and guilt hit me right in the gut. I didn't want to go up to breakfast to sit at the same table with his wife, and his daughters.

I felt so guilty right up until the night he came again. He helped replace my guilt with such sinful pleasure and because he never worried about his wife waking up and finding him gone from their bed, I stopped worrying about her, too. How do you live with shame? You keep to yourself and that's what I began to do. My only release was when I was able to lose myself in books.

I don't know why but one day he ended it. He slapped me hard across the face for not washing a pot well enough. In a way, while he no longer came to me in the night, easing the guilt that was piling up inside of me, his new hostility toward me was more acceptable. It was the way things should have been in the first place. The bad part was I couldn't undo what I had done. After that he ran the household, me included, with an iron fist. Everything had to be just so. And I fell in line with the rest of them.

One nice thing Dr. Coran did was to make us warm milk every night. He said it would help us sleep better. The first time, Queenie brought the cups to the table. When she set mine down, I saw that her baby finger was missing, and I wondered how that happened.

The taste of boiled milk was disgusting, but I drank it in the beginning because I liked him. After he became mean to me, I tried to figure out how to avoid drinking the milk. We each had to rinse our cups, and then Darcy had to remain behind to wash and dry them along with the saucepan. Some nights I fell asleep right away and slept through the whole night. That was unusual for me, but in spite of it, I would feel drowsy and sluggish for most of the following mornings.

On Sunday mornings Mrs. Coran and Darcy went to early Mass so they could be home in time to prepare dinner. In all my other foster homes, only the man had a car or a truck, but the Corans were so rich they had two shiny new cars. Dr. Coran, Queenie, and I attended the eleven o'clock Mass. Many of the people we met going into the church knew the doctor and everyone respected him.

School gave me a sense of release from the constant silence in the house. Not that I was a fun person, myself, but I did like some noise. And I liked having access to all the books in the school library. In addition to my homework, Dr. Coran took an interest in the books I brought home and criticized my choices, so I started bringing ones I didn't like, just to show them to him. Doing homework was preferable to reading the Bible and religious books they had, so my grades were better than ever before; in fact, I became an A student. I didn't dare skip out on school.

My case worker, Miss Branzil, returned for a visit and was impressed that the family had had such a positive influence on me. I really missed Leona and I wanted to show her how good I was doing in school, too, so I asked Miss Branzil if she could arrange a visit. She said she would, but she seemed preoccupied with other thoughts. It dawned on me that she had a crush on Dr. Coran. When she left, Dr. Coran walked her out to her car while Mrs. Coran took the coffee tray into the kitchen. I watched them stop at her car to talk and Miss Branzil dropped her pen. Dr. Coran stooped to retrieve it for her and as he straightened up, he touched his fingers to the inside of her ankle and ran his hand right up her leg past where her skirt ended. I jumped back when Dr. Coran turned to stare directly in my direction. Upon his return, he didn't say anything or act differently, and I never knew whether he had seen me or not.

In each one of my foster homes, I had periods of being deeply suspicious of the parents, mostly because I didn't know why they had taken me in. I figured they had to have had a motive. My suspicion flared up one night as I was sipping my milk and wondering why a man, especially one like Dr. Coran, would make hot milk for us. But I quelled the suspicion by thinking that because he was a doctor he must know what was best for us.

Then one day, it became clear to me why Mrs. Coran and his daughters feared him so much. We had just returned from church, and Queenie and I were about to set the table. Darcy and her mother were preparing dinner, when Dr. Coran called to Darcy in a chilling tone of voice that I had never heard before, "Darcy, come down here right now."

Darcy went down the stairs and, curious, I followed her. Downstairs, I was responsible for cleaning my room, the laundry room, and the basement where he kept exercise equipment. Darcy was responsible for the downstairs bathroom. Somehow he had discovered that my toilet wasn't clean enough. Why he'd even look in there was a mystery to me. He berated Darcy and then grabbed the back of her head and made her kneel in front of the toilet.

"You don't see that filth? Look at it. Take a good look at it." And saying this, he shoved her head right into the toilet bowl.

By this time I was at the bathroom door. I wanted him to stop, so I said, hesitantly, "I made that dirty."

Still bent over, holding her head down, he turned to me, and gone was all the pretence of being kind and caring. "You! You have your own duties

95

to fulfill. This bathroom is Darcy's job. She is responsible. Not you. From now on, you will all do the duties I have assigned to you, is that clear?" His voice rose, so by the end he was shouting. He released Darcy's head as I nodded meekly.

"Clean that up," he snarled at her. When she came up, the top of her head was wet and her hair looked funny, so a smile flashed across my face. Dr. Coran turned to me and maybe he caught the smile. Approaching me, he growled, "And you," he stopped in front of the sink to pick up the bar of soap, "you wash your mouth out."

Having backed out of the doorway to let him pass, I looked from the bar of soap to his eyes. I was shocked to see he was serious. "You think I don't know you just lied? You wash your mouth out now or I will wash it out for you."

He was crazy if he thought I was going to wash out my mouth with soap, and I said so, "You're crazy."

Darcy gasped. I turned to walk away but his hand grabbed me just under my mouth and he yanked me back, close to the sink. He turned on the tap, wet the soap, and shoved it into my mouth. I struggled to get free, trying to keep my mouth closed, but he was too strong. When he was finished with me, I stomped up the stairs and marched towards the front door. More with astonishment than shock, I felt him grab my arm and yank me back. "Where do you think you're going?"

"I'm getting out of here. And when I do, I'm telling what you did." As soon as I said that, I wished I hadn't because it sounded so babyish.

"Telling what? That you lied and I had to clean out your mouth? It's done all the time."

"I'm telling what you just did to Darcy."

"Darcy, come up here," he said.

Darcy came up the stairs quickly. He said to her, "Darcy, did I mistreat you in any way?"

"No, father. I disobeyed you. I'm sorry. I should have been more responsible."

He looked at me, a gleam of triumph in his eyes. "I want to show you something." He latched on to my arm and dragged me towards the rolltop desk, letting go of me to dig some keys from his pocket to open a drawer. He brought out a case, opened it and removed a kind of knife with a sharp, shiny blade. Since I knew he was a doctor, I figured it must be a scalpel. Afraid, I took a step back, wondering if I could somehow get outside before he stopped me.

As if reading my mind, he said, "Oh don't worry. I'm not going to use this on you." Raising his voice slightly, he said, "Queenie, come here. You too, Mother."

When Queenie and Mrs. Coran came into the living room, fear jumped to Queenie's eyes as soon as she saw the blade. Taking a small stainless steel tray from the case, the doctor placed it on the desk and said in a low chilling voice, "Come here, Queenie."

Incredibly, she obeyed, advancing until she stood at the other side of the desk.

"Put your right hand on there."

Queenie looked at me with terror in her eyes but she placed her right hand on the tray.

"Spread your fingers apart," he said. The way he said that reminded me of the nights he had told me to spread my legs apart. There was even a perverted kind of excitement in his voice, and it was in his eyes too.

Queenie's hand was shaking so much she could barely keep her fingers flat on the tray.

Relenting, I said, "Okay, okay, stop. Don't hurt her. I'll do whatever you say. I'll never tell anyone anything."

Trance-like, he touched the blade to her finger, very slowly, very deliberately.

"I said stop. Please stop. Please don't hurt her." My voice was hysterical with panic.

Despite my pleadings, blood began to ooze from the cut.

"I promise. Whatever you want."

He looked up at me and said, "You made me cut her. You see that? You made me do that."

I started breathing again only when he had removed the blade from her finger. He looked at it and said, "This is dirty." He handed it to

Queenie and said, "Go clean this up. Sterilize it."

To his wife, he asked, "Is dinner ready?"

She nodded right away.

To me, he said, "Go set the table. We're going to eat now."

Eat? The only thing I wanted to do right now was puke. But that would get Darcy into trouble again. Swallowing back bile, I joined Mrs. Coran in the kitchen, wondering why she hadn't said anything to protect her daughters.

I may have only been thirteen, but I realized that I was trapped here. And that I wouldn't be getting any help from outside. Leona was twenty, and I didn't know where she was. My mother couldn't have cared less about me, and Miss Branzil had her crush and would probably do anything he asked. He had turned the others into zombies by terrorizing them. It seemed that he wanted zombies around him. Well, from now on, I would be a zombie too.

One day Mrs. Coran and Queenie went shopping for school supplies, and Dr. Coran and Darcy were at his office. For the first time, I was alone in the house. Taking some cleaning supplies from the kitchen, I went upstairs. If anyone came home unexpectedly, I would say that I only wanted to surprise them with some extra cleaning, a feeble excuse since everything was meticulously cleaned every morning. The two doors on my right led to bedrooms slightly larger than mine, and the door on the left was to a very large bedroom. On one of the nightstands was a phone. All this time I had thought there was no phone in the house, for I had never heard it ring.

I had no idea what to look for, but maybe I would find something that was incriminating. Maybe I would know what it was if I saw it. I was just about to start searching when I heard the sound of a car in the driveway. A chill ran up and down my spine and I raced back out, glad that I hadn't touched anything, shut the door, and ran down the stairs back to my room.

At the doorway of my room, I saw the doctor's trousered legs as he passed by. I heard him move around in the kitchen. He rarely came home during the day, and then only for lunch, but it wasn't lunchtime.

Suddenly I remembered I had left the cleaning supplies in the upstairs bathroom. Oh my God! I thought. I had to get them or there would be hell to pay. Slowly, I ventured down the hallway, testing the floor and the stairs for squeaks and staying close to the walls. The sound of the kettle whistling made me jump, but I was quick enough to move with its sound and I was able to get to the cleaning supplies. Should I go into one of the bedrooms or try to make it back to my room? I didn't know. I didn't know. Mrs. Coran and Queenie might come back and I would be caught in one of the girls' bedrooms. Then I would be the one to lose a finger. Swallowing hard, I decided to go for the safety of my own room.

I was just starting back down the hall when Dr. Coran passed right in front of me, carrying his cup of tea. Had he been looking up, he would have seen me. As it was, he was looking down at his cup. He went down the stairs. I heard the sound of keys, and then a door opened and closed. He had gone into his study, so I moved forward. I put the cleaning supplies away under the sink in the kitchen, and then indecision set in again. Should I go downstairs to my room or outside for a walk? The doors had automatic locks, so I wouldn't be able to get back in. I decided to get back to my room and, should I be discovered, pretend I had been sleeping. I'd get hell for that too, but I wouldn't lose a finger.

At first my feet didn't want to move, but once I forced myself to take the first step I gritted my teeth and kept moving. As I was passing the closed door on my left, I heard some noises. It sounded as if the doctor was having sex or something. Maybe he had brought a nurse home. No – just one cup. I made it to my room, closed the door quietly, and lay down on my bed. My shakes stopped only after I heard the doctor leave. As soon as I was sure he was gone, I got up and went to the door across the hall to try it, but it was locked again. It didn't matter. Elation hit me as I thought I was one up on the doctor.

But then that night during supper, the doctor questioned his wife about her shopping trip, "How did your shopping go? Did you have enough money?"

"Yes," Mrs. Coran answered.

"And did you get everything you needed?"

"Yes," Mrs. Coran answered.

"And Christine, you got some things, too?" His eyes were on me.

"No."

"Why not?"

Mrs. Coran was going to tell him I hadn't been with them, and he was going to cut my finger off. I froze.

Thankfully, Mrs. Coran cut in and said nervously, "You didn't give me the money from Children's Aid."

"You still could have bought her something. We're not poor, you know."

"I'm sorry."

"Don't say you're sorry to me. Say it to Christine."

Mrs. Coran looked at me and said, "I'm sorry, Christine."

Dr. Coran's chair scraped the oak flooring as he got up, walked over to her side, and said: "Being sorry means nothing. Poor Christine! How do you think she felt watching you shop for yourselves and get nothing herself?"

Mrs. Coran had put her fork down and was now looking down at the table. She said, "I really thought you wouldn't want me to."

"I would appreciate it if you'd look at me when you talk to me."

She looked up at him and was about to repeat what she had said when—whack—he slapped her hard across the face, leaving a bright red impression on her smooth white cheek. I opened my mouth to confess, but her eyes met mine for just an instant and I got the impression she wanted me to stay silent. What was the point? Somehow, he knew I had not gone with them. I must have left some evidence that I was here today, alone.

He returned to his chair and began eating again as if nothing had happened. The other four of us had stopped eating and resumed only after he ordered us to eat our food. When we finished, he thanked God for the food we had eaten.

I wanted to say I was sorry to Mrs. Coran, but the look in her eyes told me not to say anything at all. We cleaned up the kitchen in silence and then went into the living room for his Bible reading. For a few days after that we were jumpy, because we didn't know if he was going to pursue the shopping trip further. The doctor had slapped his wife for not buying me anything, but he also would have slapped her if she had bought me something.

Gradually, he relaxed his guard against me and, at night, I managed to spill half the milk into the sink as I was rinsing out my cup. One night I was running water and pouring the milk down the drain when Queenie gasped. I hadn't realized she was right behind me. Our eyes met and I saw just a tiny flicker of life in them. We both knew she had to tell on me. I was so petrified of the expected onslaught from him that I started drinking all of my milk at night. Finally, I couldn't stand it anymore and, when Queenie and I were alone, I asked her, "Did you tell your father about the milk?"

After staring at me for a moment with her doleful eyes, she shook her head no. Sighing with relief, I said, thanks.

Almost immediately, I took to dumping my milk again. In the past when had I dumped most of it, I began waking up during the nights more often. There were lots of noises upstairs, like doors opening and closing and the shower running. The water and drain pipes ran close to my room, so I knew when someone upstairs took a shower or bath or flushed the toilet.

What I didn't know was why. One night I woke up and thought it must have been from some noise, perhaps a door closing. After lying in bed for a while listening to what sounded like a bed squeaking, I finally got out of bed to investigate. I sneaked up to the main level. Upstairs, everything was dark; no lights shone from under the cracks of doors. A door on the right side opened and I guessed Queenie or Darcy was going to the bathroom. Suddenly, the bathroom light went on and I saw Dr. Coran. He was completely naked! He closed the door and I was in darkness again, but I heard him taking a shower. The doctor opened the door before he shut the light off, and I saw that he was now wearing his pajamas. I heard the door on the left open and close.

His daughters? Maybe I had just been something new to try out—but his own daughters? That was incest. That was evil. He was evil, a very evil man. And I had wanted him? I felt a need to throw up. I went down to my room and spent the rest of the night trying to think of a way I could make up for what I had done. Another thought came up. Was he drugging us? Why else would he make us drink warm milk every night? And that's why he wasn't worried about the noises he made. We were all supposed to be sleeping, except for the one he was with. Or did his daughters sleep through it? Did he do it to me while I slept?

I realized then that I couldn't stay there. I'd have to run away. Then it occurred to me that if I ran away, he'd blame his wife for my getting away and he'd do something horrible to her and probably to Darcy and Queenie too. How, I wondered, had I come to care about what happened to them?

The next day I decided that I needed some kind of proof of what he was doing. If I ran away and they found me, they might just send me back here. I had to get back into his study and find proof to take with me.

As it happened, the opportunity to get his keys came in a completely unexpected way. Sometimes Dr. and Mrs. Coran went out for the evening to fancy places, and the three of us were locked inside the house. One Friday night, I awakened when the front door slammed shut. Dr. Coran was yelling at his wife and from the noises he was beating her, too. I opened my door a crack. By now they were near the kitchen. Then she raced by for the front door. He threw his keys at her, yelling that if she left she was not to come back. They were words only, because when he passed by he got hold of her and dragged her back. They went up the stairs and once their bedroom door was slammed shut, his voice was muffled. I went up to see if he had forgotten his keys. The moonlight came through the windows above and beside the door and I could clearly see his keys lying in a little heap.

It was my opportunity but I was suddenly too petrified to move. He might have been yelling at her, but his rage scared the wits out of me. I looked upward, back over my shoulder to where an ominous silence now hovered in the darkness. Maybe he had planned this. Maybe he had quietly come out and was standing there in the dark, watching for me. I wouldn't put that past him, so I went back down and waited and listened and waited some more.

Setup or not, I finally decided to go up and get those keys. Once upstairs, I checked the kitchen and dining room to make sure he wasn't lurking about, and decided that if he were, I would say I thought I heard a noise. Returning to the keys, I made sure they didn't jingle when I picked them up. Downstairs, I tried one key at a time, and it was the last key on the chain that made the lock click.

My eyes had to adjust to the darkness and, when they did, I crossed to the window and pulled open the curtains. The moonlight flooded the room and that was good, because if I turned on a light he might have seen it from his bedroom window above. Some kind of medals and framed pictures of what looked like army people hung on one wall. A framed photograph sat on his desk, and I took it closer to the window where the light from the full moon was better. It was a wedding picture of him and Mrs. Coran. They were younger, and she was smiling up at him with adulation in her eyes. It occurred to me, once again, that I had not once seen Mrs. Coran smile with pleasure, not her or her girls. When that picture had been taken, she must have thought he was quite a catch.

Opening the drawers to the desk, I found nothing of importance in them, and in the top three filing cabinet drawers there were only file folders containing what I guessed were old medical files. But the bottom one contained magazines, and I took one back to the window and discovered it held pictures of naked women. Some of the pictures were of half-naked men doing it to naked women who were tied up or blindfolded. One big picture in the middle showed a naked blindfolded woman with her legs and arms tied to four bedposts. A man was shoving some sort of stick between her legs and she looked as though she was screaming in pain. Sickened, I closed the magazine and put it back where I found it. The doctor was a pig, a sick, disgusting pig. Sorry, pigs. I mean he was a pervert, a monster, a mean, slimy, evil monster.

I eased the drawer of the filing cabinet closed, with hands that were trembling. I wanted to get out of this room, yet I had to do some more snooping. Up on the shelves behind his desk chair were more books, and then I spotted a jar. I reached for it, took it to the window, and almost dropped it when I realized what was in it. A finger bounced around in some liquid. Queenie's baby finger! This could be my proof but if I took the jar and those magazines, would they prove anything? Besides, the way it was displayed, the doctor would notice the missing jar immediately.

I put the jar back on the shelf, anxious to get out of there. I made sure that all the drawers were closed securely. At the doorway, I spotted a garbage can at the other end of a leather couch, but when I checked, it had only used tissue paper. I walked out of his study, wondering who cleaned up in here. The key turning in the lock now seemed so loud. I tested the door to make sure it was locked. Then I went up the stairs to the front entrance and placed the keys as I had found them. Once I was back in the "safety" of my own bed, my breathing gradually returned to normal, but the shivers stayed with me.

Sitting cross-legged on my bed, I wondered what I could do next. If I did run away, got caught and was sent back here, he'd have a whole bunch of jars with fingers in them. The thought of that gave me the willies. Unable to resolve the problem, I lay down and tried hard not to think of dirty magazines and jars with baby fingers. I must have been on the verge of sleep when a thought jumped out at me. If that shelf had been dusty, the doctor was tall enough to see that the jar had been moved, and the same with the wedding picture on the desk. In bright daylight, he would immediately see disturbed dust. His keys had been out in the open, so he might check around in his office just because he was by nature an extremely suspicious man. And he was also a clean freak.

Unsuccessfully, I tried to convince myself that he wouldn't put up with dust, gave up, and got out of bed once again. Up the stairs I trudged, looked up the other staircase, and then around the corner to the foyer. I blinked. The keys were no longer there. I looked again. Still no keys. A line of panic surged through my centre. It had been a setup. I tiptoed back down the stairs and paused at the door to his study but couldn't hear anything. I returned to my bedroom, wondering if he was somewhere behind me, in the basement, perhaps, watching me.

The next morning I went upstairs and played the innocent, trying hard not to think of my nocturnal activities. It seemed that people always picked up on what was on my mind. Mrs. Coran was wearing a bruise on her cheek. She was the only one who got hit in the face.

Dr. Coran was reading the morning paper as he ate. Without looking at me, he said, "Did you have a good sleep, Christine?"

The basement, I thought. I hadn't checked the basement, and that's where he had been, watching me and waiting. Plotting. That's why the keys weren't there the second time. His way of letting me know that he knew what I was doing. That was the moment I remembered I hadn't closed the curtains, and I felt like throwing up.

When we ate, we made sure our cutlery didn't hit the plates, because that disturbed him. I had once gotten a fork thrown at me because I forgot. Now the silence grew, if that was possible. That was when I knew the girls were aware of what their father was doing to them. They knew. A tremor came to my hands, and I put down my fork and knife and swallowed bile.

"I asked you a question, Christine," he said, and I knew he knew I'd been in his study.

"Yes," I mumbled. And I forced myself to look at him.

"You don't miss my visits?"

That question made me look down. I hadn't expected this move.

"Yes, Christine is a little whore. That's the way they are. What do you think we should do with her? Janice?"

"Janice, I'm asking you a question. Please have the courtesy to answer me."

I heard his wife say, "Just send her away."

"Just send her away. So she can tell lies about me? She doesn't care about what happens to you or Darcy and Queenie. Do you, Christine?"

"I wouldn't tell anyone anything."

"And how would you explain your missing finger?"

I'd been staring so hard at my toast, I didn't hear him get up and now he was right behind me. Instantly, I knew what that meant and I tried to get up and run, even though I knew I wouldn't be able to get out.

He let me run but cornered me at the front door, like he had done with his wife last night. Behind him I saw her and her daughters go upstairs.

He slapped me hard across my face, and then he was punching me in the stomach. The punches brought tears to my eyes and made me want to puke. When he got me back in the living room, he threw me forward and, tripping on the leg of the chair at the rolltop desk, I landed hard. He was down on top of me right away, with a crazy lunatic look in his eyes. I thrashed around trying to avoid his punches, fighting to get free. When the fight had gone out of me and I lay still, he kissed me hard on my mouth. Just before I squeezed my eyes shut, I saw Mrs. Coran at the top of the stairs with Darcy and Queenie looking down from behind her.

The thought that they might help me made me renew my efforts, and I squirmed some more until my head was under the rolltop desk, which would prevent him from kissing me again. But that was right where it seemed he wanted me. With his weight holding me down, he got his keys from his pocket and unlocked the drawer where the black case was stored. With one hand he fiddled with the lock and, with his other, he gripped me by the neck, choking me. My alarm at seeing his intent gave me strength I didn't know I had and I bucked, making him lose both his grip on my neck and his balance. Instead of trying to flee again, I tried to scratch and bite at him, so he found it hard to get another good grip on me and get at his case. I yelled at those women to help me. The doctor now had the case on the desktop, but he stopped trying to get his scalpel out as he again focused his attention on getting a firm grip on me. Repeatedly, he hit me across my head, back and forth, and he said, "You think I don't know you went into my study?" And then he was tearing at my clothing and his hand was grabbing at me between my legs.

"You like that, you little whore? Oh yes, I know all about you. You squaws like to play so, so coy, don't you? And what you really like is for us men to jam it into you. Isn't that what you want, my little brown whore?" He didn't say these words all at once. He said them between gasps and hard breathing. And the hard breathing didn't come because he was exhausted from the fight. It came because he was sexually aroused. Instinctively, I knew nothing would stop him from raping me.

He stood up, forced me to my feet, and dragged me towards the stairs like I was a child's rag doll. When he noticed his wife and daughters at

106

the top of the stairs, he hissed, "Go to your rooms. Right now."

When they didn't move, he yelled, "You want to watch? Huh? Is that what you want?" In a lower tone, he said, "Filthy whores, that's what they are. Filthy, filthy whores!"

Then he was dragging me down the stairs, down the hallway to my bedroom. He threw me on the bed and, as he started to undo his buttons, I tried to get out. He easily pushed me back, taking the time to give another hard slap.

The doorbell buzzed and, in quick succession, it was followed by the sounds of someone pounding on the door and a muffled voice saying, "Police. Open up."

A stricken look came over Dr. Coran's face, but he quickly recovered and hissed at me, "All five fingers."

He raced back upstairs, re-buttoning his shirt. I followed right behind because I wasn't going to stay here tonight or ever again. If I had to attack a policeman to make them take me with them, I would. Before he went to the front door, he glanced around, saw the case on his desk, took the scalpel from the case, slashed himself a few times, on his arms and across his stomach, and tossed it on the floor nearby. After that, he went to the front door. Two policemen barged in, and the first thing they saw was the blood all over Dr. Coran's shirt and arms. Their hands went down to their holsters as their suspicious eyes fell on me.

By this time Dr. Coran was saying, "I'm glad to see you. You've got to take this girl away. She went after my wife with that." He pointed over to the scalpel lying on the living-room carpet and continued his spiel, "She went completely berserk on us. Just like that."

While he was talking, I was thinking with delicious satisfaction that since Mrs. Coran must have called the police, she and her daughters would tell the truth. I was about to get another surprise.

He turned to his wife and gently asked, "Are you all right, dear? Did she cut you anywhere?" He looked up at her, full of loving concern. To the police, he said, "I'm Dr. Coran. I have a medical practice in town."

Seeming puzzled, one of the policemen looked up at Mrs. Coran and asked, "Is that right, ma'am? Did she take that knife to you?"

We all looked up at her.

She very deliberately took hold of Darcy's hand, held it tightly, and looked straight at me. She wet her lips and then she nodded yes.

The policeman next to me said, "You'd better come with us. Nice and easy, now. Could you get her coat?"

Dr. Coran got my coat from the back closet and, as he was handing it to the officer, he said to me, "We went out of our way for you. And this is our reward." To the officer he said, "Don't be too hard on her. She's had a difficult life, going from foster home to foster home and she's told us some fairly strange tales. I'm not a psychiatrist, but I would diagnose her to be schizophrenic."

While he was saying this, I put on my coat. They handcuffed me and one of the officers led me outside to a police car, with its lights still flashing.

Dr. Coran was talking to the other policeman, as neighbours gathered, wondering why a police car was at the Coran house. I heard someone ask the doctor if everything was okay, and their eyes full of concern, went from his bloody shirt to me and changed to disgust. None of it mattered. Although I was in a lot of pain, I was just happy to be getting out of that madhouse. I bet not many people thought that getting arrested was like getting their freedom.

Miss Branzil came down to the police station where I was being 'processed', and the first thing she said to me was, "You've really gone and done it this time."

She set down her large purse, retrieved a notebook from it, and, with her pen poised above the paper, she asked, "What on earth got into you to pull a knife on Mrs. Coran? My God, that poor woman. The doctor says she almost had to be hospitalized, you traumatized her so much. And slashing the doctor? That's a very serious matter. What happened? What set you off?"

"I want to see Leona." I said.

Thinking of Mrs. Coran's last silent plea to me, combined with the doctor's last threat to me, I knew I could say nothing. Could I ever convince anyone of what was going on in the Coran house? I didn't think so.

---

That was how I ended up in reform school. I had lots of time to keep the guilt I had for going to bed with such a man alive and that guilt was still alive, even though he was dead. My conscience for such immorality never let it go, probably because I had never told anyone about it. I had always had this feeling I needed to cleanse myself so I wouldn't be evil anymore.

Now it was all too late. The only reasons I had had for attempting to cleanse myself were gone. And I had to join them. My life was worthless.

# 8

## RESISTANCE

Howard was peeved. Ever since Thursday night, Peter had ignored his visits. He hadn't touched any food, and all he had done was sit or lay down. It was time to take the boy to him and stir him up a little. If Peter reacted as expected, it meant he'd been faking a breakdown. There was no fun in trying to play with someone who didn't want to play.

Archie had taken Adolph for a visit to Christine the night before. That dog of hers, Lady, had survived his Rottweiler's attack. Archie said he had to get Adolph away when Christine had come running out. A smarter woman would have considered her own safety over that of a dog. But Christine, being a half-breed, couldn't be expected to think normally.

Archie had come up with another plan and even though he had thought it up for his own fun, Howard had approved it. He decided he would be on hand, after Archie and his men were finished having their fun, to pick up the pieces. There would be time enough later for him. In the meantime, he went to get the boy.

Peter was lying down, facing the wall, when he heard the panel slide open. He heard Howard's voice, "Peter, wake up! I brought a surprise for you. Look, I made a mistake. I didn't kill Todd after all."

Peter slowly turned over. He pretended to be groggy and confused as if he were slowly coming out of his stupor. He slowly sat up and rubbed his eyes, ignoring Howard's voice.

"Peter come over here. Look, here's Todd! You do remember your son, Todd, don't you?" Howard moved so Todd could peer into the small room. "Look, Todd, there's your Daddy."

"Daddy! I want my Daddy." Todd began screaming. He grasped the bars and leaned in towards his father.

It took all of Peter's will power to ignore his son. Still sitting, he slowly looked over, as if his memory was slowly returning. Finally he said, "Todd?" He allowed only a little of his excitement to show through, as if he didn't quite believe that he was seeing his son. Then he stood up and slowly approached his son and reached out as a man hallucinating might do. "Todd," he whispered.

Just before he could reach his son to touch him through the bars, Howard said, "Well, enough of this. Say good bye to your father, Todd." And he yanked the boy back and slammed the panel shut.

Through the door Peter could hear his son screaming for him. Knowing a camera must be on him, he only reacted in a dazed confused way. Inside, he was elated. His son was alive! Amazingly, believing it in his mind was different from actually seeing him. Now if only Howard would buy his act, he might yet be able to escape. Somehow he would find Todd and reclaim him from this madman.

He returned to his cot, sat down and looked toward the door as if he might be wondering if he'd really seen Todd. Then he began sending mental messages to Chris over and over again, because even though that probably didn't work, it gave him hope.

# 9

**M**y first thought when I woke the following morning was to wish that I didn't have to go through another day. Why should I wait? I now had no doubt that Peter and Todd were dead. Just because the RCMP hadn't found them—well, that no longer gave me hope. Once they found them, I'd have to bury them. I knew I couldn't live through that. I'd have to leave it to Peter's parents.

I spent some time wondering what it was like to be dead. Was there another world? Would I join Peter and Todd? That idea helped me make up my mind. Since I knew now they had not gone to Leona's, they had to have gone into the Peace River. It seemed the police had based their suspicions on the lack of skid marks, but there could have been a reason for that, and not a suicidal action on Peter's part. That was just a week ago. And if this is how I was feeling now, I knew I would never recover. Time wouldn't heal my pain. It would only get worse, and I couldn't hang around just for more. I had to end it.

Just before noon I looked at the rifles again but I was unable to decide if I should use the .22 or the .30-30. The kickback from the .30-30 might make me jerk and make me miss, but not completely. I decided on the .22 and prepared my mind for the event. Then I heard Lady outside, sounding out an advance joyful greeting.

Shutting my bedroom door behind me, I went outside just as Amber, Mona, and Kit rode in on horseback. Mona was dressed in jeans, a sweatshirt under her denim jacket, and cowboy boots. She looked like a younger version of her usual self. Seeing the look of surprise on my face, she knew immediately it was because of the way she was dressed.

"You're wondering what an old lady like me is doing on a horse." Chuckling, she eased down. "How is everything?"

"Okay," I lied.

"We brought you some stew. I made extra last night. I said, 'Chris is probably not eating anything.'" She indicated with her chin that Kit had it with him in his pack. "I hope that's okay with you."

I nodded. Internally, I was peeved at having my plan disrupted, but I added that I was glad they had come. Kit dismounted and took down the food cooler and carried it inside. He got wood and put on a fire in the stove while Mona messed around in my kitchen. Considering my state of mind, lunch tasted really good.

Eating one last hearty meal was a fine ritual. I told Kit about the wolf and the pups for something to say. "I know it's probably not a good idea, but I fed them."

"That was Wapan you saw, and those pups? They're not hers. She was from last year's litter," Kit said. Seeing that none of this meant anything to me, he explained, "Wolves aren't like dogs. They don't breed until they're at least two years old."

That still didn't mean anything to me, but I asked, "You know the wolves around here?" Kit and Mona never ceased to amaze me.

He smiled, but it was a sad kind of smile. "I knew them. Okimaw, he was the big boss, and Neka was his wife and the mother to Wapan and those two pups."

"What do you mean was? Come to think of it, I haven't heard them howling lately. But with everything going on, I wouldn't have noticed."

"I found their carcasses up in that valley," he said, sighing and showing me which direction with a tilt of his head. "When you were away, the government people, they came in with their helicopters or planes and shot them all. At least I think it was government people. They say it's to thin out the wolf population, but it's the oil companies behind it. The governments have these studies done for environmental groups, eh. And if there are no animals in the area, the oil companies can move in and do

113

their thing. So they get rid of the animals before a study is done."

"All for money," I said. "Colin wanted to lease our land for oil explorations."

"Yeah, they can just come in and . . . 'cause they and those mining companies, they can stake your land for, uh, for mineral rights and that, and landowners don't have those rights when they buy property. They only find out later after those companies move in, and they can't do anything about it anyways."

"Peter told me about that because Colin asked him about leasing our land. But I didn't know about the environmental studies."

"Maybe with you and Peter being writers, you've got more influence than most landowners."

"Peter said that wouldn't matter. How many other wolves were killed?" I asked. My curiosity was strange given that I was planning on joining the dead ones.

"Three adults. Otakosin, Kanatan, and Nimis. There were two others. Oskinikiw, he got shot last fall and Kehte-aya. Her, I think she died of old age, earlier this year. She was the mother to Okimaw." The way he talked, it seemed like he knew them all intimately.

"Did you tame them or something?" I asked.

"You don't tame wolves. They're not like dogs. Never make pets out of them."

"Yeah, but that one wolf I saw, it didn't seem scared of me," I said. "It was like, only fifty or sixty feet from me. And that one puppy, it came and licked my hand. Scared the shi- . . . wits right out of me."

Amber contained a snicker as smiles flickered across the faces of the elders. I shrugged an apology.

"That must have been Wapan you saw. Maybe she sensed you're like her," Kit said gently, and I knew instantly what he meant. We had both suffered the loss of our families and on top of that they were starving. "She was at the den, watching the pups when the killing happened. I heard her calling for her family. There were six pups, so I guess there's only the two left now."

"One's grey and the other one's black, and all three were really scrawny-looking, which is why I fed them. Is it bad to feed them?" I asked, watching Kit's face closely for his expression.

"No, it's only bad to make them dependent on you. They hunt in packs, so that's why they're hungry," Kit said.

"I've got meat in the freezer that I won't eat. I was going to offer it to you, but now it can go to them," I said. I felt Mona's eyes on me, so I added, "Peter's the one who loved rabbit stew." I sensed that Kit felt we should let Nature take care of its own, no matter how harsh or tragic the results might be. But then, it wasn't Nature who had forced the loss of Wapan's family.

I remembered the phone call I was supposed to make about Michael. If he knew Peter and Todd were gone, he wouldn't want to stay with me anyways. Letting Leona down by not taking him would be the last disappointment I would cause anyone.

After they left, I tidied up because I didn't want to leave a mess for anyone else. I went to our office area at the other end of the living room, got a bullet for the .22 from the filing cabinet, and went to my bedroom to take the rifle down from the wall. I sat on the bed, positioned the rifle, and then it occurred to me that I had just cleaned up so as not to leave a mess.

Taking the rifle with me, I went out and sat on the porch steps, considered hiking further into the mountains, but the moment came over me. I had the nerve to do it. If Peter and Todd were here with me, I could live with having given up my baby girl, and what I'd done with Dr. Coran. I'd lived with it so far. But I could not go on without them. I couldn't live with this deep, deep depression. I needed for it to stop. I had just put on a pretense that everything was okay. Nothing was okay. I wanted to stop with the pretense, all the pretenses in my life.

I loaded the bullet into the chamber. I tilted my head and put the barrel of the rifle under my chin. Then I put my thumb on the trigger. Now all I had to do was press.

What if Kit and Mona came back—no, worse—what if Amber came riding along by herself and found me here—I took my thumb off the trigger—could I do that to a young girl? Give her an ugly memory that would stay with her for the rest of her life? Could I? Yes I could, because what did I care? I was a person who cared for no one. To hell with whoever found me. My thumb returned to the trigger.

Damn it, I did care, I did care. Caring was what had gotten me here in the first place. Covering my face with my hands, I began to cry. At first I cried because I wasn't dead yet and I didn't even know if I could ever pull that trigger. I was too scared to do it and too scared not to. More bleak thoughts and feelings whirled around inside me. Most of all I was crying over my loneliness for Peter and Todd. I was crying over the guilt I had for not having loved them enough when they were with me. I was crying because I had too much unbearable pain inside and I clawed at my face, wanting to replace the pain inside me with outside pain. A flash of Todd, with a hurt, bewildered expression on his face because I had scolded him for nothing, for something that was trivial, minor, silly—and now I could never take it back, never undo it.

"I'm sorry, Todd. I'm so, so sorry. I love you so much and now it's too late. It's too late!" I made a high, keening sound and rocked back and forth. The ache, the pain, it was so, so bad. I wanted it to stop. With my eyes shut tight, some of the pain was lost in pitch-black space. "All I want is to be with them. That's all I want. Just to be with them. Please."

Through the haze of my emotional turmoil came the sound of a low whimper. Lowering my hands from my face, I opened my eyes to blinding sun. A large muzzle opened and a tongue licked the tears from my face. Without thinking, I buried my face in the wolf's neck and continued wailing. The animal stood patiently, allowing me to do this, waiting until my wailing subsided into half-sobs. Finally, I straightened up and sat back. My grief was so consuming that it hadn't occurred to me that what was taking place here was unbelievable. This had to be the wolf Kit called Wapan—a wolf who had more heart than I, a wolf who took care of young ones not her own, a wolf who gave comfort to a half-crazy, grief-stricken woman in the wild.

The depth of wisdom and compassion I saw in Wapan's amber eyes completely humbled me. And there was more. The viruses that had wiggled and squirmed inside me were being vanquished and stilled. The emotional and spiritual maggots that had gnawed away at my heart, mind, and soul were somehow being destroyed, as if an invisible blood transfusion were infusing antibiotics—infusing life into me. Wapan was sharing her power—a clean, pure, healthy power. We were not touching now, only our eyes were locked onto each other's, but I had no doubt I was being empowered.

She must have sensed the new feeling in me because she released my eyes, lowered her head, and sighed, as if to say, There, it is done. As she slowly began to turn away, she glanced at me sideways, the expression in her eyes changing to one of humour. And now it seemed she was saying, Get on with life, for life is sacred.

Tentatively I ran my hand along the side of her neck, and she turned back to me again. She put a paw on my leg. "I'm okay now. I'll be okay." My voice went shaky, as though I was going to begin bawling all over again. "Thank you, Wapan."

The wolf removed her paw, licked my face once more, and turned to leave. She trotted away and then stopped to look back over her shoulder. I nodded and watched her leave.

A strange feeling settled over me once Wapan was gone. I stood up and found that the invisible oppression that had been weighing me down was gone, and I felt, oh, so relaxed. Looking down at the rifle, it occurred to me that maybe I had used it, that maybe right now I was dead, and maybe the passage to the other side was the vision of a wolf. No, her paw prints were right there, on the ground in front of me. My hands still had the feel of her fur, and my face still tingled from the roughness of her tongue. If I were dead, I would be in another dimension and, surely, nothing would seem the same.

Bending to pick up the rifle, I noted that my body still operated the same. Even though I saw a bullet in the chamber, I still wasn't convinced I was alive. Unloading the rifle, I walked, not floated, into the cabin to put it away and turned on the television as I was passing by. If I were a ghost, I wouldn't be able to do that either, yet still I was unable to shake the strange feeling because I knew that what had happened between Wapan and me was impossible.

I finally found the phone number of Leona's friend in the pocket of the jacket I had worn the day before and drove over to Mona's place.

First thing I told Emma was that I'd love to have Michael come live with me and asked if he'd be able to come tomorrow. I asked her if Leona was going to get out on bail and she said no, because she had no way of coming up with the money. I asked for Leona's mailing address. Because she didn't have it, I asked for a phone number for the Remand Centre. Then I asked if Michael was there. When he got on, I told him I'd pick him up in Fort St. John, and I'd call Emma back with the details. I thought of forewarning him about Peter and Todd but he already sounded down about his mother. Besides I couldn't talk about that over the phone.

It turned out he had his mother's address, but he didn't know about her lawyer. After I finished talking with them, I made a few more phone calls. I arranged for Michael's flight, and called Emma back with the details. I couldn't get through to anyone at the Remand Centre so I'd have to return here first thing Monday morning.

When I got back to the cabin, I wrote to Leona. While I was more at peace with what had happened to Peter and Todd, I still wanted to know the circumstances surrounding their deaths. The most pressing question I had for Leona was about that phone call to Mona. Since Colin hadn't made it, I wanted to know who had, and why. Then I needed to know why she had assaulted someone, and who her lawyer was and I also wanted to arrange bail. I thought she could come live with me while she waited for her trial date or whatever was to come next. I forgave her, and in forgiving her, I recalled that she was the one who finally made Dr. Coran pay for what he had put me through.

---

My experience at Dr. Coran's house should have made me more badly behaved, a "handful" to deal with in reform school, but instead, I became a model "inmate." Probably because all the fight had been taken out of me. I tried hard not to think about Queenie and Darcy. Their lives were much, much worse than mine.

It was months later, almost Christmas time, before Leona came to see me. After some initial small talk, Leona explained that Children's Aid finally got ahold of her and told her all about my situation.

She said, "I don't believe a single word they told me. So what did happen?"

"I can't tell you anything."

"What do you mean you can't? Of course you can. Or is it that you just won't?"

I eyed her. Telling her anything wouldn't solve problems; it would only create new ones. But more than that, I truly believed that if Children's Aid went to see the doctor because of me, he would do more outrageous things. And get away with it because he was a doctor and a real smooth talker. He was going to keep his daughters living at home forever, and no one would ever know what was happening to the women in that family. But then the idea of them living there like that just didn't seem fair, either. Damn it, what did I care? That they were prisoners was their own doing. Well, that really only applied to Mrs. Coran. She had a car. She could have taken her daughters and left him. I had thought about that a lot and I just couldn't understand why she stayed.

"Chrissy, this stuff is going to go on your record. You must have had a reason for taking a knife to that woman and for slashing that man."

"If you really think that I did that, would do something like that, then you don't know me." I said, and my voice wavered.

Leona leaned forward and said, "Then tell me what really happened. I promise you I won't tell anyone else if you don't want me to. But tell me, okay?"

"Leona, I can't. Someone else could get hurt."

"What does that mean?

I stared at her long and hard. I did want to tell her. I wanted someone else to know the truth but I just didn't know what to do. I sighed and then said, "You won't believe any of it."

"Try me."

I did tell, all of it except for the part of my going to bed with the doctor. That was one secret I could tell no one.

When I finished, Leona whispered, "Oh my God! Oh, Christine! That's just horrible!"

"I know. I was there," I said, wiping tears from my eyes.

"We have to do something about it. I'm going to tell your new social worker— what's his name again?"

"You promised me you wouldn't tell anyone else. You promised me!" I pushed my chair back, got up and stormed out of the visiting room.

The next time I saw her was around Easter time. She had come many times before, but I had always refused to see her. This time she had been adamant about seeing me, relaying a message that she had something urgent to tell me. I had been so happy to see her last time and then she had lied to me. I'd had time to think and I'd come around to thinking that maybe she had been right. Maybe we had to try to do something. Besides that, I was lonely for her.

"Chrissy, you're going to hate me," she said after our preliminary small talk.

"I could never hate you."

"Then why wouldn't you see me before this?"

"Well, you did lie to me," I replied. "So why am I going to hate you?"

"Because I told your social worker and his supervisor what you told me, and . . ."

"You really did lie to me," I interrupted.

She smiled and said, "Yeah, unlike you, I do lie. But hear me out." Her calm reaction made me very curious. "The important thing here was that it would have been a crime not to tell the proper authorities. You see that, don't you?"

"Coming from your side of the table, I guess I can see how you would see that."

She got a serious look then, took hold of my hand, and said, "You couldn't let that man get away with what he had done."

"So? Please continue," I said.

A smile replaced the serious look, her eyes dancing and sparkling with merriment: "So you're getting out of here. Unfortunately you won't be able to come and live with me yet. They said you're too young."

I asked, "So what happened with Dr. Coran?"

"Well, I went to your previous social worker, Branzil, and her supervisor."

Skeptical that Miss Branzil would have listened to the story, I raised my eyebrows.

Leona's next words told me I was right. "Afterwards, Miss Branzil said you had a history of problems and that lying was one of your bad habits. When the supervisor seemed like he was going to believe her, I threatened to go to a reporter and that wouldn't look good for Children's Aid. Miss Branzil seemed so uptight about it, like it was her fault."

"I think she was having a thing with the doctor."

"Oh, so that's probably how he knew they were coming."

I was somewhat surprised she wasn't shocked by their committing adultery, but asked, "What do you mean? Who was coming?"

"The supervisor, Mr. Bancoates, he finally decided to get a court order or something. Your new worker, Mr. Carruthers, since Branzil's gone, he told me they called in the cops, got a court order, and went to visit the Corans."

"How come they never came to me?"

"I don't know. Mr. Carruthers did say that you would have to testify against the doctor. You are up to that, right?"

"Testify?" I asked. "Did they arrest him?"

"From what I last heard, no. He wasn't at his office, him or his daughters, so maybe Branzil warned him. And now that you told me about them, maybe she went with him. Anyways, only Mrs. Coran was in the house. She broke down and she's been placed in care. She's in a mental institution now."

"And he and his daughters disappeared?"

"And Branzil, too. According to Mr. Carruthers, she walked away from everything she owned. Imagine having an affair with a foster father? Too much!"

"Poor Mrs. Coran went crazy, and he got away."

"I'm sure they'll catch him. And even if they don't he's lost everything—

his house, his practice—everything. So in a way, that's justice."

Sighing, I said, "I suppose so." But I would have been happier if he had ended up in jail.

---

Now all three were dead. Dr. Coran deserved that but his daughters didn't. They'd been victims for most of their lives. Victimhood—I knew what that was all about. To think I was going to abandon Michael for the sake of succumbing to victimhood. I couldn't believe how selfish and self-pitying I had been.

What I had to do next was going to be emotionally difficult for me. Michael was going to have Todd's bedroom so I would have to pack Todd's belongings. I packed his clothing, books, and toys into our suitcases because I didn't have any boxes. As I worked, I thought of Wapan. I might have imagined the expression in her eyes, imagined what she was thinking, and imagined that she had caused a change in me.

My mother must have been a superstitious woman because she'd had me baptized as a Catholic when I was a baby. As far as I knew she'd never practiced the religion, but one of my first foster homes was Catholic. We had been taught that man was created in the image of God and, therefore, we were superior over all other creatures. Animals could not think or feel the emotions we did, and they acted only on instinct, always for their own benefit. While I had to listen to these teachings, outside, I let the animals teach me differently.

Kit had once told me that Indian people saw things differently too. Animals and all other creatures and living things did not need people and could do very well without us. We humans needed the forests and the meadows and the rocks and the animals. We needed water from the rivers, and we needed our air to be clean and fresh. Yet we fooled ourselves into believing that we were the superior beings. Today, I'd been like the child I once was. Wapan had confirmed Kit's bit of wisdom and regardless of what I had imagined and what had been real, I was alive and I had plans, not only to exist, but to live. I now knew I had to begin a journey of self-healing; not just the healing from the deaths of Peter and Todd, but from all the negatives in my past life which had allowed those viruses inside me to fester and eat away at my soul. I had to do that for Todd and for Peter. Today, Wapan had empowered me and, even if that was only my perception of what had happened, I now looked forward to all the tomorrows to come.

As I packed up Todd's things, I would come across a particular toy and remember how delighted Todd had been with it. Or, I'd look through one of his books and hear Peter's voice reading it, Todd nestled comfortably against him. When I was done, I took some of the suitcases into my bedroom. We had a pull-down staircase to the attic and I struggled to get the rest of the packed suitcases up the narrow stairs. Maybe in a year or two I would take Todd's things somewhere so another child could use them, but right now I could not part with them. Up in the attic I looked around for a good place to store them. That's when I spotted an open laptop under the window that overlooked the porch. Why would Peter have a laptop up here? I wondered. I looked closer and saw a thin white cable running from the laptop down through a hole in the floor. I pulled at the cable but it got stuck. I unplugged the laptop and after finding a spot for the suitcases, I took the laptop downstairs.

Downstairs just above the door, I saw that the thin cable was attached to the fire alarm. Now why would Peter rig this up? Both fire alarms worked with batteries. Whatever he rigged up, I had just unrigged by disconnecting the laptop.

Later that night Kit and Mona came over in their pickup. Amber had gone babysitting so they thought they'd come over and keep me company. Kit brought in some meat pies and such, saying that Mona got into a baking spree and made more than what could fit into their freezer. While he unloaded the packages to store in the freezer, Mona and I chatted and made tea. When it was ready, Mona said, "Let's have a campfire tonight."

By the time we went to the lake to light a fire, the sun had gone down and dusk had turned to night. Kit sat on a log and picked up one of the sticks we had once used for roasting wieners and marshmallows. Mona was in a chair, and I was sitting between them on the ground. We were all facing the lake. The loons' last calls of the day echoed across the lake and, when the birds had gone silent, the frogs, crickets, and the mosquitoes began their symphony. The fire, crackling, snapping, and sizzling, mesmerized us.

In the sandy soil, Kit was marking a pattern of a circle divided into four parts. He murmured, "It's the Medicine Wheel. A likeness."

I looked up from the circle on the ground to his weathered face. For a moment, it seemed that a total hush descended on us, and even the crackling of the fire stopped.

Kit's words broke the silence. "We need four basic things to be in balance for our well-being."

When I looked back at the circle, he had written four words, spirit, mind, heart, and body. I looked back up at him, for I had not seen him move to print these words.

"The Spirit, that's our way of life. It's how we are all related to each other and to everything here on Mother Earth."

Gazing into the dancing flames of the fire, I waited for him to continue, wondering why he was telling me all this.

As if he had read my mind, he continued in a low voice, "I tell you this because you could do more with your writing. The centre of the circle, that's where we are, each one of us. From us, our way of life spreads out from the centre and it has an effect on others. Put yourself in the centre and think about it."

Out of respect, I obeyed, imagining myself at the centre of a large circle, but at the same time I was thinking this concept was simplistic: what I did, what I wrote, could spread out and affect others. Even my death could have had an effect on others. And the actions of others could have had some kind of effect on me, even if I hadn't known at the time what it might be. Since I couldn't control the actions of others, what was the point of thinking about this?

I looked back up to Kit's face to see if he expected a response from me and caught a movement beyond him. Wapan had joined us and was lying down in the grass, maybe a hundred feet back. The outline of her ears was barely visible, but her eyes reflected the flames of the fire. Turning to Mona to indicate the wolf's presence, I saw she was already staring at Wapan.

As if he also knew Wapan was there, Kit said, "In Cree, wapan means 'It is dawn.'"

Looking down at my hands gripping my cup, I told them about the day before. "Yesterday, I was going to shoot myself. And then she came." Tears rolled down my cheeks and I moved my cup so my tears wouldn't fall into my tea.

Mona put her hand out to me. Awkwardly, I reached out to hold it. She said quietly, "Sometimes we have to go to the top before we can get to the bottom."

I looked up at her, puzzled. At first she had this wise, deeply serious look on her face, then a twinkle came to her eyes, and a smile cracked her face and, finally, she was chuckling loudly. By then I was laughing too.

Kit was grinning and he shook his head. "She always gets those sayings wrong."

I went to bed that night feeling special because I had these special people close to me, and one very special friend from the wild. I realized I did have something that was strong and good in me, something that could not be taken away from me.

# 10

BEYOND REACH

s soon as Howard walked into his study he noticed that the
monitor showing the inside of Christine's cabin was black.
That meant that the connection to his laptop in her attic wasn't
working anymore. He suspected a computer glitch at first, but he prided
himself on thinking of all possibilities. What if Christine had found it?
What to do? First thing would be to destroy everything on the laptop so
nothing could be traced back to him. He keyed in the instructions and
as he pressed the enter button, he realized too late that he had deleted
everything that had been taped yesterday. That angered him and he had
only one person he could take it out on right now. He stormed out of his
house and marched over to the compound that housed Peter's cell.

He opened the panel of the door and said, "Good morning, Peter. Had
your breakfast? I sprinkled some rat poison on it. Feeling the effects, yet?"

He wanted to go inside and talk face to face with his captive but
Peter had a powerful build and could prove dangerous if he was faking a
breakdown. Later, he would really drug Peter's food and then go in, but
for now all he could say from outside the cell was, "Guess where I was
last night? I took your wife out. And then we spent the night in your bed,
Peter. Nice set of rifles you have on your wall there. Oh, and she turned
that picture of the two of you down on the dresser. Thought I didn't
notice. I guess she didn't want you watching us. That woman sure knows
how to make a man feel terrific. I guess you already know that."

Still there was no sound from inside. "Peter, are you awake? Can you hear me? I said I had your woman last night. And again this morning. She has the smoothest skin of any woman I've ever had. Do you miss that, Peter?"

Howard began to worry that something might really be wrong with Peter. He could see him lying there facing the wall. Ever since he'd told him that Todd was dead, the man had gone listless on him, unresponsive. He hadn't even reacted yesterday when he'd brought Todd over. Could a man break this soon?

"Did you even notice your son yesterday? That wasn't an illusion. Here I thought your son passed away, but he didn't. He's alive. Like Lazarus. It's a miracle."

"Peter, are you listening to me? Your son is alive." Howard decided that he would come by later with Archie and the rest of his men and if nothing was wrong with Peter when they went in, something would be wrong with him by the time they left.

Peter didn't stir for quite some time, not until he was absolutely sure that Howard had left. Aware that there might be a camera on him, he sat up slowly. At one time, he thought that Howard might possibly have overdosed Todd. But seeing him and hearing him the night before had made him all the more determined to escape. And just now Howard had revealed something else: Chris was alive. She was not being held captive. But could Howard be believed?

One thing Peter did know was that she would never let herself be attracted to another man, let alone go to bed with him, not even if she was somehow convinced that he would never come back. Did she really believe that Todd and he had died in an accident? How did Howard know something so intimate as the feel of her skin? Oh God, he didn't rape her, did he? Even though he had written eight murder mysteries, thought up countless plots, he had never believed that a man like Howard actually existed and that he could ruin two lives forever. And for what?

Peter was heartened by one thing. He had noted a tinge of worry in

Howard's voice and thought, "Worried I'm beyond your reach, are we,

Howard?" Maybe if he continued like this, Howard would eventually come in to check on him. And if he did that, it would be his chance to escape.

# 11

Sunday morning, I felt good about myself. If Peter and Todd were really gone, I knew that even though the sorrow would always be with me, I would be able to handle it.

Midmorning, Colin came to visit and, thankfully, Howard wasn't with him. He suggested we have our coffee out at the lake since it was such a beautiful day. Once we settled with our coffees at the picnic table by the lake, he asked how the investigation was going. Nothing new there, I told him. But I did have news of Leona and it wasn't good.

"Apparently, she was arrested for assault and she's in the Remand Centre in Winnipeg. She doesn't have money for bail, can't afford that, so I'm going to offer to cover that for her. Then she could come here until her trial, or whatever is next," I said.

"She won't be able to leave the province." Colin said. "They'll make it a condition."

"Oh. Are you sure? I was hoping she'd be able to stay with me."

Colin appeared to be thinking of something else and he said, "Listen. Let me go there. I'll arrange for the bail and I'll get her the best lawyer. She probably only has a legal aid lawyer. And all they do is make deals with the prosecutors. So will you let me do that for her? Please."

"You really love her."

"I do. I've done stupid things in my past. The worst is driving her away. I've missed her since she left and I really want to see her again. When does Michael arrive?"

"I'm going to pick him up at the airport this afternoon. How soon could you go for Leona? Because even though she won't be able to come here . . . you're really sure about that?" He nodded and I continued, "Anyways, I want her out on bail as soon as possible."

"I'll leave as soon as I can arrange a flight. Maybe I'll see you at the airport this afternoon." The gratitude in his eyes made me adjust my opinion of him.

At about three p.m., I left to pick up Michael. I worried that he might have decided not to come; although Michael and I had never really bonded in any way, I was looking forward to having him here. Another disappearance wasn't something I wanted to handle. Thankfully, he was out front waiting with his luggage.

I had wondered what we could talk about. I made a point of sounding thrilled to see him, but he sounded as despondent as he had on the phone. Maybe he was resentful because of his mother or because he'd be going to a new school, the third one in a school year. I was counting on Amber to help with that adjustment.

Unlike Peter, I had never had the knack for easy conversation. Peter genuinely liked people, whereas I was distrustful and suspicious. I always found myself racking my brain for something appropriate to say, always without success. Peter told me once I should try to think of common interests and just relax. Michael and I had only his mother in common, and right now I didn't know what to say about her. All I could do was to try to relax.

Michael plugged his earphones into his ears and started listening to music, so I didn't have to force conversation after all. I still had to tell him about Peter and Todd, but it didn't seem like the right time. Midway home, he took out the earphones and asked, "You like Michael Jackson?"

"Yeah. I've got his Thriller CD in there." I indicated the radio/CD player. "When I'm alone, I blast it really loud."

"Peter doesn't like him?"

"He prefers folk music. He likes Buffy St. Marie. And Neil Young."

"What about Elvis Presley? You like him?"

We talked on. Music had broken the ice and it seemed to soothe him.

We drove on, listening to some of his music. Sometimes he'd tell me things about the singer or the band before he played them, almost like he had done when he showed Peter and I the katas from his karate classes.

By the time we reached Dodging, dark clouds had moved in as if the skies were in sync with what I still had to tell Michael. I slowed the truck to a crawl because I wanted to look at him, "I have to tell you something. About Todd and Peter."

"How come they didn't come with you?"

"They had an accident." I almost came to a stop. "And both of them might be dead."

For a while, he didn't say anything and then he asked, "What happened?"

"Peter's truck went into the Peace River. The police haven't found them yet but they think they were carried away by the currents."

Michael said in a low voice, "I'm sorry."

After that we kept our thoughts to ourselves. By the time I pulled into our yard, raindrops began to hit the windshield. I walked in through the porch and opened the door. Right away, I saw that something had been inside and had ransacked the cupboards. Flour, sugar, molasses, syrup, and other torn packaging lay scattered across the floor. Michael, still behind me, tapped me on the shoulder and I turned to look at him.

"Is that your idea of a bear rug?" he whispered, pointing towards the other end of the living room near the desks.

Puzzled, I turned to look in that direction, and saw a chocolate-brown mass of fur.

The grizzly looked kind of groggy, or maybe that was my impression because it hadn't come charging right at us.

We both stepped back out in unison and then dashed for the truck. I drove around the cabin to the front and saw that the wind was making the front door swing back and forth. I thought the grizzly must have smelled the food inside and forced the door open to get at it.

"I think we should go get Kit to help us evict it."

I backed the truck up to turn around and Michael said, "Look, it's coming out."

131

Not knowing if it could get at us inside the truck, I drove out of the yard. Michael watched it out the rear window. "It's leaving. The other way."

I stepped on the brake, prepared to drive on if necessary and we watched it saunter off around the cabin and towards the west.

"So. Welcome back to our cabin, Michael." My smile was kind of shaky. I drove as close as I could to the porch steps.

After waiting for a while to make sure the bear didn't return, we left Michael's luggage in the truck and quickly went into the cabin. I rushed to the front door and closed it, puzzled that I was still able to lock the knob and turn the bolt. Neither was broken so how had the bear gotten inside? Then I looked at the mess and tried to decide where to begin on a major cleanup. Some of the cupboard doors had deep gouges or been torn off their hinges and one was broken in half.

Showing Michael to his room was easy, so that's where I started. At least I had closed the bedroom doors to keep the mosquitoes out. I wondered how the front door had gotten unlocked because I had been careful about locking up the cabin. Looking on the bright side, I was thankful that the bear hadn't relieved itself before it left. I returned to the kitchen to start a fire and heat up some water. Through the window and the foliage, I saw the flashes of headlights, and Kit's old truck rolled into sight. Watching for the bear, I went outside to greet them. Kit, Mona, and Amber all got out and I told them right away that we had spotted a grizzly bear.

"Come in, and I'll see if I can find some tea." I led the way back in, embarrassed to let them know that a bear had breached security.

All four of us silently took stock of the chaos with me acting like this was the first time I saw the mess.

Kit said, "I came to tell you a young grizzly's passing through these parts. Looks like he stopped in to say hello."

Amber walked around, taking care to step only in the clean spots. "Boy, you must have thrown one heck of a welcome home party."

Michael came out of his room and said hello to Kit, Mona and Amber.

Amber continued stepping around, looking at the mess. "Either that, or you are one lousy housekeeper, Mrs. Webster."

"It's good that you can joke about it, 'cause, as a good neighbour, you won't mind helping to clean it up," Kit said with a mischievous twinkle in his eyes.

"Well, on the other hand, it doesn't look half bad in here after all," Amber shot back.

"Too late," Kit said, turning to me. "We thought we heard you drive by so we came over to let you know about the bear."

"Must have been the meat I left out for the wolves," I said.

Kit responded, "Don't worry. He's probably miles from here already. He won't be back."

"Take a look at the door. It didn't force its way in, unless it had a pick."

"Could have had a Visa card," Amber joked.

As Kit had a closer look, I said, "That door was locked."

Kit turned to us and said, "For sure, it wasn't forced open."

"Did you hear anyone drive by?" I asked

"No, and we didn't go anywhere. But we don't always notice, either."

Kit went outside and studied the ground while we decided where to start cleaning up. When he returned, he said, "Can't tell if there are strange tire tracks cause of the rain and our trucks."

Now apprehensive, I looked everywhere to see if anything was missing. Looking over at our desks, I noticed that my copy of Peter's manuscript was gone, just like Peter's copy. "Peter's manuscript is missing and I know I put my copy right there. First Peter's copy goes missing and now another copy. What's going on?"

"We still have the copy that Peter gave us."

"He gave you a copy?"

Mona said, "When you were away . . . he wanted Kit to have a look at it. Because it's about this area."

"I think it's the best one so far." Amber said. "Do you want it back?"

"No, you keep it at your place. I think it's safer there. The good news is that the bear didn't waltz through a locked door. The bad news is that someone else was in here. Someone else with a key."

My words, as I said them, sent chills up my spine. Knowing that Peter was not involved, I could only wonder who was doing this, breaking into my cabin and taking the copies of his manuscript. If they had a key, then maybe Peter was somehow still alive and they had some kind of contact with him. Just last night, I'd gotten this overwhelming feeling that they were still alive but then I had thought it was only wishful thinking.

Weird things were going on and I had to take time to think it all out. While Mona prepared supper from all the stuff from the fridge or freezer that hadn't been breached, the rest of us cleaned the house, and by the time supper was ready, everything was pretty much back in order. Kit took down the ruined cupboard doors and said he would repair them at his place. He and Michael brought his luggage in.

Before they left, Amber asked Michael, "Hey, want to go horseback riding tomorrow after school?"

Michael looked at me and I nodded. "Cool." To Kit, he asked, "You sure that bear's gone?"

"Yeah, you'll be okay. But always stay alert. They can wander great distances."

As if to show there was no need to worry, Amber said to me, "I'll bring him back here so you won't have to pick him up."

In the middle of the night I woke, alarmed, and wondered what it was that had roused me. I got out of bed to check the front rooms. The doors were locked, but that didn't mean much now. I had meant to ask Kit if he could change the locks, but the package I'd bought at the hardware store was still in my truck. Returning to my room, I heard groaning sounds come from Michael's room. Listening closer, I thought I could hear him pleading, "No, no, get it off me. Get it off."

When I asked him about it the next morning, he said he couldn't remember having a dream. From the way he looked, I didn't believe him, but I didn't push him for more.

On Monday morning, we picked Amber up because I had to enroll Michael in school. Lady came along for the ride. I missed her so much, but I couldn't think of a way to ask Amber if she could come back home. Besides, with wolves and grizzly bears running around my place, I thought she'd be safer at Kit's, just because he had all those animals.

Amber teased Michael about different things to do with school, making me smile almost all the way there. In a way, she reminded me of Andrea, the friend who had introduced me to Peter. Amber had a good energy about her, and I found it hard to believe she'd gotten into serious trouble when she was living with her mother. On the other hand I could see it. She was fearless and she'd probably gotten into trouble on a dare.

After I enrolled Michael, I went to the grocery store and post office and found the same hostile attitudes still in effect. The woman who worked at the post office would probably tell Mrs. Springer about my letter to Leona at the Remand Centre. I had written her a new letter the night before to tell her about Colin and to let her know Michael was now with me. I left out tales of grizzlies and missing manuscripts.

I dropped Lady off at Mona's and she took her inside. Being a collie, Lady had a tendency to wander off. She used to go visit Amber and now she might try to come to my place. Ever since she'd been attacked, I was nervous that she might run into something she couldn't handle, and Mona knew how I felt.

Back at the cabin, I searched for the missing binder very carefully without success. I sat down at the computer and made a list of all the weird stuff that had happened over the last week or so. I now felt so utterly foolish for having suspected Peter of betraying me. Although he was the only one who'd be interested in having all the copies of his manuscript, he wasn't the one who had sneaked in to steal them back, otherwise, he would not have given Kit and Mona a copy. He and Todd were in the Peace River somewhere.

A man calls Mona, a week ago Friday, and asks Peter to go to Fort St. John for Leona's sake. Why? To get him out of the cabin? To wait and cause an accident on the highway—but why no skid marks? I stopped typing. I was coming up with more questions than answers, so doing this wasn't really going to help. I made myself keep typing anyway.

That Sunday, I had come home and, yes, I'd been depressed that Peter had gone to Leona's. But did I really cut my own hair? Did I really drive the truck somewhere? How would anyone have been able to do that to me with Lady there? She would have woken me up. And why was I so tired? Like I'd been drugged or something. I'd experienced that kind of tired before, from the anti-depressants I'd been given when I first tried to commit suicide. And before that at Dr. Coran's house. But how could I have been drugged? Who would bother with such a thing and why?

Colin? He'd been bugging Peter about leasing our land since last summer. Was that a motive? Kit said the same thing as Peter, that if a company wanted to explore for oil, they would just come in and start drilling. So, really he didn't have a motive. But he was in love with Leona and if he thought, like I had, that Leona wanted Peter, he might want to get rid of Peter. But Todd? Not likely at all. Colin said he'd done some stupid things in his past and now I wondered what kind of stupid things. Like how did he know Leona wouldn't be able to leave Manitoba as being part of bail conditions? In the end, he just didn't strike me as a crazy, crafty psychopath, and that's what it would take to murder a child with premeditation.

Little things—I had to think of small details—details that had seemed meaningless when they happened but were actually very meaningful. I sat there, drumming my fingers on the top of my desk, my mind a blank. I went to take a sip of my coffee and my cup was empty. I got up to put the kettle on, but the fire had gone out and I noticed that I would soon need more firewood. Then that one detail about Peter's note to me returned—to Christine and signed, Peter. It was definitely his handwriting but was it a clue? He had once told me that clues to loved ones don't look like clues to strangers. I thought about it some more. He could not have been angry with me, so why the 'Christine'? Why the 'Peter'? Maybe somebody had forced him to write the note? But why?

And the police—they thought there was something fishy about the accident scene, didn't they? I got the impression they felt it was staged. But I had only thought about Peter doing that. And then there was the stranger who called it in. Why wouldn't he leave his name? Was it because he had caused the accident? And then the manuscripts went missing. How did that fit in? I had thought Leona might have gotten someone to make the call for her because Mona would have recognized her voice. But so what? She could have called herself, if she had even been in Fort St. John.

My whole conception of what had happened the week before had all been marred by my own stupidity, my suspicions, and my distrust. What if I had trusted Peter right from the beginning? What would I have thought? For one thing, Peter's note to me would have given me my first clue that something wasn't right.

I worked at trying to rethink everything; trying to figure out the "who." Someone, I thought, had something against Peter, probably something to do with his books. I decided I'd have to read all of them again.

Later Amber and Michael rode in on horseback and they both looked excited about something.

"Good ride?" I asked.

They looked at each other guiltily and said yes in unison.

"What?" I asked.

Michael dismounted and handed his reins to Amber. He looked up at her as if to ask permission to tell me what was up.

She shrugged and dismounted, and said, "Well, I read Peter's manuscript. And that place, NAK-WAN? Well, Peter's compound made me think of that place, so I've been kind of watching it. And I took Michael there today."

"Yeah and we saw armed guards," Michael added, "except they were in fatigues. What kind of guards wear fatigues?"

"And they had this huge Rottweiler with them."

"Oh, it's just a laboratory of some kind," I said. "Sergeant Trolley knows all about them. He said they're above board. Sorry to disappoint you. Must be really high security, though, if they have armed guards."

"They sure are. They've got that high fencing with all these keep out signs; you'd think it was a jail," Amber said. She didn't seem convinced it was above board.

"Did they spot you?" I asked.

Michael answered, "No, they were too far away. The dog didn't even know we were watching them."

"Anyways, we came out on our road just north of our place. So the way their road winds, they're north of us." This came from Amber.

"And the other thing is that we found ATV trails. Down in the gulley that runs between us and them," Michael said.

"I think everyone from town comes back here to do their riding." I said, "In winter, it's snowmobiling. You can hear them because of snow and there's less foliage. Anyways, you should stay away from that place from now on. We wouldn't want you hauled in to the police."

Amber crinkled her nose and said, "Ah, you spoil all the fun." To Michael, she said, "Later." With that, she tied the reins of Michael's mount to the saddle horn and mounted her own horse.

We watched her ride away, both amazed that the other horse just followed along.

After she left, Michael split some wood and I carried it in. As I was picking up the short logs, I got that feeling I was being watched. I'd had that feeling a few times before when I was outside and usually it was nothing. This time I looked around and saw Wapan and the little black pup sitting near the edge of the woods, and I swear she had a smile on her face. When I called to her, I was amazed that she came trotting towards us. I dropped to my knees and let her make the first move. After she had nuzzled my hands and sniffed at me all over, I noticed Michael staring at us with an open mouth.

"That's a wolf!" he finally exclaimed in a low voice.

"It's the mystical, magical wolf of Shadow Lake. Kit named her Wapan. It means, 'It is dawn,'" I told him.

"You guys have tame wolves around here?"

"No. They're wild. And free."

Wapan's head turned to Michael and her tail-wagging paused.

"Don't be scared."

"I'm not scared," Michael said.

"No, what I mean is that wild animals can smell fear."

"Well, I'm really not scared."

Like me, Michael dropped to his knees so he was at face level with Wapan. She approached him, sniffed him and then she left.

"That's one of the pups she looks after."

"What pup?" He looked in the direction she had taken but both were gone.

"There was a black one over there. I never touch them because they should be afraid of us. There's another one, a grey one. It licked my hand once."

Michael was grinning from ear to ear.

"I read that wolves always avoid people," Michael remarked, staring at the now vacant tree line.

"Wapan's special, unique."

"Yeah, but how come she came when you called her?"

"Because I'm special and unique," I said, jokingly. "No, I fed her last week."

"That's all you did? Was feed her?"

"Yeah, but we're not really supposed to."

"How come?"

"'Cause if they think we'll feed them, they'll always come around, and then some day they might hurt us. Or we might hurt them. Kit told me that some hunting guides feed black bears at one spot so the bears get used to going there. That way they can guarantee hunters that they'll bag a black bear."

"That sucks. Is she the one that hurt Lady?"

"Kit said it wasn't a wolf, and I can't see Wapan doing that to Lady. Even if she did, her family lived here long before we came, so we're the trespassers. See, we're supposed to let nature takes its course, meaning that I was supposed to let them starve to death. I couldn't do that. People shot her family; otherwise she and the pups wouldn't have been starving in the first place."

"Why can't they hunt on their own?"

"They hunt in packs. And Kit thinks government people killed her family. So if they overrule nature that way, then I don't feel so bad about having fed them. Besides, she helped me a lot more than I helped her."

"So that's why Amber has Lady now?"

"Yeah, partly that. And I didn't think I'd be staying here for long." Another thing I felt foolish about now.

Fortunately, Michael did not ask how Wapan had helped me, and I turned the conversation to the pups. "Those pups, I hope they learn to hide from us, or hunters will get them for sure."

Michael resumed his work and he was smiling to himself. Between Amber and Wapan, he seemed to have forgotten his resentments.

That night over supper, Michael said to me, "I did have a dream. More like a nightmare." He paused as if it was a struggle to talk about it. "I woke up in my dream and a man was leaning over me. Mom came up behind him and stabbed him with a broken beer bottle, and his blood was all over me. It's like she went crazy. She just stabbed him."

"Dreams can be pretty weird sometimes." That was all I could offer.

"But I think she did that for real. And that's why she's in jail. She just went crazy."

"Did you talk to her about what you think?"

"No. I don't really want to know. If she is crazy."

"One really good thing she did was to have you take Karate. Did you keep at it, in Fort St. John?" I asked.

"Yeah, Mom found a place there."

"And did you get your green belt?"

"You remember?" he asked with a look of surprise.

"Of course. I was impressed with your Karate demonstration. So was Peter. He was going to add another character to his books, one who knew martial arts."

"I thought you weren't even interested. Do you want to learn some?" he asked enthusiastically.

"Okay. Show me some good defense stuff."

"It all comes in sequences. You have to start with the basics."

Michael was going to take his teaching seriously so I decided to be a good student. We spent over an hour at it and he was a good teacher. By the end of our session, I learned the proper way to block, punch, and kick. My teacher told me repetition was key, so I decided I would practice those movements whenever I could.

That night, I dreamt that Peter and Todd were alive. Even though

I wasn't able to talk to them, I felt such joy. The joy vanished when I opened my eyes.

As I drove Michael to Kit's for the school bus, I felt an urgent need to get back to my computer to work on my list.

I'd had another thought; it was to do with the blood spots on Todd's runner. If the truck had gone down the steep embankment, Peter and Todd would have gotten knocked around a lot more and blood should have been in the rear jump seat where Todd's seat was instead of just on his running shoe. How would he have gotten out of his chair? True, Peter could have undone the latch, got Todd out, and maybe succumbed to the water before being able to escape. I'd have to ask the police about the blood. Maybe that was one of the reasons they suspected the accident wasn't really an accident.

I also wondered about the lack of skid marks. If Peter had swerved to avoid something, he would have slammed on the brakes. It couldn't have been a suicide attempt. Mentally and emotionally, Peter wasn't like me, susceptible to a past life of abandonment, and deceit and all the rest of a hell I'd been subjected to. His parents were solid happy people and their love and commitment to each other and their children was not something I had ever experienced. So Peter was solid and strong with no weaknesses that would make him want to take his own life along with his son's. He had inherited his smile from his mother and now when I thought about it, she had smiled at me with the mischievous part of his smile. Why I ever thought the worst about Barbara had to have come from my own insecurities and I felt just awful for having once rejected her.

I told myself to focus, but instead I got up to make another coffee and filled the sink to wash the breakfast dishes. Thinking about Peter and Todd and their possible last moments brought on the tears and while I busied myself with chores, I tried not to believe they had been in the truck at all.

What I wanted to do was hop in my truck, drive to Fort St. John and talk to the police. I really wanted to know about the blood and whether water could have washed away all traces of other blood. But what if I

141

later came up with other questions for them? I'd be driving back and forth all day. No, I had to think it all out before I went to them.

Back to the beginning: who knew about my trip and was that part of an overall plot? Since they disappeared while I was gone, maybe it was. For no reason at all, I had a moment where I was convinced they were alive—Peter had not run away; something had happened to them, something he had not planned. So what could have happened? I just couldn't seem to concentrate. The idea of practicing my Karate movements came to me and I spent an hour at it. Feeling better, I decided to tackle the wood. Exercise would keep the blues in check. Slipping my favourite Rolling Stones CD into the player, I turned up the volume and went outside to chop wood.

I soon got into a rhythm: set up the log on the base log, raise the axe, and slam it into the centre to split the log in half. My concentration was focused on the aim so when I heard a man's voice right behind me, I was so startled that the blade of the axe thudded into the ground. Three men, wearing plaid shirts over T-shirts, work pants, baseball-type caps, and work boots, had formed a semicircle around me.

"Didn't mean to scare you. You know where the Rutlands live? We're kind of lost." He scanned the area, maybe to check that I was alone.

One of the others asked, "You got a phone? Maybe we could phone them."

"I'm only the help. I'll go ask," I said, backing away towards the porch.

"The help? No. You're that writer, I saw your picture in the papers," one of them said, almost scornfully.

"The writer? Oh, yeah, people are always telling me that," I said, trying to keep the fear I felt under wraps.

"Yeah, you squaws all look alike, but we know it's you. Nice try." The guy who seemed to be the leader grinned, showing nice white even teeth. His eyes were what scared me. His eyelids were kind of pink, with a fringe of blond lashes, and the blue of his eyes was a dead, pale blue—or maybe that was his soul I glimpsed.

"Michael!" I yelled, above the music. They stopped closing in on me, as they looked towards the porch area, warily. If I ran inside, they'd kick the door in before I got a chance to lock it.

So I took that second to bolt around the front and south side of the cabin, cutting across the rear to head into the forest, north of the cabin. My initial intention was to run along our road east to Kit's place and my preference would have been to go straight east in the first place, but I didn't want one of those men throwing the axe into my back.

With their heavy boots on, they sounded like a herd of elephants stomping behind me.

Kit's was a long way off and another plan came to me. If I could get a good lead on them, I could circle back to the cabin, back to where the rifles were. Before I could change course, one of them tackled me from behind, pitching me forward under his weight. The thistles of the briar bush I'd landed on prickled painfully into my flesh. The others caught up. The one who'd tackled me stood up, grabbing a handful of my hair forcing me to stand. We stood there, breathing hard, and I saw my future—a brutal rape and then death. A shudder ran through me as I tried to think of a way to escape. And then I had help.

To our north, a low growl drew our attention. Wapan was about seventy feet away, her head lowered and the fur on her neck and back ruffled, making her appear larger than she normally was. Behind her, shaded by the foliage, two more wolves were barely visible.

"Let go of me or I'll tell them to attack," I said in a low voice.

The grip on my hair loosened, and the leader's arm went down to his side.

Backing away from them, I said, "Lie down on your stomachs."

"They'll attack," one of them grumbled.

"No, they'll only attack if you don't do what I say."

The three men sank to their knees and did as they were told. When I looked to the north, the wolves had disappeared, so I turned and ran back towards the cabin. Once I was at my road, I increased my speed, fearing they might cut across and stop me from getting to the cabin. Because I was concentrating on the area to the north to my right, I didn't see the man rushing at me from my left. Suddenly, an arm went across my midriff, stopping me from running. Yelping once in terror, I punched wildly at the body now blocking my way.

A voice I recognized was asking, "Hey, hey, hey, what's going on?"

"Howard!" I stopped to catch my breath, then said, "Three men—I've got to get to the cabin." With that, I ran ahead and he followed.

"What is it?" he called after me.

At the cabin I ran into my bedroom, then to the filing cabinet to get some bullets, loaded the rifle, checked that the safety catch was on, and went back out, ready to face my attackers. Howard followed me around, trying to find out what was going on. While I looked towards the woods north of my driveway, I told him of the three men chasing me and began to tremble. Seeing me tremble like that, he took the rifle, hugged me, and led me back inside.

"It's okay. It's okay. You've had quite a fright, but I'm here now and everything's going to be okay," he said soothingly. "I'll go out and take a look."

"Be careful," I said, and then I moved to the dining-room window where I could see to the north.

He returned a while later, saying he couldn't find anyone or anything, and then he put the kettle on the stove to make us coffee. He spooned two teaspoons of sugar and lots of milk into my coffee and asked again exactly what had happened. When I'd finished with my brief account, he said, "I didn't see any vehicles along the road when I came in."

"Maybe they hid it or something. But they were here."

"Oh, I believe you. I'm just wondering why they would have taken the trouble to walk in. That's what they must have done because there aren't too many places to hide a vehicle on your road. How'd you get away from them?"

"A distraction," I said, not wanting to tell him about Wapan. "I should go to town to phone the police. But I don't want to leave here. Michael might come back while I'm gone. And those men might return, too."

"Michael?" he asked.

"My nephew. He's staying with me. I don't expect him till later," I should have kept that to myself so I added, "but he might come back early. I don't know." The clock on the wall showed that it was only almost

1 pm. "Could you go phone the police for me?"

"Of course. Are you going to be okay, here, alone?" he asked, as he got up.

"Yes, I'll be fine."

"Okay. Because," he said, looking his watch, "I did have an appointment in the area, but I can cancel it and come back."

"That's okay. You don't have to come all the way back here. I'll be okay."

"You're sure?" He took hold of my hand and, this time, I found his touch comforting.

I nodded, and he walked to the door, pausing once more to say, "You lock these doors and close those shutters."

As he drove away, I locked the doors, closed all the shutters, and moved a chair up to the dining-room window, so I could sit there and watch the driveway and woods to the north. The rifle on my lap gave me a small sense of security in that I really didn't want to use it. Now that I was alone, I could replay the event in my mind.

Wapan had saved my life. Without her intervention, nothing would have stopped those men from raping me. And because they were not wearing any kind of disguise, it meant they intended to kill me once they were done raping me. They hadn't picked up my axe, as I imagined; so they might not have been armed, but they could have strangled me. Yes, Wapan had saved my life, once again.

Because of their suspicious attitudes, I was not looking forward to talking to the police again but I did have a question of my own this time. At three-thirty I decided to go to Kit's. Michael and Amber had planned to go horseback riding again, but if those men were still in the woods, that could be dangerous for them. Since the police hadn't shown up, I began to suspect that Howard was a part of what happened, but all my scenarios did not include a motive for him.

While I was at Kit's telling them briefly what had happened, I heard a car go by and thought it must be the RCMP. I told Kit I had to go back to talk to them. On the drive, I mentally apologized to Howard.

Inside, Sergeant Trolley made me recount what had happened, and instead of telling them that wolves helped me get away, I said it was a pack of stray dogs. That part of what happened sounded so far-fetched I would have understood their skepticism, this time.

True enough, Sergeant Trolley asked, "Stray dogs. Where did these stray dogs come from?"

"From the woods," I answered. From the look he gave me, I continued, "I fed them before because they looked scrawny and I had meat in the freezer I wasn't going to eat. And one of them was friendly."

"Can you show us where everything happened?" Constable Cormier asked, pausing from writing in a small notebook.

Sergeant Trolley apparently wasn't ready for that yet, so he said, "Before we do that, there are a few more questions I have. I wonder if you had any other thoughts about your husband's disappearance."

"Yes, I do. I want to know if blood was found in the jump seat or anywhere else inside Peter's truck. Because it doesn't make sense that a few drops would land on Todd's runner and nowhere else. So was there?"

That seemed to take Sergeant Trolley by surprise, and it was Bob who answered, "No, there was no other evidence of blood. And that raised questions for us too."

"Could the water have washed away any other blood stains?"

"No, they tested the interior with luminol. In spite of water there would have been evidence of blood."

"Then Peter and Todd were taken. Someone's been coming into my cabin. First they took Peter's manuscript. Then they came back and took my copy of it. And Peter's note was to Christine and signed Peter. All his notes to me before were always to C and signed P."

"And you still don't think Peter had anything to do with this?"

"No! Definitely not. These past few days, I've been thinking through everything that happened, and I think he and Todd are being held somewhere. And the other thing . . ."

Sergeant Trolley interrupted me, "Mrs. Webster, I understand you're loathe to blame your husband for leaving you and staging an accident to make it look like he and his son drowned. And if someone's coming into your cabin, he's the only other person with a key, isn't he? Who else would want his manuscript? He just forgot about them and he wants them back."

Hiding the disgust I felt for Sergeant Trolley, I looked from him to Constable Cormier, and he asked me, "What was the other thing? What were you going to say?"

"He gave Kit a copy, as well, while I was away. Because he got the idea for this novel from that NAK-WAN place and he wanted Kit to check it for authenticity of the area, and he's introducing an Aboriginal protagonist."

"We should check that place out," Constable Cormier said to Sergeant Trolley.

Sergeant Trolley said, "I know the place and the people who run it. They're above board and there's no sense wasting our time there."

"Then what is that place?" I asked.

"It's a private laboratory."

I must have wanted it to be some sort of rogue oil company because I felt disappointed. A laboratory would have no interest in us. So that was a dead end.

Then I told them about the laptop I'd found in the attic. I got up to get it and handed it over to Sergeant Trolley. "Peter didn't put that up there." Then I pointed to the new fire alarm above the porch door. "And I'll bet he didn't put that extra smoke alarm up there, either. A wire or cable was attached to the computer and it's attached to that fire alarm."

Constable Cormier got up to take a closer look and then he pulled a chair over. Because he was taller than me, he was able to reach it. "Do you have a screwdriver?"

He got the fire alarm released from the wall and examined it. "It looks like a camera in here," he said.

Sergeant Trolley said, "Maybe your husband put it in while you were away, for security reasons."

"And then staged an accident?" I asked.

Sergeant Trolley almost growled, "I don't know what your husband was planning."

I shook my head in disbelief. "He didn't plan anything. Something has happened to him and Todd."

Constable Cormier said, "Let's have a look outside and see if one of those men left anything behind."

As we went out the side door I glanced back and saw that Sergeant Trolley remained at the table to inspect the laptop. I asked Constable Cormier, "Do you need to see where I ran, exactly?"

He nodded, "They might have dropped something."

Retracing the route I'd taken, we came to the spot where they had caught up with me. Constable Cormier examined the area thoroughly. "Do you believe me, about Peter and Todd?"

From where he was kneeling, he looked up at me and said, "I met Peter a few times in Fort St. John. Kit had told him about me being a constable. He kind of interviewed me for the novel he was writing. So I never believed he staged an accident, but I had no idea what could have happened. From what you've told us today, maybe I'll come back and we can brainstorm."

"I've been trying to do that. Kind of point-by-point but I have more questions than answers and it's really frustrating. I just go around in circles. I write children's books. Peter was the mystery expert. I really miss them." Tears came to my eyes and I turned away.

Constable Cormier stood up and put a hand on my arm. "Hey, we're going to figure this out."

Finally, I thought. Finally I had an ally and the tears threatened to spill over again, I was so grateful. I felt distanced from the terror I'd experienced earlier.

"One more thing," he said, "I'm good friends with Kit and Mona, and I liked Peter. So call me Bob."

As I showed him where I had run into Howard, we heard the rumble of a vehicle coming up the road, and soon Kit's pickup rolled into view. He slowed and came to a stop. Michael and Amber jumped out from the passenger side, and Kit got out as well.

"What happened?" Michael asked, rushing to us.

"Three men came here and they were, um, up to no good," I said, not wanting to just blurt out the word rape to kids their age.

"Hey, you're one of the instructors at the Karate school," Michael said, looking up at Bob.

"And you're Mike," Bob said, "I wondered what happened to you. And here you are."

Kit reached us a few minutes later. Nodding a greeting to Bob, he asked, "Find anything?"

Before Bob could answer, Michael asked me, "Do you think it was the same ones who let the grizzly in our cabin?"

"The grizzly?" This came from Sergeant Trolley who had finally come out to join us.

Amber explained. "Yeah, when he first came here. On Sunday. Someone with a key left the front door open and a grizzly got in."

"That's when I found Peter's copy of his manuscript was missing," I added, noticing that Sergeant Trolley's eyes were boring right into me.

Even though I had not lied, I felt uncomfortable. As far as I was concerned, I had given them all the information they needed, and now Michael and Amber were complicating matters for me.

"Do you think those men will come back?" I asked.

"They might. Strange that they knew who you were. If I were you, I would seriously consider staying at the motel in town for a while. Without a phone, you're really isolated out here," Sergeant Trolley said.

I didn't say anything. I was thinking that from now on, I'd be on guard. No one was going to sneak up on me again and no one was going to drive us out of here.

"Could you come in to the station to look at mug shots?" he asked.

"It'll have to be tomorrow. I'll come in as soon as I can," I answered.

Before they left, Bob said they would come out to check on us more frequently. Alone with Kit, I said, "I told the police that stray dogs saved me. It was really Wapan with two adult wolves. I didn't see them clearly because they were farther back in the bush, but I'm positive they were adult wolves and definitely not the pups. I thought it was only her and the two pups."

"Could have found herself a mate. Sometimes young ones will leave their packs to start new packs in another territory. Or she could have been accepted into another pack and they've taken over this territory."

149

"Does that mean they would have killed the pups?"

"No, they're social animals. The only time might be if food was scarce. As much as I watch them, I don't know how they think. The tie Wapan has with you—that's very special."

"I know."

Amber had brought her homework with her and she and Michael had settled at the dining room table to work by the time I entered the cabin. I went to work on preparing supper. Kit was going to get Mona so they could join us. I was so grateful for their company. I glanced over at Michael and Amber. They reminded me of the times Peter and I had sat there, going through our manuscripts, and I thought, "What a lovely domestic scene they make."

Michael looked over at Amber and said, "That Warner, he's pretty friendly, eh?"

"Yeah, he is. Just like Marla, huh?" Amber responded, without glancing up at him.

Michael grinned. "So you did notice."

"Okay. You got me on that one." Amber smiled to herself. She finally looked up, still smiling. With the sunlight shining on her face from the west, Amber's greenish, tawny eyes sparkled, and her face seemed lit up from inside. I thought to myself, "My, my, I think that girl's got a major crush." Then, "whoa, they're only kids." I cleared my throat to break the magic of the moment but I was pleased to see the normal, sassy, impish look return to Amber's face. Feeling better, I snickered to myself silently.

Amber said to me, "All the guys at school are crazy about this Marla." She pronounced the name with emphasis. "She's new in town. Like Mikey here. She's real hot stuff. Right, Mikey?"

"I wouldn't know," Michael said, glancing down at his books. He looked up again and said with a mischievous grin, "But I could find out."

Amber made a face at him and said, "Up yours."

The magic of the moment was broken when we heard the sounds of distant rifle shots. Right away I worried about Wapan and her family and hoped they were far away and safe.

With Kit and Mona there, I was able to put the earlier trauma out of my mind over supper. Afterward Michael and Amber continued with their homework at our desks. We had tea at the table. I told them that Bob Cormier was going help me go over everything that had been happening so far and see if we could figure out a connection. They told me that they had known Bob since before he became a police officer.

"When he started out, he was a Special Constable. He was more of a liaison between the reserves and the RCMP. He told me he was kind of like a paralegal among lawyers." Kit said.

"He's got a third-degree black belt." Michael piped up from across the room.

"His wife, she came from my reserve," Mona said. "But she died of cancer a couple of years back."

"Did they have children?" I asked.

"No. No children and he never remarried."

Kit said, "The RCMP officers around here, they used to have this idea that, in our communities, if we wanted to punish people for wrongdoing, we cut off their fingers."

"What?"

"Yeah, some of them had some strange ideas about Indian people."

"I was in a foster home once, with a white family. Dr. Coran, he was my foster father and that's what he did. He cut off one of his daughter's fingers and he almost cut one of mine off."

"Ugh." That came from Amber.

"Sounds like he was a very sick man," Mona said.

"He was. He got me arrested and I . . ."

"You got arrested? Mom never told me that," Michael said from across the room.

At the table, we grown-ups exchanged smiles. "Your mother is the one who proved I was innocent of what Dr. Coran accused me of."

"Maybe this doctor is behind what's happening now." Amber joined in.

"No. He died. Along with his daughters. Those three men that came today, I think they have something to do with all this. That reminds me, no horseback riding around here, okay?"

They both protested in unison.

In the morning after I dropped Michael off at Kit's place, I returned home with plans to sit at the computer all morning and do brainstorming on my own. My afternoon plan was to go to Fort St. John to look at mug shots so I wanted to have all my questions ready.

My only disruption was Howard who apologized right off for not being able to stay with me the day before. I told him I was fine now and that I'd be going to Fort St. John to look at mug shots this afternoon. Now that I was safe, I found I was back to not appreciating his company and felt badly about it. To make up I told him that Constable Cormier had offered to come over to brainstorm everything that had happened recently, to try to figure out what and who was behind all the weird things that had happened to me since Peter and Todd's disappearance.

"Disappearance?" he asked.

"Well, I'm not so sure they drowned and neither are the police. For one thing, they would have found their bodies by now."

"Unless they got hooked up on something in the river. A branch or a rock."

"I thought of that, but both of them? Besides, the currents should have released them by now . . ."

Tears sprang to my eyes and I wondered what I was doing, talking to an almost stranger, about my loved ones. "I'm sorry, I can't talk about them."

"It's okay, I understand." He made a move as if to come over to my chair so I offered him another coffee. He was facing the kitchen and my back was to him as I made him another coffee. I could feel his eyes on my every move, and the idea that he might like me in an inappropriate way made me feel uncomfortable once again.

He finally left and I returned to the computer. I sat there for a while trying to concentrate, to figure out the answers to the questions I had. Now the three men became my prime suspects, but I needed to figure out how they could be involved, and why? As I sat there trying to come up with answers, I nodded off for a few minutes at the computer. Thinking that it was all the stress of the past week that was making me so drowsy,

I decided to go lie down for a catnap. When I woke up, it was after one and I figured a round trip would take about three hours. I would have to pick Michael up so I'd have no time to prepare questions. I hurriedly got myself together and left.

At the police station, I looked through books of mug shots but I wasn't able to pick any of the three men from them. The disappointment I felt was so distressing because it meant I'd have no idea of where or how I could find Peter and Todd.

I stopped at Kit's, talked to them for a while and then drove home with Michael. As soon as we drove in the yard, we saw something at the foot of the porch steps. Michael jumped out and ran over to the dead wolf that was lying on the ground. I rushed over and I groaned. Our beautiful Wapan had been placed there, her rich grey and tan coat soaked in spots with blood and mud, now dried.

Michael was standing over her, staring down wide-eyed. Tears rolled down his cheeks. Even though I knew she was dead, I leaned over her, calling her name. Wapan, the beautiful, mystical wolf of Shadow Lake was dead, and I wept for her. We both stroked her body, even though we knew she couldn't feel anything anymore.

# 12

REVELATIONS

Wapan's eyes were glazed and her body was stiff. In death, she hardly looked like herself, except for her tan and grey coat. Simultaneously, I was filled with grief and rage. Whoever had brought her here might still be out there, and perhaps we were in their sights right now. Gently, I eased away from Wapan, saying, "Michael, I'm going in for the rifle. You should come inside. They may still be out there."

Michael shook his head, no, and said, "Let them shoot me. I don't care."

"I do. Come on in. We're going to go to Kit's but I have to get some things."

I put my hand on his shoulder to comfort him. Inside, I told him to find the binoculars as I got a box of bullets for the twenty-two. Before we went outside, I scanned the area very carefully through the windows on all sides of the cabin and once more through the dining room windows. Michael was crying the whole time, while I could barely breathe. I handed him the rifle and said, "I'm going to move the truck closer and I want you to stay low and get in."

"What about Wapan?"

"We have to go Kit's and call Constable Cormier. Then we'll come back."

I went out first, got in the truck, aware the whole time that another bullet could stop me. My biggest concern right now was Michael. When he had the cover to get in, I leaned over and called to him.

Once inside, Michael looked up at me with a tear-streaked face. "It's your fault."

"I know," I said quietly, and I began to drive away, even though I was as reluctant as Michael was to leave Wapan's body. "I need you to keep watch with the binoculars. And the rifle is only to scare them off."

As I drove to Kit's, watching both the road and the woods on either side, tears ran down my face. With my horn blasting, I drove into their driveway, and the noise drew them all out immediately. Jumping out of the truck, I told them that Wapan had been killed. Kit phoned Bob, who said he was on his way.

Michael looked at me. "I'm sorry for what I said, Auntie Chris."

"It's okay, Michael."

"No. Wapan was a great wolf. She wouldn't go around blaming anybody else for bad things."

Kit said, "She was right at your doorstep? Something very bad is going on."

I nodded. "It's got to be those three men from yesterday."

Less than an hour later, Bob drove into the driveway in his own vehicle. He was off duty but he had called Sergeant Trolley.

We all went back to Shadow Lake, Bob with Michael in his SUV, me in my truck and Kit in his. Mona and Amber stayed behind. When we drove into my yard, we saw right away that Wapan's body was gone.

The only evidence that her body had been there was some tufts of fur. There weren't even any blood spots. "The blood was dried," I said, "those shots we heard last night. They must have been shooting at the wolves." A cold chill ran down my back, a familiar feeling these days, but this time it came from knowing they had been watching us. "Why didn't they shoot us?" I wondered out loud.

Bob asked if I remembered anything more about the three men. Unfortunately, I could tell him nothing new.

"Listen, Christine," he said. "Those men are dangerous. It's not safe for you and Michael to stay way out here alone."

"They're not going to drive me away. Shadow Lake is my home."

"Think about Michael."

"I want to stay here too," Michael added.

"I'm sorry, Michael," I said, "whatever is happening is most likely because of Peter. And if they're coming after me like this, then . . . then Peter and Todd must be alive! Those three men must have them somewhere. Yesterday, I was positive they were going to kill me. They'd had a chance, but they didn't take it. So why not?"

"Can't be about ransom because they wouldn't have staged an accident, and they would have already made their demands. You have no idea at all of what this is all about?" Bob asked.

"Not a clue. Only speculations. And some of them were pretty stupid at that."

Just then Sergeant Trolley's police van pulled in.

Bob said to me, "That brainstorming I said we'd do? I think we better get to it today."

Kit said, "We can do that at my place. And Michael, you could stay with us until this is all over." He looked at me and said, "It will be all over, and soon."

I nodded and in spite of the great loss of Wapan, I was filled with a new hope that made this latest reason for grieving less painful. Todd and Peter were going to come home.

I said, "Well, right now with all of us here, we should be safe. And since I think our place might be the source of everything, we should do it here. How're your computer skills, Michael? While we brainstorm, you could check Peter's computer because maybe he has something on it."

He said, "I'm not very good, but Amber is."

That made me think of her and Mona's safety. "If we were being watched, do you think they might go to your place, Kit? You and Bob should go get them right now."

They agreed and they left just as Sergeant Trolley joined our group.

Bob told him they'd be back shortly with Mona and Amber.

After they were gone, I asked Sergeant Trolley if they had any idea who those men were.

"We've got nothing. No sighting of any vehicle, no tire tracks. And you weren't able to pick out their mug shots. I even stopped in at NAK-WAN, and the director there said they have no personnel fitting the description of any of the three men you saw. I'll check the woods around here and see if I can find anything."

I followed him. We came across nothing that revealed where the men might have been hiding themselves from our view. Sergeant Trolley left, after everyone, including Lady, came back.

We all went inside and Amber and Michael went over to Peter's computer. Our desks were back to back so that if we were both working we could easily talk to each other. Plus they took less room that way. Bob got a kitchen chair and took it over to my computer, so Michael got himself a chair as well. Mona made coffee and sandwiches, then she and Kit settled on the couch. Before I settled in, I showed Amber the word processing and spreadsheet programs that Peter and I used; they were very basic.

"No Internet?" Amber asked.

"No landline." I replied.

"Oh, yeah. That's why you e-mail from our place. Gee, you're missing out," she said, and started looking through Peter's lists of files. "There's nothing in these files. They're all empty."

Bob and I got up to look. Sure enough, file after file had been deleted. The last date they'd been modified was the Saturday that Peter disappeared.

"He always saved everything now on those USB things."

"Flash drives," Amber said, "we just heard about them at school."

She slid her chair back so I could look in the drawers of his desk. I suddenly noticed that all his backup drive disks weren't in their usual place, but I found a few USB flash drives among his pens and pencils. His publisher had a computer whiz on staff and he was always telling Peter about the latest technology in computers. Amber inserted one of the flash drives. The file for his last manuscript wasn't in the list, so she inserted another one. This time we got lucky. I was amazed that even though she'd never used one before, she could just click her way around and figure it out.

"Why would he delete everything in the files?" Amber asked.

"I don't think he did," I answered, "because if he had, he would have taken the flash drives with him. He always kept the backup disks in there and they're not there now."

To Michael she said, "Okay, you write down the files and I'll look at them one by one."

Back at my own computer, I went to the spreadsheet where I had begun to brainstorm. Oh crap, I'd forgotten I had put such personal thoughts and information like my suicide attempt in there so as we both read it, I was thoroughly embarrassed that Bob was seeing my most private secrets, recent secrets.

When he was done, he looked at me and said, "We'll talk about this later, eh?"

I nodded and said, "I wasn't thinking right." Well, if I wanted to get Todd and Peter back, I had to let Bob know everything, sooner or later. Bob had pulled out his small notepad and made his own notes.

He said, "That's okay. You think you were drugged?"

"I've never blacked out before and I've never walked in my sleep. Peter would have told me. And once I knew someone was coming in here, I figured I must have been drugged because I wouldn't cut my hair like this. I hate it. And I had no place I wanted to drive to that night. I just wanted to wait for Peter to get home."

"And who is Dr. Coran?"

"He was my foster father when I was thirteen. He was evil—a very evil man. But he's dead."

"He wanted to cut her finger off," Michael said.

Bob looked at me. I nodded.

"And he got her arrested," Michael added.

"I was 13. Michael's age. That was a long time ago."

"Mom proved she was innocent." Michael said.

"Yeah, she did. But that time has nothing to do with now," I said.

"Okay, did anything unusual happen before you went on your trip to Manitoba?" Bob asked.

"Not that I can think of. Well, Leona came here last summer. From Winnipeg."

Michael looked over at me, so I added, "With Michael."

Michael said, "And she met Colin."

"Michael, pay attention. Did you get this one?" Amber asked him.

"Right." I said, "She met Colin and almost every time he came, he asked Peter if his company could lease some of our land. So I guess I should move that one up. But I'm positive now that he doesn't have anything to do with this."

"Why's that?" Bob asked.

With Michael right there, I didn't really want to tell him that Colin was in Winnipeg trying to help Leona get bail, especially if he hadn't told Amber about it. I looked at him, then over at Michael, and Bob nodded that he understood. Mentioning him made me wonder if he had gotten Leona out on bail by now. If it was true that Leona wouldn't be able to leave Manitoba, maybe he had decided to stay with her for a while.

Bob interrupted my thoughts, "Could be someone who works with him. Does he still come to visit?"

"He came by with Howard Norach, but he's retired. I think he used to work in the oil business."

"You should include his name."

"Okay, but I think he's just a lonely old man."

"With time on his hands," Bob added.

"Then I found that laptop. Did you find anything on it?" I typed that in.

"No, that was a dead end. Nothing on it."

"Had it been working, do you know?"

"It might have been, but Sergeant Trolley said it had been wiped clean."

"Like no fingerprints?"

Bob smiled and said, "No, they have viruses and worms. Something wiped out the programs that might have been in it."

"So you'd have to have computer smarts to do that, right?"

"You'd have to be a computer geek," Amber said.

"Peter wouldn't set up a camera without telling me. That's really creepy. Someone was spying on us." I added all this to my list. "I just thought of something else but it would have to do with why things happened to me only. But no, it doesn't make sense."

"Let's talk it out." Bob said.

"Mrs. Springer, the reporter for The Peace Valley Voice, wrote an article on Peter and Todd, saying I was a person of interest. I guess people think I was involved, and now no one in Dodging likes me. I thought at one point that maybe a fan of Peter's might be trying to get even with me. But her article didn't come out until after things already started happening."

"Right, I did read that. A lot of suppositions. Her source didn't come from us," Bob added, "Include that anyways."

From the couch, Kit asked, "How are they getting in and out without us hearing them?"

Mona answered one part saying, "We've been gone weekends to my sister's. Remember, I took that phone call and you went to Peter's and then we left?"

"Okay but what about those three men? How'd they get in? We were home that time." Kit responded.

Michael answered that one, "Maybe they had ATV's. We saw all those trails in the gully north of here. They could have parked and walked in. Maybe we can go look and see where they lead to."

"Not now, you can't," I reminded him.

"What if we all went?" he asked.

Bob said, "I'll go look tomorrow. Kit, Christine, you could come with me."

"I can't think of much more, except to add Wapan. I think those three men killed her just to get even. Nobody else knew about her and what she did. They're the only ones connected to her. And they're probably behind everything else. Because they already knew who I was when they first came."

"That's right. We really need to find them. I think we should have Mrs. Springer put their descriptions in the paper. Put her to good use."

The way he said it, I got the impression he didn't think highly of her reporting ethics.

Before printing out my list, I asked Bob, "You're not going to have to give this to Sergeant Trolley, are you?"

"No, but print one out one for yourself and make the changes you want, just in case. And I'll take those flash drives with me for safekeeping. Are there any more?"

I looked through the drawers again, including mine and found one in mine. After we were done, I said to Michael, "You should get some things together for tonight."

He seemed to have forgotten he would be staying at Kit and Mona's place. "Couldn't I just stay here tonight?"

"Michael . . ."

"You're going to be here all by yourself," he said, "and if someone is after you, well, they'd think twice if we were both here. I'm not a baby and that's what you're making me feel like." At that, Amber snickered. "I should be here."

"And what are you going to say tomorrow?" I asked.

"I'll think of something new." Michael grinned.

"Okay, just for tonight." He was probably right about anyone trying anything with the two of us here. And the idea of spending a night alone after what happened yesterday and now today was not something that appealed to me. On the other hand, I had wanted to be alone because so far I'd been holding my grief for the loss of Wapan in check for Michael's sake.

Bob said, "I'd offer to stay but I have to go to work soon. I'm filling in for someone."

"If anything happens, fire off three shots and I'll be here in a jiffy." Kit offered.

"Don't forget to call me first," Bob said to him.

With that, we said our goodnights to each other, and I went outside to see them off. It was already dark and it was starting to drizzle. When I went back in, Michael was sitting at Peter's computer. As I began going around shutting all the shutters, I was still amazed that Wapan's death had such an impact on him because he'd met her only once and so briefly.

She must have been on both our minds because he asked, "How could anyone do something like that? How?"

After I was done with the shutters, I put the kettle on for hot chocolate, tidied up and began shutting off most of the lights. I made sure to leave the side and front lights on so if anyone was out there, they would know we could see them clearly.

Once we had our cups of hot chocolate, I sat in the easy chair that faced Peter's desk. I felt we needed to talk but had no idea how to get him to open up. I considered telling him about how Wapan had saved my life, but he was so young.

"Do you think my mother's crazy?" Michael asked, "for stabbing that man? That is what really happened."

I tried to think of something that would provide understanding. "I used to wish I had your mother's name because it reminded me of lions and cougars. Mother lions protect their cubs any way they can, and while I don't know what happened. Her being charged with assault? I bet she did it to protect you."

"That man she stabbed . . ." Lost in the memory of that night, he didn't say more.

In a way, I was still a stranger to him. Why would he be open with me? I decided to confide and I told him about me, about how I was going to kill myself partly because I couldn't bear to live without Peter and Todd and partly because of just being the person I was. I couldn't have sunk any lower.

"I guess I was living on self-pity," I said, "and once I decided to do it, it took priority over everything else. That was the day before I talked to Emma, and she asked if I could look after you. At the time, I wouldn't commit because I thought I wouldn't be around. On the day I was going to shoot myself, I sat out on the porch steps there with the rifle ready and I changed my mind. I thought of Amber. The day before, she had taken me horseback riding, and I thought if she came over by herself and found me, what a horror that would be for her. That's when Wapan came to me. We were face to face and in a blink of an eye, she changed me . . .

my way of thinking. She empowered me. She gave me the courage to live."

I hesitated. "There was so much I wanted to tell Peter and I never did. Since it was all in the past, I thought it would never affect our lives together, but our past is part of us. If the past has messed you up, you have to deal with that. We can't just leave it behind because it does shape us in some way."

After a few moments of silence, he said in a low voice, "That man that Mom stabbed, he wasn't just standing over me. He was bent over me. He was touching me." He swallowed a few times and his chair creaked as he moved to get some tissue. In a stronger voice, he continued, "Yeah, he was touching me."

"Were you angry with your mother for bringing that man into your life?"

He nodded slowly. "Yeah, I was. She was drinking and partying and bringing strange men home with her. So it was all her fault."

"The one thing I know for sure is that your mother loves you. You two have a bond that I wanted to have with Todd. Give her a chance."

"I miss her."

"I know." I got up and walked over to him and gave him a hug. "It's late, you should get to bed."

"Now you sound like Mom." He smiled as he got up and went to prepare for bed.

# 13

## HOPE LOST

rchie left Howard's office after updating him. Howard hadn't liked his incentive on taking the helicopter out to shoot at wolves but he did like the results. Archie was in charge of the hunt and he wanted to use bows and arrows on Peter and Christine. Since the police had recently begun cracking down on poachers, Howard agreed that it could be a part of future hunts—archery training. Yes, that could lead to competitions. It might be fun. After all, once Christine and Peter were gone he'd have to find something new with which to occupy himself. The hunt would be the last stage of the plan and Howard was almost sorry to see the end approaching. He had enjoyed this game tremendously.

He would have to step up his plan because now she had gotten the police on his doorstep, asking about Archie and his men. The worst was that she had somehow figured out that her family had disappeared. That was a shock. Damn Peter with his latest manuscript. Well, he had everything on it now, including the backup discs. If he hadn't done his homework on Peter, he might have missed what was in his last manuscript. And if it had been published, the locals would have looked at this place in a new light and they would have come snooping around.

He had gotten word from Colin that the charges against Leona would be dropped and he'd be bringing her back tomorrow or the next day. Howard gave him simple instructions for when they did get back. He hadn't decided whether to include Colin and Leona in the hunt or get rid of them beforehand. Decisions, decisions. But what he did know for sure was that tonight Archie and his men would take something else that was precious to Christine and tomorrow, or the day after, she'd be here at the compound. People would simply think she'd moved away. The only other decision to be made was how long to keep her before giving her, and Peter, up to the hunt.

Archie had wanted to put the wolf in her bed tonight but now there'd be no time, not if all of them were gathering at her house. He wished that he had listened to Archie about bugging her place, but now he felt the risk was too high. Peter might have installed a laptop for security reasons but bugging devices? No. Still, it would have been nice to see if the gathering was social or if they were up to something.

Archie's plan was a little tricky, and Howard warned him that if Christine didn't come out alive, no place would be safe for him and his men. Archie was beginning to get out of control and beginning to challenge him. He'd begun to talk as if they were equals. His plans might even include taking over the running of his compound. Well, that wasn't going to happen. He'd have to deal with him. Maybe getting rid of Archie and his men would become a future project.

He still couldn't decide if Peter was faking or not. No matter. He wasn't going anywhere. Today one of the member compounds in Washington had asked him to give a keynote speech next month. He'd come up with an idea he might use, and he needed to get back to it. His draft began:

*Loss . . . that's what it is all about. If you want to control people, take the most meaningful things from their lives. Oppressive governments, like our Canadian and American governments, have manipulated the Native people successfully. In the past they did their jobs beautifully, and we can learn from those times.*

*Take their languages. Take their so-called traditional religious practices. Take their land, their homes, and their food. Isolate these mud people. Take their children. Split their homes and families apart. Take, take, take. Make them into total losers. They will never recover. The proof is in the state that they remain in today. They are the poorest of our country, the most uneducated, the most defeated. They have never recovered.*

*In return, give them the drugs that confuse them and daze them. Give them firewater. Give them their crack cocaine. Then throw them in jail. Take their freedom. They will never recover. They will turn on themselves with murder, suicide, and crime.*

*Today our governments are giving them too much. They have convinced the voters and the taxpayers that they need equality. They need justice. In the East, governments are caving in to them. We must unite with our Eastern brothers to fight this miserable turn of events.*

*Real democracy belongs only to the privileged. Real democracy belongs to us, the North American Aryan Nations!*

While Howard worked at his speech, Peter was laying on his cot, bruised and sore. He was disappointed with himself. His ploy had worked but not in the way he wanted. Howard had finally come into his cell, and as expected he had brought three armed men with him. He had checked on his vitals almost as if he knew that Peter was faking, saying, "Peter, I'm not fooled by what you're pretending to do. If you don't eat your food, I'm going to have to punish your son. And my punishments can be quite disfiguring."

Even with those men hovering over him, Peter had thought he could try to escape. But with this threat to Todd, he realized he had no choice left.

"Don't hurt my son." He began to sit up.

Howard said with great satisfaction, "I knew it." He turned and walked out, saying, "I want him in good enough condition for the hunt."

The three men began using him as a punching bag.

Now he was pondering Howard's last comment, "I want him in good enough condition for the hunt." Could that mean they planned to hunt him down? Was the purpose of the high fencing and barbed wire twofold: to keep strangers out and to keep human prey in? And when was this hunt going to happen?

For the first time since his imprisonment, Peter lost hope. He felt he was going to be killed.

# 14

CLOSING IN

In the early hours of Thursday morning, I woke to the howling of a wolf. At first I thought I had been dreaming, but then I heard it again. I looked out and saw only blackness because of the clouds. I got dressed so I could go outside for a look around. Hearing movement from Michael's room, I called softly, "Michael, are you awake?"

He said, "Yeah, I heard it."

"It sounded like it was right under my window, but I can't see anything. I'm going outside."

"Wait for me," he called.

We were going to get our jackets and head out through the porch doors, but we saw moving lights through the cracks of the dining room shutters to the north next to the porch, then to the east. Suddenly they were on the outside of the kitchen shutters to the west. Michael looked out one of the living room shutters and immediately realized what was happening. He grabbed my hand and pulled me towards the front door, saying, "We have to get out."

He unlocked and opened the door to a wall of flames and the smell of gasoline. He slammed the door shut again. I wanted to get the fire extinguisher, but he pulled me towards Peter's desk, to the south window, the only window that opened for cross breezes. Just as he was opening those shutters, another fire flared up, blocking our way out.

Leaving me, Michael raced into my bedroom, came out carrying the twenty-two, and got bullets from the filing cabinet. Seeing him do that,

I yelled, "Michael, forget the rifles! We have to get out!"

A picture of Peter and Todd hung on the wall beside him and, while he raced to the front corner window behind my desk, I grabbed the picture. The smoke alarm went off. If it were not for the smell of gasoline, I would have thought a forest fire was about to engulf us.

Michael was trying to move my desk closer to the window, and I hurried to help. When it was close enough, he lay on it and kicked out at the windowpanes, breaking only glass. Like me, he wore running shoes, not very effective for breaking through fir window casings. The windows that might have been designed to keep bears out were now keeping us in. As he kicked again, more glass panes broke, sending pieces flying about.

While he carried on, I ran to the kitchen to soak some dishtowels, but the water ran out too soon, and I only got one towel dampened. Michael tied it over his mouth and nose and then lifted my chair onto the desk. Standing up on the desk, he slammed the chair against the wooden frames. I sat on the floor, out of his way, clutching the picture close to me. Little by little, the wood splintered and gave. By now, more smoke was swirling around, and I remembered reading that most people who died in house fires were killed by smoke. Although I was sitting on the floor, I was finding it difficult to breathe. I couldn't imagine what Michael must be going through. He was amazing. The fire was inside now, lighting up the interior. Embers of burning paper and cloth floated about the room, riding on the draft from the broken window.

Trying to keep the smoke out of my lungs, I covered my nose and mouth with my hands. Then I felt a stinging sensation on my back. Panicked, I lay back and rolled back and forth to squelch the fire. That's when the acrid smell of singed hair came to me and, looking up at Michael, I knew I couldn't afford to panic. My eyes and my throat stung from the smoke, and my ears were ringing from the high-pitched screech from the smoke alarm. I didn't want to turn to see how far the fire had advanced because I didn't want to know. Shutting my eyes to keep the smoke out, I heard Michael hitting at the frame, again and again. He jumped down from the desk and crouched down beside me. "Someone's out there. When you get out, get down and take the rifle. Ready?"

Nodding, I climbed up on the desk and put the picture down so I could slide backwards. Feet first, I went downwards and out through the small hole. One jagged end of broken glass still in the upper frame scratched along my back and snagged in the collar of my sweatshirt. Michael tore it loose and handed me the rifle. Crouching down immediately, I turned to give him cover if anyone began shooting, not that I could have seen anything, I was blinking so much. The smoke alarm went silent, but the ringing in my ears continued. Michael was taking too long and, looking around one last time, I was about to go back in when his foot poked at my head. My heart started beating again as he slid out. Taking the rifle from me, he signalled for me to follow him towards the darkness of the lake. A loud explosion came from behind us and I turned to look. The garage for the ATV and snowmobiles had become a huge bonfire. Michael grabbed at my wrist and we kept going.

At the edge of the lake, we took cover in the tall damp grasses and crawled over to an outcrop of boulders. Watching the flames shoot out from the windows of the cabin, I realized only then that I had forgotten the picture on the desk. Inside the burning cabin were all my memories of Todd and Peter. Gone. All my things, all of Michael's possessions. Gone. Tears ran down my face, but I didn't openly weep. Michael tapped me on my shoulder and pointed in the direction where we had parked the truck. A man in dark clothing was putting a torch to a rag stuck in the gas nozzle and he raced for cover up the road, where we could see two others waiting at the back of a white van.

Michael aimed the rifle at them, but I stopped him.

"But they tried to kill us!" he yelled.

"We're not in danger right now," I said calmly. "Besides, they're probably more armed than we are."

Michael lowered the rifle just as our truck burst into flames. Beyond that the taillights of the men's van disappeared around the first bend. Through the branches, I thought I saw another set of taillights as well.

Turning my gaze back to my truck, then to the cabin that was now beginning to cave in on itself, I said, "On the other hand, I should have shot them myself."

170

"No. You were right." Michael said. "They must have had rifles. They must have seen us getting out, so why didn't they try to finish us off?"

All I could say was that I didn't know. Everything that had happened so far was incomprehensible. Without the adrenaline pumping through me, the intense pain of the fire and the cut on my back was screaming and I groaned.

Michael moved to wash the smoke out of his eyes, and I thought of doing the same, but I had no energy to budge and certainly no inclination to touch icy cold water.

"I should signal Kit." Michael said.

"You think they've passed by his place yet? We don't want him running into those men."

We waited for what seemed like an eternity, and then Michael shot into the air, counted to five, and shot once again, then a third time. He suggested we begin walking to Kit's in case they hadn't heard.

"I don't want to leave here," I said.

"There's nothing we can do here. We'll come back tomorrow if you want. Come on." He stood up and held a hand out towards me.

"Let's wait until the last of the embers die," I said, not moving.

"But Auntie Chris, that might not happen until tomorrow. Unless the rain picks up."

"Oh." I smiled at the tone of his voice and reached for his hand, saying, "Okay. Let's go."

My body was stiff, my back stung, my throat was sore, and I was cold. We had just lost our home. Other than that, I think I was okay.

"Michael, did you get hurt? How are you feeling? Did you get cut?"

"I'm okay. My throat hurts a lot, but I'm okay."

Michael helped me walk a bit, until I could get some of the stiffness out of my joints and legs. Sitting on damp earth and grasses hadn't helped. As we headed for Kit's place, the smell of burned wood mixed with gasoline stayed with us a long ways down the road.

Sniffing, I said, "I can still smell the smoke."

"That's because it's on our clothes and in our hair," Michael said casually.

His matter-of-fact tone made me smile. "You were right on, Michael. The way you reacted and everything. How did you know it wasn't a forest fire?"

"When I looked out, I saw a man run towards the back from the fire. We were lucky they didn't shoot at us."

"I wonder why they didn't. They must have known we'd try to get out."

"Probably busy carrying cans of gasoline. If the wolf hadn't howled, we'd most likely have burned to a crisp. We would have been sleeping when the alarm went off."

"That warning, that's something that Wapan would have done," I said through chattering teeth.

As we walked on towards Kit's place, we suddenly saw two lights bobbing in the distance. We stopped. "They're coming back!" I whispered. "Get in the bush!"

We dove into the underbrush at the side of the road, getting scratched by branches and thorns in the process, and Michael was about to put the rifle in position.

"Give me the rifle, Michael." He handed it to me and I asked, "Why would they come back?"

"Maybe they forgot something, something incriminating. Hey, look. It doesn't look like headlights. More like two people walking. See how the lights move differently. Like they're carrying flashlights."

Suspicious, I watched as the lights approached. Even after we heard the sounds of horses snorting and treading over the ground, I had a hand on Michael's arm to hold him back. If the riders were Kit and Amber, they would have had Lady with them. When their identities were unmistakable, I sighed with relief, jumped up, and ran over to them, yelling "Kit!"

That must have given Kit quite a shock, for he dropped his flashlight. I had startled the horses, too, and they almost bolted, but their riders got them under control. Amber was able to hold onto her flashlight and her reins.

"Sorry, she didn't mean to startle the horses," Michael said.

"You okay?" Kit asked, with a testy edge to his voice.

"Yeah," Michael answered simultaneously as I said "No."

I babbled on, "Those three men came back and this time they burnt us out. Even the truck. We were coming to your place. Where's Lady?"

Amber was the one who answered. "Kit said to keep her in the house. I thought I heard your signal, so I woke them up. And the truck's not working, so we had to get the horses saddled up."

"Didn't want your dog saying hello to strangers," Kit explained. "Here, give me your hand."

Michael got up behind Amber, and Kit helped me get up behind him. Now that I was safe, my trembling increased. Forcing myself to relax, I'd stop for a while, but then the tremors would come again and again, until I could no longer get them under control. By the time we rode into their yard, I was really having the shakes. While I couldn't control the shakes, my mind remained vaguely aware.

Kit stopped in front of the house and helped me off. Amber and Michael headed for the horse shed, but Kit called them back. Both of them dismounted and ran back to us. I still had the presence of mind to be amazed that they could just leave the horses untied in the yard. Michael looked stricken when he saw how violently I was trembling. His eyes moistened, so I said, "I'm just really cold, Michael."

"Get a blanket, Amber," Kit said, as he asked Michael to help me inside. "Don't look so worried, it's just a delayed reaction. Shock. But we have to get her warmed up, quickly."

Mona appeared at the door, and Amber ran back out with a blanket. They put it around me. I tried to walk normal, but I really just wanted to lie down. In the light of the living room, Amber's mouth opened in horror when she took a good look at me. She later told me that a few burns had gone right through my sweatshirt and that blood from a long gash down the right side of my back had seeped through the material and that a lot my hair had been singed. Some soot had blackened parts of my face and she thought they were burns too. I looked much worse than I really was.

Assuring me that Michael was fine, Mona left for the kitchen and returned with some tea. I tried to drink, but I couldn't keep my hands steady and it slopped over. Amber held the cup so I could drink from it. When I was done, Mona helped me take my top off so she could work her medicinal magic on my back. Air hitting the exposed wounds sent a shock of excruciating pain through me and I cringed.

Mona said in a quiet, calming voice, "It's okay. We have to clean all this first." Mona washed my back with a nice warm watery solution that greatly muted the pain, and I began to relax.

Amber left and returned with a clean pair of pajamas. Finally, I was lying down under some warm blankets, the tremors gone. Unable to sleep, I listened to the others in the kitchen. Kit was telling Michael that they had called Bob and that he was on his way. Lady came over to me and licked me a few times on my face, just as in the old days. Then she lay down beside the couch, and I put my arm down so I could pet her.

From the kitchen, I heard Mona order Michael to take off his shirt, and Kit said, most likely to Amber, "Come on, we'll go and put the horses away." For some reason, that phrase, put the horses away, struck me as funny.

Mona said, "Don't pull away. You got glass in there."

A little later I heard her say, "I can't get it."

Michael said, "I can get it out later."

"No, it might go in deeper."

Amber and Kit returned and Mona said, "Amber, go get me your tweezers."

Amber said, "Why? You giving him a facial?"

That too struck me as funny.

By the time Bob came, I was sound asleep. No one disturbed me.

When we were having breakfast the next morning, Michael told me everything that had happened. Bob and Sergeant Trolley had come first, followed by more police officers, and he and Kit had gone with them to the remains of the cabin. They had taken pictures of almost everything.

"Want to know what they didn't burn?" Michael asked. "The outhouse. Bob said they had a really warped sense of humour."

"Next time, I'll know where to put my valuables," I chuckled. My own sense of humour could be pretty warped too.

"They found their footprints all around the buildings. And they found the wolf's tracks too. It was right outside your bedroom window, Auntie Chris." He took a big bite of his toast and continued, "I told the cop who found the wolf prints that if it hadn't woke us up, he'd of been looking for murderers right now."

"What did he say?"

"He asked if it was a pet."

That cracked me up too. "No, I mean did he believe you that they tried to kill us?"

From the look that Michael gave me, I knew he thought I was acting very strangely, but I couldn't help myself. He shrugged and said, "He didn't say anything about that. Just asked if the wolf was a pet."

"How are you feeling?" Kit asked me.

"Much better, physically. I want to go to the cabin," I said.

Kit and Mona looked at each other, and I guess they figured there was no sense trying to talk me out of it. I looked to Michael to continue.

"So this cop asked if the wolf was going to be a problem when the others come. And Kit told him they would never see it."

"What others?" I asked.

"The fire inspector or something. Oh yeah, and Bob said you should call your insurance agent."

"Did you get any sleep at all?"

Michael said, "No. I couldn't sleep."

Amber joined us and said to Michael, "You look a mess. You'd better get ready for school."

"School?" Michael asked. "I can't wear these to school. They're all dirty."

"After what you've been through, I think it would be a good idea for you to skip school anyways. You should get some sleep. If you feel up to it after lunch, I can always drive you." Then I remembered we had no vehicle anymore. "And then again, I'm going to have to rent a car or something."

Kit said, "Which reminds me, I have to take a look at my truck.

Strange it didn't work during the night." He left with Michael following him.

When we finished breakfast, I stood up, thinking I should go get dressed. Mona and Amber took me upstairs to find clean clothing. Amber was too slim for me to wear any of her jeans, so I had to tie a belt around a pair of Mona's. I was taller than Mona, so the short pant legs made me feel weird, but a sweatshirt of hers was fine. When I came back down, I heard Sergeant Trolley's voice in the kitchen.

Sergeant Trolley looked at me when I entered. "I'm sorry about last night. How are you feeling today?"

"Fine." Mona's medicines had worn off and although I was sore and stiff again, the pain from my back wounds was bearable.

Mona said to Amber, "The school bus is going to be here any minute."

"Oh, can't I stay home, too?"

Mona gave her a look that said no, and Amber made a face and collected her lunch and school bag and headed outdoors, just as Kit and Michael came in. Kit went to pour himself a coffee as he said, "We found the problem. Someone took a spark plug out of my truck."

"When did you last drive it?" Sergeant Trolley asked.

"Last night. We got back here about . . . it was dark already."

"It was about 9:30," Mona said.

The officer looked at me and said, "Mrs. Webster, I know we're beginning to sound like a broken record, but by now you must have some idea of what's going on."

"I don't. Only that it was those same three men. They could have killed us but they didn't."

Michael said, "Why don't you fingerprint Kit's truck? You wouldn't wear gloves to take out a spark plug."

"We'll do that," he said almost dismissively. To me he said, "It's too bad you can't tell us more about these men." He seemed edgy, maybe because he resented Michael telling him how to do his job. I had reacted with resentment to his adversarial approach and I had noticed the way he seemed to talk down to Bob. Being in a highly suspicious mood, I put him on my list of suspects. Next time I saw Bob, I would ask him about

Sergeant Trolley in private.

"Maybe they're just racist," I said, eyeing him closely.

"Personally, I think that's a charge that's overused."

We stared at each other. Because I might need him to get Peter and Todd back from wherever they were, and because I had just added him as a suspect, I didn't want to totally alienate him, and I kept my retort to myself. I backed down and looked away.

"Well, none of this is not very useful," he said.

In my mind I told him that was a double negative.

He looked at Kit and added, "I'll send someone to fingerprint your truck." Then he left.

Michael said, "Auntie Chris, I don't think he likes you."

Later that day, Kit drove us out to Shadow Lake, where Sergeant Trolley and others were already poking around and another man was photographing this and that. They didn't want us creating new footsteps before they had taken more pictures in the daylight, so we went down to the lake to wait. Another police car drove in and Bob, in uniform, got out from the passenger side and came directly to us to offer me his sympathy. No time like the present and I drew him aside and asked, "Do you trust Sergeant Trolley?"

"Yeah, sure, why do you ask?"

"Probably just the state I'm in. Drawing at straws kind of thing."

"You suspect him of something?"

"Well ... yeah."

"He's been with the RCMP for over twenty-seven years and he's gotten all sorts of commendations. I think he rubs most people the wrong way."

"Commendations don't mean much to me. I just had to know if he's trustworthy."

"Yeah, I think he is. He's just frustrated with not getting anywhere with everything that's happening to you."

"You mean he cares?"

"In his way, yeah. With him it's a matter of catching the bad guy." Bob smiled and I took Sergeant Trolley off my list of suspects.

We left shortly after that, mostly because there were too many people there, and Kit and Mona took me to Fort St. John while Michael stayed behind to get some sleep. There, I took what was left of our clothes to a Laundromat and then went over to our vet. The receptionist checked to see if Peter had brought Lady in recently and he hadn't. After that I met Mona and Kit to have lunch with them.

In the diner, I was putting sugar in my coffee, when I remembered that in comforting me after my escape from the three men, Howard had made coffee and put two heaping teaspoons of sugar into my coffee. Ever since Peter's joke in front of Colin, I had prepared my coffee at the counter. I had never fixed it in front of Howard, so how did he know to do that? It had been too sweet since I had cut down on the sugar and I hadn't finished it. Colin could have told him, but why would he?

That made me wonder why Howard aroused in me a sense of . . . was it disgust? Well, whatever it was, it was something yucky. What was it about him? Maybe it was his eyes, the way he looked at me? What if he were a stalker-type? Why not? Something about him reminded me of someone else, someone younger, probably some actor who'd played a stalker.

Something else: Before Peter disappeared, and when Colin and Howard dropped by, Lady had had no reaction to Howard. Afterward, when she should have been more protective of me, she had growled and retreated from him.

Mona interrupted my thoughts. "You know, you could stay at our place with Michael."

"Wouldn't that be crowded?" I asked.

She smiled and said, "I grew up in a two-bedroom house with eleven brothers and sisters. That was crowded."

I smiled at her and then asked Kit, "Do you know Howard Norach?"

"No, I don't."

"What about Colin Sayers?"

"That's the one that was with your sister?" I nodded and he said, "I only met him that one time. Why?"

"I was just wondering how close Colin is to Howard. I think they might have worked together. When you get back, could you call Bob and ask him to check both of them out? Here, I'll write their names down. I think Howard's last name is spelled like this."

"You think they're in this somehow?"

"Just a thought. That's why I only want Bob to do a check on them."

"Maybe he's at the station now. We could go over there."

"That would be good. I don't want to go there, though. If I ran into Sergeant Trolley he'd think my reasons are silly. And, maybe they are. Anyways, I'll go rent a car. Do some shopping—we need jackets, and I'll meet you back at your place later. If Michael's still sleeping, I want to go back to my place."

"I could come with you. You shouldn't go out there alone."

"I don't think they'll come back. With the police troops out there, I think they're long gone. I'll take Lady with me." The reason I wanted to be alone at Shadow Lake is that I wanted to say goodbye to the place I had come to love, and if I got emotional I wanted to be alone.

Later that afternoon, after I changed, I left Michael sleeping and went back to Shadow Lake. With the police having been out there, I thought it would be safe, but just in case, I took Lady with me. She jumped out of the back and ran towards the cabin. There she came to a dead stop, sat down, and looked back at me. She seemed to be puzzled by the change that had taken place. Then she went to work sorting out the new scents in the yard, sniffing and blowing. When she approached the rubble of the cabin, I thought of all the broken glass from the windows. I called her back to me and made her get back in the car.

I finally got out and walked around, looking at the ash-laden debris that had once been a comfortable safe home to my family and me. Now it was all gone, including all my mementoes. They hadn't been happy with taking Peter and Todd, they had to take my . . . Whoa, I thought, this was bordering on self-pity, and I was finished with all that. Did I really believe they were alive? I did. I really did. I was going to find them and we were going to make new memories for the future. There, that was better.

What if I put this place up for sale? Would that make those men do something more? Flush them out as they say. The NAK-WAN laboratory was north of Kit's. What if Peter and Todd had been taken there? Lady had wanted to go into the woods north of Kit's the day I came back from Norway House, when normally she would have been beside herself to see me. But maybe she had followed them being taken there and had returned to Kit's to tell someone—me. Could she be that smart that she wanted me to follow her there? That was a big supposition. What about those strange wounds on her? Who had stitched her up? Not Peter because considering his books, I had always been amused by his phobia about needles. No way would he touch her with one. Plus there was that rope burn around her neck as if someone had tied her up and she'd fought hard to escape.

I returned to the car and said, "Lady, talk to me. You know more than what you're saying." She wagged her tail and licked my face. I started the car and as I pulled out of the driveway, I recalled seeing a flash of light, like the sun reflecting on glass on the morning I left for Norway House. Were those three men watching us even then? Nobody would be out driving ATV's that early in the morning, unless it was hunting season, and that wasn't until fall. As I headed back to Kit's, I intended to tell him to call Bob and have him meet me at the NAK-WAN laboratory. It was time for us to check them firsthand. A white van coming towards me appeared around the last bend, and I couldn't believe who was in it.

# 15

A DEADLY GAME

Colin and I each brought our vehicles to a stop, and I jumped out and rushed over to Leona who had also gotten out. We hugged each other and then she dropped her smile and told me how sorry she was about Peter and Todd. Just seeing her so unexpectedly and her offering of condolence made me emotional, and for a minute I couldn't say anything. Through the tears that rimmed my eyes, I told her that Michael was at Kit's and we could go back there. Because we were so close to Kit's, I let Lady out and told her to go "find Michael." She trotted off towards Kit's place.

The only way to turn the van around would be to go back to Shadow Lake so I hopped in the back seat. I was startled to find Howard sitting behind the driver's seat. I'd been so focused on Leona that I hadn't noticed him.

"Hello Christine. Very nice to see you again. I'm sorry about your cabin."

As I asked him how he knew about the fire, Leona asked me, "What about the cabin?"

To her I replied, "It burned during the night." I turned back to him and, trying to keep accusation out of my eyes, I waited for his answer.

"Everybody's talking about it. Peter Webster's cabin burned down," he replied.

From the way he looked at me, I knew he wasn't a stalker. He was something else, something more menacing than a stalker. I turned away from him so he couldn't see the suspicion and apprehension in my eyes.

About five minutes later we drove into my yard. Leona got out as soon as she saw the debris. "Oh Chris, I'm so sorry. Are you and Michael okay? Did you get hurt?"

I got out too, saying, "We're both fine."

"How did it happen?"

I didn't want to go into details in front of Howard so I told her quietly it was deliberately set, but we didn't know by whom or why.

We both turned to get back in the van just as Howard and Colin came around the van to join us. I figured now was as good a time to tell them, especially Howard, that I was going to sell the land and move back to Winnipeg. I started by asking Leona, "Are you planning to move back to Fort St. John?"

She was about to respond but the look on her face changed from meditative to one of wide-eyed, open-mouthed horror as she looked over my right shoulder. I turned and saw Howard advance towards her with a scalpel in his right hand. His intent seemed to be to slice open her neck.

"Neither of you are going to be moving anywhere," he said.

To his right, Colin yelled, "What the hell are you doing?" He seemed so shocked that he couldn't move.

I reacted instantly and with the palm of my hand I punched hard at the inside of his wrist, and the scalpel dropped. Before he could react, I stepped in front of Leona to face him and as forcefully as I could I punched him in the throat. Without Colin and Leona there I wouldn't have had the guts to do something like that. To my amazement, it worked. He clutched at his throat and began to gag.

"Let's go! Let's get out of here," Leona screamed to Colin, and she jumped into the van.

We were both shocked when Colin shook his head, no. To my right, Howard suddenly lunged towards me. I didn't realize he had stooped down to pick up the scalpel until I felt a stinging pain at the tip of my left middle finger and saw blood spurt onto the ground between us. I kicked out at Howard and was satisfied to see I got him in the face. I grabbed Leona's arm, pulling her from the van, and we raced for what

I hoped was safety in the forest. Behind me, I heard Howard ordering Colin to stop us.

We crashed and stumbled through the underbrush. The pain from my finger on my left hand seemed to intensify each time my feet hit the ground. "Leona, slow down," I whispered, loudly. In her panic, she had raced ahead of me and we were going nowhere fast.

"Why are they doing this? It doesn't make sense," she whispered, studying the landscape to our south. I wrapped my bleeding finger with tissue I had in my jacket pocket. "He got you!"

As we both looked towards the south, I said, "Just my finger. Today, I just figured out Howard might be part of what's going on. But I didn't know about Colin." I turned to look back but they didn't seem to be following us.

"What are we going to do?" Leona asked.

"Remember that cave Michael found? We'll go there but we have to move quietly. We're making too much noise. Come on."

We listened for a moment to make sure there were no other sounds. Surveying my surroundings, I picked out landmarks and, once I knew where I was, we moved forward carefully toward the gorge ahead of us and then east along its basin. Once we got to the spot I remembered, I studied the southern wall of the gorge until I recognized the rock on which Lady had stood to bark out that she had found Michael's hiding place last summer. We took a moment to listen but the only sounds were of birds going on with their usual business. That meant we were probably alone. For now!

The mouth of the cave was five feet up from the ground and getting to it meant a few seconds of exposure. If we were seen, it meant we would be trapped in a hole. I braced myself and clambered up into the hole. Turning, I studied the surrounding area closely and then signalled for Leona to climb up. The mouth of our cave was well hidden by bushes.

At first, we breathed heavily. "Don't worry," I whispered. "Someone will come looking for us." I whispered.

"Are you sure?"

"Yes. A lot of weird things have been happening and when Lady shows up without me, they'll know something's wrong. Kit will call Bob—he's a police officer, and he'll call Sergeant Trolley, and so on. We've got them right where we want them," I said, smiling. In spite of our predicament, Leona smiled back. But then I thought to myself that if Michael was still sleeping, she might just settle down beside him. Her job was to "find him," that was it.

We stopped our whisperings for a few minutes and thought we could hear the distant sounds of ATV's from the northeast. The sounds increased. At first I thought help of some kind was coming but then there was silence and only the normal sounds of the forest returned. I had my right hand tightly wrapped around my left-hand fingers, trying to stop the flow of blood and to stop the air from getting at my wound.

Eventually, Leona whispered, "Let me see how bad it is."

"No. I don't want to see it." I pulled my hands back protectively.

"Listen!" I whispered. Suddenly, we could hear movement out there, branches snapping.

Howard's voice rang out in the distance, and it had a madman's sing-song quality to it. "Christine, where are you? You know we're going to find you. It's just a matter of time. My men are going to track you down. So come out of whichever hole you've crawled into."

Leona and I looked at each other silently, and we both must have had the same thought: we were not going to get out of this alive. Howard had just said his men were going to track us down so now I knew for sure that besides Colin, those three men had been working for Howard all along. Howard was behind everything, from taking Todd and Peter, to this. But why kill Leona? And if he wanted me dead, why had he not already killed me?

Time passed while I tried to figure out the whys. I gave up and turned to thinking about how we were going to get out alive. Maybe what I had told Leona only to comfort her would happen. Lady would somehow get Michael and Kit to find my car still on the road. I had left the keys in it, but then Howard knew of the car and probably had it moved. They'd still have to go past Kit's place but I didn't think they'd risk that. If I knew what his plan was, I would know how much time he figured he had to carry it out, because he hadn't counted on us escaping.

"Oh shit," I whispered.

"What?"

"No, it's okay."

"What?"

"I just realized that he was probably going to take me to where he had Todd and Peter."

"You think he has them?" She seemed both surprised and doubtful.

"Yes. And I was just thinking I should have let him take me there."

"Right." She stretched the word out.

"Wrong. Because he was going to kill you first."

"Oh, yeah," Leona flopped back. "But if you get another chance to find them and it comes down to a choice of it being me or them, I want you to . . ."

"No, Leona. For one thing, he could have already . . ." I couldn't bring myself to say the worst out loud, not for Todd and Peter. "Well, we're definitely alive," I said instead. "Let's keep it that way."

Leona nudged me gently and pointed to the outside.

Leaning forward over her shoulder, I could see a man in fatigues, a rifle hanging from a sling on his back. He was poking a long stick in among the bushes on the other side. Then we heard the sound of rustling leaves as someone approached on our side. When the man came into view, I recognized him as the leader of the three men who had attacked me. He, too, had a rifle in a sling. Leona flattened herself to the ground, and I leaned back against the wall, wanting to watch but not wanting to be seen. He paused right in front of our hideout to study the embankment. Muttering to himself, he moved on. The ATV's we'd heard had been theirs.

The cave was barely big enough for the two of us. Changing position, I bumped my wounded hand and fresh pain shot up my arm, making me want to cry out. The tissue was already soaked with blood. It was leaking through my fingers, so I raised my arms, hoping that would slow the bleeding. My heart was racing again, and common sense told me that meant more blood was being pumped into the rest of my body. I tried to have calming thoughts—Peter and Todd out on the lake; Peter fishing; Todd napping; me reading; Wapan's visit. Suddenly the thoughts weren't so calming anymore; all the good times in my life really had come to abrupt disastrous endings. And now men with rifles were hunting us and there was nothing we could do. To distract my mind from the pain and my thoughts, I asked Leona, "How'd you get out of the Remand Centre?"

"Colin. He came to see me and I told him the whole story. Then he went to my lawyer, and after that he learned what he could about Frank, the guy I stabbed. Turned out, he was a pedophile, and my lawyer got the charge dismissed."

"Why didn't you just tell the police what Frank had done in the first place?"

She turned over to face me and whispered, "I didn't want anyone knowing what might have happened to Michael. And I didn't want it in the papers, that's for sure. Did he talk to you about it?"

"Yeah."

"How does he feel?"

"He's going to talk it out with you. You've got quite an impressive son, there. He's been teaching me Karate. And last night, if it weren't for him, we wouldn't be here now."

We both realized the here was not really a good place to be in and we both smiled. I said, "Rephrase—we wouldn't be alive right now. Anyways, he has a lot of courage. You did good."

Tears came to her eyes and she said, "I'm not going to see him again."

"Yes you are."

This time my question was to distract her from her thoughts. "Why'd you leave Colin in the first place?"

"I found a membership card for an Aryan organization and some pamphlets and junk like that. He was a racist!"

"Maybe that's what this is all about. Peter's manuscript is about one of those organizations. Maybe he was on to something and didn't even know it. I was going to go to this place, NAK-WAN. That sign on the road past Kit's place? It's supposed to be a laboratory but I'm beginning to have the same thoughts Peter had in his manuscript. Why didn't you let me know you were leaving?" I whispered.

"I knew you didn't want me around. I was surprised when Emma told me you agreed to take Michael."

"I got rid of my stupidity."

"Colin told me about Peter and Todd first thing. I felt just awful for you and I wanted to come to you and tell you how sorry I was, am. And here, he had something to do with it. You know, I did love him. When he came to me in Winnipeg he told me he got in with an Aryan gang while he was in prison for embezzling. After he got out he met Howard. Howard changed his life. And then he met me. He told me he quit with the Aryans but he owed Howard so much."

"If he confessed about Howard, why would he bring you back here?"

Neither of us could figure that one out.

Eventually Leona said, "He did love me. Maybe he was just torn between his love for me and his loyalty to Howard. It's almost as if he had Colin hypnotized." She turned over again to watch the outside. We must have been on the same wavelength because she turned back to me and whispered, "Who the hell is that man?"

"With that scalpel, he reminds me of that Dr. Coran."

"Except that he's dead. Maybe he had a brother."

"That's it! That's got to be it. Howard always reminded me of someone else. He's not as tall as Dr. Coran and he doesn't have that hooked nose or that mole, but his eyes always seemed familiar. I thought it was the way he looked at me. He made me feel yucky. The last name's not the same, though."

"Could have changed it," Leona suggested.

"I don't remember Dr. Coran having family, but maybe. And maybe he's looking for revenge for his brother's death. As if we had anything to do with that."

Leona turned to look out again. The late afternoon sunlight brightened as clouds lolled by, and the sun's slanting rays from the west lit up our interior.

Just then, three things happened at once. I heard a dog barking in the far distance, and, although faint, it sounded like Lady's bark. I heard gunfire coming from the far west. And Howard's grinning face appeared at the entrance.

"Come out, ladies. I don't think I have much time, so move it."

We heard him go back down and then I crawled over Leona to climb out of the cave first. Howard had a revolver in his hand and he pointed it at Leona.

Colin, just behind him, deflected his aim, shouting "No!" Howard fired at the same time and Leona grunted and fell over. While the two men struggled with each other, I looked around and found a short, solid branch nearby. I knew she had been hit and I wanted to see how badly, but I kept my eyes on the men, hoping for a way to get that gun, hoping Colin would wrestle it from Howard, because he was the lesser of two evils. The gun went off again and a pained, surprised expression appeared on Colin's face. Howard pushed him away and he fell onto his back.

The circumference of the bloody stain on his shirt quickly expanded, spreading across his midriff. "You think I don't know you saw them come here?" Howard snarled at him. "You wasted all this time for me. Your usefulness to me has just come to an end."

As Howard aimed the revolver at him once again, I forced myself to ram the end of the branch full force into his face and then slam it down hard on his gun hand. The revolver dropped to the ground. I bent down to grab it, and he kicked at me, catching me in the side. From a kneeling position, I jabbed him again with the branch, aiming for his crotch but getting him in his leg. Then I got hold of the handgun, expecting that he would just jump on me.

I stood up quickly, backing away from him. We heard more gunshots, some sounding like a succession of quick snaps and some sounding like shotgun blasts. Glaring at me, Howard pressed his hand to his bleeding right cheek, and after a quick downward glance at Colin who was lying on his back with unseeing eyes open to the sky above, he said "He's dead. And you, I'm still not finished with you." He smiled, clicked his tongue and winked. "When you least expect it, I'll be back."

The smile turned to a sneer and he glanced to the west of us, where gunfire continued sporadically. He turned and began limping away from me, following the gorge eastward. He knew I wouldn't shoot him in the back. Leona was still, and I needed to have a look at her, but I couldn't just let him leave. He might have Peter and Todd.

I raised the gun, lined up the sight on his back, and then—and then all I could do was watch him walk away. I couldn't bring myself to shoot so I lowered the revolver. He was quickly putting distance between us. I looked up towards Leona and back at him. I thought that maybe he was going for Todd and Peter. If he got to them, he'd kill them. I raised my right arm again, steadied it with my left hand, and aimed for his left thigh because I'd already hurt his right leg. Knowing I was crossing the line, I squeezed the trigger. A red spot appeared on the back of his thigh just before he stumbled and fell forward. Satisfied that his progress would be reduced or maybe even stopped, I dropped the handgun and climbed up the embankment to help Leona. She had fallen back onto her side and blood stained the front of her blouse and jacket. But she was breathing.

Just then Lady came into view, her tail flying high. She saw Colin and sniffed at him. "Leave it," I called down to her.

"Leona, can you hear me? You're going to be okay, you hear?"

Her eyes fluttered open and she moaned, "It hurts."

"I know. Lady's here. The others must be close. I'm going for help, okay?"

I removed my jacket so I could cover her. Lady whined anxiously from below and, when I called for her to come to me, she had to circle around the area before she found a place where she could climb up. As soon as she reached me, she wanted to lick my face. She must have smelled the blood and sensed how desperate we were, because when I told her to stay, she settled right down beside Leona.

I climbed back down and holding back my repulsion, I went to Colin's body to rummage in his pockets until I found the keys to his van. I knew I had no choice but to leave Leona there and not really knowing if anyone was close, I'd have to drive to Kit's and get them to call for an ambulance, and the police.

As I left, Lady whined, but didn't attempt to follow me. Wanting to get an immediate overview of what was going on, I climbed straight up the south side of the gorge. The gunfire was still coming from the west, but I couldn't see anyone. When I got to the very top, I looked out and was horrified to see that Howard had gotten up and, with the help of a stick he seemed to be dragging his leg behind him. His progress was so slow that I was positive he wouldn't try to return to Leona. Besides, he'd think I was there with his revolver.

The sun would go down soon, so there was no time to linger. I headed for the road and was almost there when Michael's voice came to me. "Auntie Chris! What's going on?"

"Michael! I need you to go call for an ambulance. Your mother's been shot. Here's the keys to Colin's van. We're near that cave you found."

"Mom is here?"

"Yes. She's here, but Howard Norach shot her. And he killed Colin."

"Colin? What's going on?"

"No time to explain. Hurry! I've got to get back to your mother."

Taking a step, I paused and called back to Michael, "Who's doing all that shooting?" After all the whispering Leona and I had done, my voice sounded unnaturally loud.

"Kit and Bob. Someone started shooting at us. I just came back from calling for more cops."

"Okay. Go back and call for an ambulance and tell them your Mom was shot in the chest and she's bleeding really bad." I said that part so that the medics would hurry, but Michael's jaw dropped and tears came to his eyes. To comfort him temporarily I said, "Michael, she'll be okay, but tell them that so they'll hurry. Okay?"

He ran off and I hurried back to Leona. When I got there, I called Lady back down so I would have room. Once by Leona's side, I found the entry wound about two inches down from her collarbone on her right side. Because she had fallen over onto her left side, the blood had oozed downwards, soaking her across the chest. I covered the wound with my right hand and pressed hard. Leona groaned, and I began talking to her, telling her that Michael was going for help and that everything was going to be okay. I'd had to change hands to keep the pressure on Leona's wound, and that had renewed the pain in my left hand.

Silly thoughts about why all this was happening had gone through my mind, but one remained with me. As soon as Leona was in the ambulance, I was going to go to that laboratory or whatever it was to the northeast of us because Howard was heading in that direction. Having read Peter's manuscript, I was sure that was Howard's lair. Maybe it was heavily equipped with guns, and Howard was planning to make his last stand there.

Dusk was upon us now. The shooting was still sporadic, but then came the welcoming sounds of sirens and men shouting in that authoritative tone that cops use. The whirling buzz of a helicopter overhead soon drowned out the voices.

A little while later, from my vantage point, I saw flashlight beams, like search lights, crisscrossing the gorge. Michael called out and I answered, so they could locate us quickly. A man carrying a medical duffel bag was the first to climb halfway up to us. I had to climb down to make room for him. I watched him perform quick, efficient movements, then the other men lifted a stretcher up. One man climbed as far as he could, helped place Leona onto it, secured her, and, with the help of the other men who had gathered, brought her down. Michael led the way as others with flashlights lit a pathway up the steep slope. By now it was completely dark and much colder.

Some of the men remained behind with Colin's body, and I saw flashes from the photographer's camera. Sergeant Trolley came up behind me and started asking his incessant questions. So far he had done nothing for me, and I decided I was going to be in charge for myself from now on. Besides, I was desperate to talk only to Bob, so I ignored his questions and asked where Constable Cormier was.

"He's with the prisoners. Now, could you please tell me exactly what went on here?" Sergeant Trolley demanded, provoking even more hostility from me.

"I need to talk to him. He's not leaving, is he?" He was the only one I wanted to explain everything to; the only one who'd understand what we had to do.

"They should still be there . . . shit!" That last word meant he had

191

tripped. He got up and, right away, resumed the questions.

Annoyed, I blocked his path and said, "Okay, Howard Norach shot Leona, then he shot Colin Sayers, and then he headed to the east." I was about to say that I shot Howard in the leg, but stopped because I might get arrested on the spot. "Like I said, he was heading east, and then I think he'll go north, because I think that so-called above-board laboratory is his place. That's all I know. Now I'm going after him." With that, I turned and hurried on as fast as I could.

Sergeant Trolley caught up to me again when we were on level ground and said: "You must have the eyes of a cat. You know you can't go after him. That's what we're here for."

"Well, I won't stop you. He shot my sister, killed Colin, and he had his men shoot Wapan and probably her family."

"Who's Wapan?"

"She was a good friend. But she was a wolf, so that wouldn't matter to you."

"Hey, slow down, Mrs. Webster, I'm not your enemy. I want to help, but I have to get an idea of what's going on."

"You're right, I'm sorry. But I don't want you stopping me from going after him."

"You should be going to the hospital with your sister. We'll handle everything here."

Either he didn't understand any of what I had said or as with other suggestions that we made, he thought little of it, so I stopped trying to explain further. Besides, if he ordered me away, I would have to disobey. I'd broken one law already when I shot Howard in the leg, so disobeying would be nothing.

We finally came out on the road near my driveway, and the sound of the nearby helicopter drowned out further conversation. Michael and Kit were over by Kit's pickup, talking to Bob, and I rushed over to them.

Seeing me, Michael shouted above the noise, "I can't go with her, so Kit's going to drive us there."

I took hold of Michael's hand to pull him aside and said into his ear, "Tell her you love her, okay? Even if she's sleeping, tell her!"

His lips quivered as if he was on the verge of crying, but he nodded.

"I'm going to come there later, as soon as I can. But I have to do something first."

He looked at me, his eyes curious, but he didn't say anything as he got into Kit's pickup.

# 16

RETRIBUTION

I turned to Bob and said loudly, "Bob, you know that NAK-WAN place? We have to go there. Right now!"

"But I have to go back to the detachment now."

"No! It's not finished!"

"What do you mean?"

"Howard Norach was going there, I'm sure of it."

He followed me as I unthinkingly headed for Colin's van. "You can't go in that. Come to my vehicle and you can explain on the way."

I climbed into his SUV just as Sergeant Trolley caught up to me again. Before he could say anything, I looked at him and asked, "Are you coming?" And then I slammed the door and we took off.

Two kilometres past Kit's driveway, we turned north onto the road that had the NAK-WAN No Trespassing sign.

I explained what I knew and what I suspected as Bob focused on the winding road ahead. In turn, he told me Kit had called him, after our dog led Michael and Kit to the car. He had dropped everything to get to Kit's right away, then they'd gone on to my cabin, where they found the van and some blood on the ground beside it.

He and Kit were following the few drops of blood into the woods north of my cabin when the shooting began. The three men gave up when they saw reinforcements.

The mention of Lady made me wonder where she had gone. She had disappeared into the dark when the medics and police had arrived. I thought she must have gone back to Kit's. Not a moment passed before we saw her up ahead, at the side of the road, and she seemed to be tracking something. Bob slowed and then stopped. She raised her head to look at us, then lowered it again and continued in a zigzag fashion. I opened the back door so Bob drove on very slowly, and we got out at the spot where she'd been sniffing. He studied the side of the road and said, "An ATV passed here and take a look at this."

From the headlights, I saw some reddish guck on the tip of his finger.

"Was he wounded?" he asked.

"Yeah, his leg. His thigh."

"Well, your dog must have been tracking him."

"Let's hurry," I said, calling Lady to me. I felt an urgent need to move on. Earlier Howard had said he wasn't finished with me. Well, I wasn't finished with him either.

Bob spoke, cutting into my thoughts. "My boss has just joined us."

In the side mirror, I noticed the reflection of another vehicle's headlights appear and catch up to us. About fifteen minutes later, we came to two eight-foot gates, one side still open. A winding driveway led us about two kilometres further in.

Bob parked and we looked at our surroundings. Yard lights illuminated buildings of different sizes, one to the left and some set farther back. A large bungalow, with lights coming from almost all the front windows, sat on higher ground to the right. A couple of white utility vans were parked over by one of the buildings, but the ATV was nowhere in sight. Neither was a man dragging his leg. I hoped I hadn't made a mistake.

Telling me to stay in the car, Bob got out and joined Sergeant Trolley and another officer. One of them shouted "Over there!" and they raced towards the buildings on the left as if they had seen someone.

Watching them disappear around a corner of a building, I wondered why I should obey Bob's order. As I was arguing with myself, my peripheral vision caught sight of movement at the other side of the house, where the shadows were the darkest. It had been a flash of light, like someone turning a flashlight on and off. Staring hard, I couldn't make anything out. Perhaps, I thought, I should just go check it out and look in the windows while I was at it. I got out, telling Lady to stay and to be quiet; she had begun growling, a deep low rumble in her throat.

The wind had picked up and, without a jacket, I began to shiver. I was halfway across the lawn when I saw a shape move out of the shadows and then the shape came into the lighted area. A huge black Rottweiler came right at me, and there was no time to run back to the vehicle. Behind me, Lady began barking and growling, trying desperately to get out. The Rottweiler ran past me to attack the SUV, trying to get at Lady. Praying that neither dog would break a window, since a collie was no match for a Rottweiler, and wishing I could stick around to help Lady—I had no idea how—I ran towards the house. Instinct told me that the answers I needed were in that house. Someone must have opened a backdoor to let the Rottweiler out, and right away I thought Howard must have done that.

From the veranda, I peered into windows, some covered with lace curtains and others with the drapes drawn, but I could see that the large front room was empty. I tried the front door knob and, since it wasn't locked, I entered. On the right was a huge living room and on the left of the spacious hallway that led into the depths of the house was a large fancy door. I opened it and saw that the room was an oversized bedroom. On the same side further down I came to another long hallway. Light came from a room on the other side so I cautiously crossed the hallway, intending to look into that room.

"In here, Christine. I'm surprised Adolph didn't get you. Come in and see what I have here. Don't be afraid. Come on."

Howard's tone of voice sent chills through me, but I walked forward to the open doorway. He was sitting in a leather swivel chair, turned away from a large mahogany desk to face the doorway. Although I intuitively knew what he was talking about, I was still shocked. On his right leg, his good leg, Howard was holding my son. Todd's legs dangled limply between Howard's legs. Recovering from my shock, I whispered, "You murdered him!"

His eyes took in the blood on my sweatshirt and he smiled. "Oh, he's not dead. I just gave him a little something so he wouldn't come to. And when he does, you're the one who's going to be dead."

My eyes focused on Todd as I looked for signs of life. Yes, I could see his chest moving and I was filled with hope.

Howard's crazy voice penetrated through the moment. "Oh my, what am I saying? No, no, no, the reason why I didn't kill you before was that I wanted to see your face when I slit the throat of your baby."

His words penetrated through the combination of my initial shock and subsequent elation. That's when I saw the scalpel in his left hand. I play-acted and asked, with no hint of emotion, "And then you'll kill me and what good will all this do you?" I had to convince him that I really didn't care what he did. "I've already accepted Todd's death, so you can't hurt me anymore."

"I don't believe you. I saw your eyes. I see them now—the way you look at your child."

That was true, so I turned my gaze up to his face. He looked at the wall behind me on my right, studying it for a minute. Curious about what he was staring at, I glanced back. A bank of black-and-white monitors took up the wall space on one side of the door, and one of them showed two officers ushering some men out of a building. Another monitor showed a man sleeping, a blanket covering him. Another showed the front of the house. That's how he'd known exactly what we were all doing. My eyes went back to the monitor of the sleeping man and when I turned back to Howard, he was smiling crazily. "Yes, it's Peter. But is he dead, or alive?"

Another handgun, a stainless steel tray, and a coffee mug sat on the desk beside him. On the wall behind him were pictures of people, one of them of Hitler, a poster of a swastika, and some kind of emblem I'd never seen before. Howard was part of a white supremacist group, yet he had hugged me, a lowly Métis woman—the supreme hypocrite. What was it he wanted from me? And then the answer came when one of the pictures caught my eye, a wedding picture of Dr. Coran and his wife.

"You are Doctor Coran," I whispered.

"And you never once suspected who I was. You are such an imbecile. A little plastic surgery, rimless glasses—oh, the hair loss wasn't in the plan. I, on the other hand, recognized you as soon as I saw your picture in the paper. Because of you and your sister, I lost everything. Everything!" His voice rose at the end so that he almost screamed the last word, and he moved the scalpel close to Todd's exposed throat. But he got his anger under control, and continued. "You've been unfinished business for twenty years. But tonight, I'll finish with you. By the way, how is your sister?"

My breathing began again and, hiding my contempt, I stared at him impassively. Somehow, I had to get Todd away from him. I had noticed that Todd had been slipping downwards.

The doctor put the scalpel on the desk so he could adjust his grip on Todd. He talked on as he did so: "No more confiding in me? Too bad. I think I enjoyed that the most. You mud people are so pathetic."

I remained silently emotionless, so he went on, not bothering to pick up the scalpel again. "Yes, that is your husband there. I had time to administer my drugs to him and your baby, here. They are both going to die, right before your eyes. You wouldn't want your husband back anyways. He's a broken man. I did that. Easy. Play with his mind. You were harder to break. Too bad about Colin but that was your sister's fault." He made a scoffing noise before continuing. "He betrayed me. He stupidly fell in love with your sister. But enough of all this, I think it's time I took another little keepsake from you, to remember you by. Come here. Put your hand on the tray here. You remember the routine?"

I made a look of dread appear on my face, welcoming the opportunity to get closer to them, and I shook my head, "No."

"Now, Christine. I don't have all night."

I moved forward slowly, now pretending heightened fear. When I got close enough I'd watch for the right second to throw myself at him. He was in a swivel chair and had a leg wound so that made him vulnerable. Maybe he would set Todd down while he cut off one of my fingers. At his desk, I had no choice but to place my bloody right hand on the tray but I was mere inches from the gun. He was distracted by a woman's voice coming from behind me. "Father, what are you doing with my baby?"

Howard/Dr. Coran looked over at the doorway, "Queenie, go back to bed."

That second of distraction allowed me to grab the handgun, and I pointed it at the doctor's head. I said just loud enough so only he could hear, "You know I'll shoot if I have to."

With my wounded left hand, I reached behind and gingerly picked up the scalpel and tossed it across the room, out of reach of both him and his daughter. Carefully but quickly, I removed Todd from his lap and backed away from him. He made a movement as if to lunge for me, so I squeezed the trigger, aiming for the wall beyond.

Glaring at me, he sank back into his chair. At a safe distance from the doctor, I half-turned to Queenie to make eye contact, to show her I was harmless. Although she was only a few years older than I was, she had not aged well. In her nightgown and robe, she looked plump and matronly.

Using a calm voice, I said, "Queenie, I have to take Todd to bed now."

"Don't let her pass," Dr. Coran ordered. "She's going to take your son away from you."

After she eyed Todd tenderly, she looked at me to see what my intentions were, and said, almost petulantly, "Let me take him."

"Okay, we'll just put him on the couch in the living room, okay? You can watch over him," I said, without relinquishing Todd.

"Queenie, it's a trick. Don't let her go!"

I was at the doorway now, waiting to pass by her, but I didn't want to force my way out.

"He really needs to go back to bed, Queenie," I said, changing tactics. "Could you show me where he sleeps?"

"You're not going to take him away from me, are you?" she asked.

"We'll just put him back to bed," I said. Queenie turned and I followed her. Behind me, I heard the squeaking of the chair and a drawer being pulled open. At the same time the front door flew open behind me, and I turned quickly. Bob, with his gun drawn, came towards me, and I signalled for him to stop. Without saying anything, I indicated that

Howard was in the room and had a gun, even though I didn't know for sure.

He looked at Todd, questioningly. I flashed a smile and nodded. Then I followed Queenie down the hall to a small bedroom, where I laid Todd down on the bed and pulled the covers over him. As Queenie leaned over and kissed his forehead, I noticed five capsules on the nightstand beside Todd's bed. I picked them up.

"What are these, Queenie?"

Her eyes widened in fright and she tried to grab them from my hand. "Don't tell Father, please?"

"I won't, but what are they?"

"Father told me to put them in Todd's milk, but I forgot. I put one in and then he came back from putting Adolph outside."

"Did Todd drink any of the milk?" I asked, as I put the capsules in the pocket of my jeans.

"Some. Father took the milk. And I had to take Todd to him. Todd doesn't like his milk, and he was already sleeping. I drank all my milk." She was looking from the door, to me, and back to the door, perhaps nervous that she was talking to me. She didn't look at all sleepy.

"Okay. We should go now," I whispered, wanting to draw her out of the room away from Todd. I closed the door behind me. She turned to smile at me. "Isn't he precious?"

I nodded, looked down the hall at Bob and then turned to Queenie. "You should go back to bed too. I'm going to leave now."

"I have to say goodnight to Father first," Queenie said. With that, she slipped by me before I could stop her and she stood in the doorway to his office.

I expected a shot to ring out and to see her fall, but nothing happened. "Oh, he's not here," she said, and she passed Bob as if he wasn't even there and turned down another hallway.

Bob and I both rushed to the doorway and, sure enough, the doctor had vanished. Coran had turned off the monitors. I noticed the almost full glass of milk on the counter below the blackened monitors only now. Todd would be okay until we learned what had happened to Peter, and then we could all get out of here.

A small noise came from behind a bookcase on the left side of the wall, near the corner desk. Holstering his gun, Bob used full force to slide the bookcase aside. I was wondering how the doctor had managed to move it so quietly, when the whole bookcase smoothly swung open. A light was on in the small enclosure. Bob almost lost his balance as a loud snapping sound made him jump back. Holding his upper arm, he returned to me.

"Oh man, you've been hit!"

"It's okay, it's just a nick." Bob grimaced. "He's climbing a ladder in there. We've got him cornered. They had an arsenal of weapons in one of the buildings out there . . . Damn, this hurts." He spotted the blood on my sweatshirt and asked, "Did you get shot?"

"No, I'm okay. Did you find Peter out there?"

"Not yet but they're still checking the buildings. Your son—he's okay?"

I nodded. "Yes. Howard—he's really Dr. Coran—tried to drug him, but he didn't have enough time," I added, my voice quivering, "Peter is somewhere here, in a small room. It looks like he's been drugged, maybe given an overdose. We have to find him fast."

"Okay, you stay here. Don't let him out of there. I'll go look." Bob headed for the front door, and then turned to say, "More backup's coming."

I remained still for only a minute before impatience and curiosity made me advance further into the office and take a quick look in the storage room. The doctor, breathing heavily and grunting, was almost to the top of the ladder, using his wounded leg just enough to hop on his good leg upwards.

It suddenly occurred to me that if there were weapons in one of the other buildings, maybe there were some more up there in the attic. The doctor was at the top now and both his hands were occupied, one hanging on to the rung of the ladder and the other pushing open the trap door. His weight was on his good leg. All I had to do was shoot that one and he wouldn't be going anywhere. I tried, but once again, I couldn't make myself squeeze the trigger.

So I said as forcefully as I could, "Get down from there!"

His left side was to me, and the gun was in his right hand, the one pushing open the trap door. He tried to aim it at me, over his left arm, but in his haste he lost his grip and tumbled to the floor.

Awkwardly, he pulled himself up into a sitting position, moved so his back was against the wall, looked up at me, and hissed, "Go ahead, shoot."

"What kind of drug did you use on my son?"

The doctor gave me a nasty grin and said, "If he's not already dead, he will be soon."

I kept the gun aimed at him with my left hand so I could reach into my jean pocket for the five capsules. I brought them out and threw them at him. "Guess again, Dr. Coran. You've lost control. Queenie disobeyed you."

His white face turned red with rage. "We're alike, you know," he screeched. Trying to provoke me, he added, "You and me. I saw that when you were just thirteen. So sweet, so ripe."

To shut him up, I said, "Shooting you would be too easy. I'd rather see you rot in prison."

The doctor shifted and brought his left arm up from beside him. He had gotten hold of his gun again. With a flick of his wrist he could point it at me, and shoot, but it was obvious to both of us that I could shoot him first.

It appeared that the fight had gone out of him and he crossed his arm across his midriff and let the gun fall to the floor.

Just to add to his misery, I said, "My son is going to be fine. And we'll find Peter. And Leona—you only wounded her. And me, I feel really good to see you where you belong, squirming on the floor like the slimy pathetic thing you are."

Suddenly he screamed, "Damn you!" With his right hand, he picked up the gun, pointed it at his temple and fired. Seemingly in slow motion, his upper body fell over against the ladder.

Shocked, I froze. A spray of blood instantly appeared on the wall behind the ladder. I shut my mouth and being the person he was, I didn't trust that he was really dead so I went to him to have a closer look and to remove the gun from his reach. I stepped back and stared at him, fixated on the wound to his temple. It was hard to believe I had desired him at one time—young foolish girl that I'd been. And it all ended here.

What brought me out of my trance was the distant sound of a man's voice. No words, just a "mmm-mmm" that sounded like it was coming from the attic. Dr. Coran wasn't climbing to get to weapons. I saw that blood and guck had splattered the two bottom rungs, so I heaved myself up to skip the bloodied rungs. As I climbed up the ladder, I paused to look back down at Dr. Coran and make sure he didn't somehow come to life again. Then I pushed hard at the trap door and I looked into a pitch-black darkness.

It seemed dumb, but I said "Hello?"

That "mmm-mmmm-mmm" sound came again. It sounded like Peter! Yet I'd seen on the monitor that he was asleep in a lit room. The light from the closet below barely lit up the area around the trap door, and I left the handgun behind as I groped my way further into the blackness, my eyes gradually adjusting to the dark. On my hands and knees, I felt along where two-foot-wide plywood had been placed over the joists. At one point they seemed to split off in different directions, so I stopped to ask, "Where are you?"

The muffled voice came again. I moved forward trying not to rush as my excitement mounted. It absolutely sounded like Peter! I bumped my head into a metal rail. Running my hands along it, then upwards to a thin mattress, then higher, I felt a warm human body. Further along the form I touched ropes that seemed to tie his ankles to the legs of the cot. Moving my hands along, I found his hands, which were duct taped together. Rope wound around his neck, securing him tightly to the cot. More duct tape that covered his mouth went all the way around his head. With my hand on the side of his head, I asked, "Peter?"

And I felt him give a slight nod! Emotional me—tears filled my eyes as I quickly tried to loosen the tape around his wrists, but the tape wouldn't give.

"I have to get scissors. Don't worry! I'll be back as soon as I can."

Before I got back to the trap door, I heard Bob calling me.

"I'm up here. Peter's up here!" I answered and again emotion made my voice quiver.

When I got to the bottom, I saw Bob, looking at Dr. Coran's corpse.

"What happened?" he asked

"He shot himself." Then I spotted the scalpel on the carpeted floor. "This will do."

As I picked it up, I looked at him and said, "I need your flashlight. Did the others get here, yet? Peter might need help getting down."

Back in the attic with the path now lit up by the flashlight, I hurried over to Peter and began cutting the duct tape binding his hands and then the tape covering his mouth, so he could pull the tape from his face. I went to work on the ropes around his neck. Finally he was able to sit up and stretch.

"Tell me I'm not hallucinating," he said.

"You're not hallucinating," I said, cutting at the final ropes that tied his legs to the cot. As with Todd, I held back the urge to hug like crazy. "How long have you been up here?"

"Give me a hug," he said. I obliged and we hugged each other so tightly it was as if we were one. He released me and with fear in his voice he whispered, "Todd?"

"He's fine. Did Howard drug you today?"

"No. It was morning when they brought me here. Todd is really fine?"

"Yes, really." We crawled back over to the trap door and I asked, "Can you make it down the ladder?"

"You bet."

"I'll go first."

"To catch me if I slip?"

"You bet."

At the bottom, two officers helped me step across the doctor and then they helped Peter. As we walked out of the storage room, he stopped to look back at the corpse.

"Bastard!" he snarled.

"He won't hurt anyone else now," I said. "And Todd's fine. He's sleeping right now."

204

Looking at me with surprise, Peter noticed the blood on me. Before he could ask, I said, "I'm okay."

Tears came to his eyes and he said, "Well, let's get him out of here."

Turning to leave, I spotted both binders of Peter's manuscript on the bookcase shelf. "Your manuscript—it's what got me thinking about this place."

"What about my note? That was my first clue." Peter said, as we turned to walk out of the study.

"Uh, I'll have to tell you about that later." I said. As we walked toward Todd's bedroom I said, "Did you realize that when you're angry with me you use Christine?"

"Well, I'll never call you Christine again," he smiled, as we walked toward Todd's bedroom.

Bob was already there, wrapping a blanket around Todd. As Peter lifted Todd from the bed, I said to Bob, "Wait. There's a Rottweiler at your SUV."

"So that's what all that ruckus is out there," Bob said. "We'll have to get rid of it."

"You mean, shoot it?" I asked, as we followed each other down the hallway.

"We have to get out of here."

"We don't even know if it's vicious. I'll go call it from the side door. Wait here." Before they could veto me, I raced across the hallway opening the largest door. It led into a brightly lit, gleaming white kitchen, and I saw the side door that had been opened earlier. I made sure the kitchen door was securely shut to the rest of the house. The name Adolph had been mentioned twice, so I stepped outside and yelled, "Adolph! Come!"

From where I was standing, I could hear the dogs in the distance, but couldn't see them. The sudden silence meant that Adolph must be obediently coming. That was good, but once he got here, I had no real plan to deal with him. That was bad.

I stood behind the door, and he tap-danced into the kitchen and turned to face me right away. I took a few slow, cautious steps so I could back out of the door he'd just come in. I saw his eyes as he processed information—this human is a stranger. Attack!

By then, I had swung the door closed, but had to do so with my left hand. He lunged at the door, the door slammed shut, and the knob banged into my middle finger. Daggers of pain shot through my whole body, right up into my head. Gritting my teeth, I ran around to the front, where Bob was the first to come out, and I fell in beside Peter who was carrying Todd.

Police sirens were shutting off as the vehicles rolled in, one after another, and their headlights and flashing beacons lit up the yard with their colours. Two police officers came from one of the other buildings, followed by four young girls, all with blankets over their shoulders. One of them was crying uncontrollably and another had her arm around her.

Seeing Sergeant Trolley, Bob went over to talk to him. I saw them looking in our direction and, for the first time since I'd met him, I saw Sergeant Trolley smile and nod to us. He signaled to another officer.

At Bob's vehicle, Lady went wild with excitement at seeing Todd and Peter so she was moved to the compartment in the rear. The three of us got in the back while Bob sat in the front passenger seat beside the driver who introduced himself as Constable Ringer. Behind us, Lady could not stop wiggling her rear as she whined and tried to plant her kisses on our faces. Her mood was infectious and, as Peter stared into his son's face, nothing could have wiped the smile off his face.